MW01273914

PENGUIN BOOKS
REFUGE

Gopal Krishna Gandhi was born in 1945 and did his master's in English literature from St Stephen's College, Delhi University. He joined the Indian Administrative Service in 1968 and served in Tamil Nadu. He served with the Vice-President and the President of India before taking voluntary retirement in 1992.

Thereafter, Gandhi saw diplomatic service in London and was head of India's diplomatic missions in South Africa, Lesotho, Sri Lanka, Norway and Iceland. He was Secretary to President K.R. Narayanan from 1997 to 2000. He was Governor of West Bengal from December 2004 to December 2009. He is married to Tara and they have two married daughters.

REFUGE

A Novel

Gopal Gandhi

PENGUIN BOOKS

PENGUIN BOOKS
Published by the Penguin Group
Penguin Books India Pvt. Ltd, 11 Community Centre, Panchsheel Park,
New Delhi 110 017, India
Penguin Group (USA) Inc., 375 Hudson Street, New York, New York 10014,
USA
Penguin Group (Canada), 90 Eglinton Avenue East, Suite 700, Toronto,
Ontario, M4P 2Y3, Canada (a division of Pearson Penguin Canada Inc.)
Penguin Books Ltd, 80 Strand, London WC2R 0RL, England
Penguin Ireland, 25 St Stephen's Green, Dublin 2, Ireland (a division of
Penguin Books Ltd)
Penguin Group (Australia), 250 Camberwell Road, Camberwell,
Victoria 3124, Australia (a division of Pearson Australia Group Pty Ltd)
Penguin Group (NZ), 67 Apollo Drive, Rosedale, North Shore 0632,
New Zealand (a division of Pearson New Zealand Ltd)
Penguin Group (South Africa) (Pty) Ltd, 24 Sturdee Avenue, Rosebank,
Johannesburg 2196, South Africa

Penguin Books Ltd, Registered Offices: 80 Strand, London WC2R 0RL, England

First published as *Saraṇam* by Affiliated East-West Press Pvt. Ltd 1987
Revised edition published by Ravi Dayal Publisher 1989
This edition first published by Ravi Dayal Publisher and Penguin Books
India 2010

Copyright © Gopal Gandhi 1987, 1989, 2010
Foreword copyright © Kamaladevi Chattopadhyay 1986, 2010

ISBN 9780143068532

Typeset in AGaramond by Guru Typograph Technology, Delhi
Printed at De Unique, New Delhi

For
Leela Bibile

Foreword

THIS BOOK IS HARD TO DESCRIBE—A STORY? A NOVEL? A NARRATIVE? a tale? None of these familiar titles ring true. Perhaps saga comes nearest, nevertheless it eludes the very essence of this book. It is a picture of life: men and women foraging for their daily needs, plucking tea leaves or collecting rubber in driblets, the inevitable births and deaths—all this makes the sum total of everybody's life in this setting of plantations in Sri Lanka. Yet the narration is related in a most unusual language. Though the events are most commonplace and mundane, every word vibrates with a very rare richness. It were as though a finger of alchemy streaks every syllable with a bright golden glow. Every thought, every little event is pregnant with a hidden wealth that oozes out an unusual aura and flavour. As I survey the books I have browsed through, pages I have scanned, lines I have excitedly lingered over, I cannot recall anything comparable to this. My perplexity is intensified for I can't lay my finger on just where the magic button lies. I am imbued with a silent sense of fulfilment as my unusually hungry stomach would were I eating a rare delicacy, or an agonizingly parched throat would tingle with a satisfying touch of coolness at a fresh spring.

One couldn't have sought a duller and less exciting *setting* than what this provides. The life of these plantation labourers is a tale of deadly routine. Let me quote one vivid paragraph to illustrate what I am trying to say.

> The workers returned to the lines in the evening, spent for the day, not unlike the return of limp figures to their allotted boxes after the puppet show is over. In a fairy tale one can imagine the puppets rising (under the closed lids) to puissance. Something like that

vii

happened at Craigavon's lines every evening. Used up for the day by the world, the 'force' on returning to the lines became people again.

But a people known only to themselves.

These few words paint what no artist could with a swarm of brushes and a multitude of colours.

Equally vividly poignant is a tragic scene where a pregnant woman in labour is denied a vehicle by a plantation officer and as her husband watches, in helpless agony, she dies with a tree as mute witness. This is how in a few disjointed words the entire tragedy is laid bare. No laments, no crying. Yet so sharply moving. The final para shows how closely intermingled are life and death, almost hand in hand and so naturally.

Someone complains to Kandan, the dead woman's husband, about broken cartwheels and almost instantly the cartwheels of Kandan's mind begin to turn bringing back an undimmed memory of his wife's death.

They turned at first with the same momentum of any cartwheel, but were soon turning very fast, faster, until they became a rotating firework. Kandan saw and felt its pivot extend towards him, seize him, draw him into its revolution.

Raman watched Kandan go pale and turn suddenly in the direction of the estate and then run. 'Hey, Kandan!' he called out to the running figure. But Kandan heard nothing.

Kandan felt propelled, painfully, inescapably. And soon he found himself under the tree. *That tree.* The sun was about to set, just as on that day ten years ago. Quick, quick, a voice said to him. Put a screen. Kandan stripped. From that branch, yes, from that peg there. Tie it fast. Now draw the other end of the cloth. Over here. That is how. Bring it now over here, here, to this place. A little higher. That will do. That will keep the wind out. There, there you are . . . that should be better . . . better . . .

Kandan did not feel the soft earth on which his toddy-logged head dropped.

The sun set over Craigavon that Thursday evening in some embarrassment and much pain.

Some descriptions are absolutely classic. For instance, a deaf-mute is introduced to the readers as one on whom 'after seven years of sounding silence from silence, a tranquillity had settled.' I should like to quote another of the author's phrases, characteristic and uniquely demonstrative of the author's style: 'A thought, rather a fraction of a thought, crossed his mind like a familiar but unwelcome backyard cat.' The reference is to an unexpressed regret in the man's heart that the couple did not have children, though happily married.

This book is also singular in the absence of heroes or heroines. Valli, the suggested heroine, makes a most innocuous entry as an entity when a reference is made by her grandmother to her prospective marriage, soon after she came of age when a girl's serious life was expected to begin. 'For another, coming of age, marriage and child bearing—like two leaves and a bud—were all of a piece.' But for Valli it was 'a piece that lay with her mother in the dust of death.'

Into this time-worn sanctuary, which had all the cold dinginess of a rarely used room, crept in a thin ray of romance for Valli. When she and her mate first met

> primeval emotions surged within their veins almost simultaneously. Valli clung to him like a creeper . . . Soma and Valli had known only the affection of relatives. But in the daily recurrences of their lives there was a tedium, a monotony which they sought to overcome in each other's company. Each was an oasis in the other's desert. They had never felt another body as they did each other's that day . . . Their limbs, wet and yet warm under the wetness, locked . . . The rain, which seemed to intensify every minute, carried them on . . . like a storm-tossed boat moving through currents, to their destination.

The book is also singularly free from grim shades of dyed-in-the-wool villains. There are the usual shaded villains for the world is too full of them, for shadow is inevitably a part of light.

The saddest part of the story is a real tragedy and no fiction but a harsh fact: the rendering of 9,75,000 mostly estate labour 'stateless'. This stark reality in which an 'avowed' free choice or option proved a painful illusion, gave me a rude shudder after the long pages of a beautiful narrative which, notwithstanding a few fleeting shadows, wraps one into a delightful aroma. For in it the harshest events are modulated and the most stinging sounds purred into a delicate softness.

To me reading this book was a rare experience.

K. Chattopadhyay

New Delhi
27 November 1986

Author's Note

PHILIP CROWE, A FORMER US AMBASSADOR TO COLOMBO, WRITES in his memoirs: 'The estate bungalows are roomy, surrounded by really lovely gardens. Servants are plentiful and relatively cheap. Social life is mainly limited to the local club—consisting of tennis courts and a bar. There, at weekends, the planters gather for bridge, gossip, drink, billiards and tennis. Somerset Maugham might not find the makings of a great novel immediately but the pressures of life in the small tea communities of Ceylon are apparent.' I wonder if Ambassador Crowe thought of estate labour as forming part of the 'tea communities of Ceylon' on whom a novel could be attempted.

Be that as it may, this novel is based on encounters with a large number of plantation workers during a four years' stay in Kandy between 1978 and 1982 when I served as First Secretary in the Assistant High Commission of India. I was working on the rehabilitation of 'Indian' Tamils repatriating to the land of their origin in terms of the Indo-Ceylon Agreement of 1964, under which 5,25,000 persons with their 'natural increase' were to repatriate to India, leaving, 3,00,000 with *their* 'natural increase' to stay back. My office in Kandy was situated directly above the placid waters of the town's famous lake, beside which stands the sacred Sri Dalada Maligawa, or the Temple of the Tooth. Two streams of people wound their way round the lake every day: One, of pious Sinhala Buddhists, converging on the Maligawa to seek the Three Sacred Refuges. The other, converging on the mundane office of the Assistant High Commission of India, on the eve of their repatriation to India. Great numbers of these estate workers met me every day in preparation of their journey to a motherland they hardly knew. Most of them had been born on their estates in the central highlands of Sri Lanka and knew little of the world outside. They viewed their prospective journey with unconcealed trepidation. But the doctrine of karma has a strange hold on the Indian mind. And so trepidation and resignation alternated as their chief emotions. The human dimensions of this organized emigration could not be missed. I felt that I owed it to a fulfilment of my encounter with these persons, that I attempt a documentation of this experience. Others had produced excellent academic studies. My instincts inclined me to the genre of a novel. And as I heard my repatriating callers explain the story of their lives, this novel acquired shape.

I owe to the hundreds of prospective repatriates that I met and spoke to, my everlasting thanks. I would also like to reverentially acknowledge my gratefulness to the Venerable Nyanaponika Mahathera, that embodiment of Theravada Buddhism. To Florence Ram Aluvihare, Godwin Samararatne, C. Sankarakumaran, Rev. Paul Caspersz SJ, the Wijeyeratne family, and above all, the late Rev. Lakshman Wickremesinghe, Bishop of Kurunegala, I extend my thanks for helping me realize how committed the generality of Sri Lankans are to their pluralist heritage.

Shri Thomas Abraham, who was the High Commissioner for India in Sri Lanka while I was posted there, and his wife Smt. Meera Abraham, made very useful comments on the MS. So did my friends O.R. Rao, V.K. Ramachandran, Keshav Desiraju, S. Muthiah and N. Parthasarathy of the Oxford University Press, Madras.

My wife Tara and our daughters Divya and Amrita encouraged me to persist with the project despite my misgivings. I can hardly thank them enough.

And finally, to Smt. Kamaladevi Chattopadhyay who has known Sri Lanka long and intimately, I am beholden for the Foreword.

GOPAL GANDHI

THE FIRST SIREN AT CRAIGAVON ESTATE SOUNDED AT SIX IN
the morning. Velu, a compactly built light-skinned man,
was the sounder. A resident of line number seven, he
woke at five every morning by a habit ingrained in his psyche
as well as his physique. He shook sleep out of his system by doing
a somersault on the mud floor of his room. He then sprinted up
to the estate office and, still panting, waited for the office clock
to attain the perfect verticality of six. He positioned himself at a
groundswell near the building with the elan of a maestro, raised
the conch ceremoniously to well above his head, and taking a deep
breath brought the conch's mouth to his own. From the hollows
of his lungs he then breathed into the spiral hollows of the conch
a gust of life which suffused the estate. Pooum! Poooummm!

Admittedly, the sound of Velu's trumpet did not reach very
far. About half the estate lay beyond its call but by a system of
relay soundings of bells at given distances, the entire valley and
all the far-flung divisions of the estate were stirred into activity.
Velu had inherited the conch-service when he was fourteen, at
his father's death. Twenty-three now, he remembered his hearing
as having been normal until he was about seventeen, when his
eardrums began to fail him. Inside his head, a hum not unlike
that produced by the conch, toned out other sounds, particularly
human voices. Shortly thereafter this hum condensed, obscuring
other sounds even more. A point was soon reached when the
hum lengthened into a continuity. Before long Velu was in
the zone of complete soundlessness.

Blowing the conch, a dull vibration passed from the pit of his
stomach to the chambers in his cranium. Velu understood the
scale of its ascendence even as Charles Richter must have
understood *his* before giving it to the world. Velu understood
the calibration of this tremor, knew when it started, grew, reached

1

its climax. What, for the rest of the valley, was the sound of the siren at full blast was for Velu a noiseless tympanic paroxysm. After years of sounding silence from silence, a tranquillity had settled on Velu. He spectated life on the estate with an almost perpetual smile in his eyes and on his conch-kissed lips.

Craigavon estate lay in a valley. It was girt by two ranges of hills, the medium-sized Balangoda–Bogawantalawa group and, behind that, the higher Maskeliya range. The Kaluganga, Ceylon's most important south-westerly river, glistened amid these surroundings, a shiny brown vein of nutriment to the soil.

Craigavon was the foremost of the Maradeniya Group of estates. The Craigavon tea acreage was one vast undulating billiard table-top, its tea bushes lined in row by thick row of dark green. Its rubber acreage was a large but symmetrical forest of slender trees with slenderer branches plaiting the sky.

Someone not working on Craigavon or its kindred estates—a visitor or a passerby—would have been tempted to tarry and allow the beauty of the place to wash his mind clean of cares. For the men and women workers on the estate's lines, however, day-break at Craigavon betokened something else.

Every morning, after the conch-blown siren call, the lines poured themselves out in the shape of tea-pluckers, pruners, manurers, weed-removers and rubber tappers—the estate's faceless workforce. The estate then became a hive of humming activity. Into the tea slopes the women workers streamed, their wicker baskets suspended from their foreheads over their backs. Their nimble fingers plucked the two-leaves-and-bud until their baskets were full. These were then emptied for the pluck-fill to start over again until the pluckers' daily norm of output was met. The men on tea slopes fanned out with mammoties and knives and hoeing forks for tougher tasks. Similarly, into the rubber section the tappers filed, to gash and tap the white sap that filled coconut-shell cups tied to the trees and, thence, to transport the latex to collection centres and on to the factory.

This operation was supervised by a hierarchy ranging from sub-kangani, kangani, assistant field supervisor, field supervisor, kanakapillai to, finally, the superintendent or periyadorai as the workers called the olympian figure who was at once the lawmaker and enforcer. The periyadorai had a property in this workforce, a property which he controlled and invested through the supervisory grid at his command.

The workers returned to the lines in the evening, spent for the day, not unlike the return of limp figures to their allotted boxes after the puppet show is over. In a fairy tale one can imagine the puppets rising (under the closed lids) to puissance. Something like that happened at Craigavon's lines every evening. Used up for the day by the world, the 'force' on returning to the lines became people again.

But a people known only to themselves.

The lines on Craigavon estate were typical of tea and rubber plantations on the island. They had ten rooms on one side and ten on the other, back to back. Twenty families, therefore, lived on each line. The walls and floors were earthen, the roofing of zinc sheets.

There was, of course, no electricity. Did the occupants need any? This question was sometimes asked, rhetorically, by the staffers, clerical and supervisory, who lived in dwellings called quarters, not lines. Electricity meant light-up after dark. Of what use was light to a people who could not read? Lights were needed for the occupants of the quarters and, of course, for the periyadorai who resided in the bungalow.

The hierarchy of the estate was something that was given to it, rather as the hierarchy of a military cantonment is given to its khaki population. Questioning it would not be wrong. It would be absurd.

On line number seven lived about twenty interrelated families of one caste, being one of the three main castes on Craigavon, regarded for centuries as 'beyond the pale'. These formed the majority of the workforce. Most of them were second- and third-generation descendants of persons who had been recruited in the Pudukkottai–Ramanathapuram tract of Madras Presidency in the 1910s and the 1920s. They had been recruited by fellow castemen who had reached Ceylon earlier and been appointed on the labour-starved Ceylonese estates as kanganis or coolie-finders. The kanganis, having received what were called coast advances, used to scour the Tamil countryside and offer a free passage and all-expenses-paid for work on the plantations of the emerald isle. Their search for coolies was particularly serendipitous during times of drought that left their lands sharded by the deathly regularity of the droughts. Defeated by their gamble with the monsoons at home, they decided to gamble with their fortunes overseas.

Parents of those who lived on line number seven had been recruited thus by a kangani called Ramasami. Hailing from Pudukkottai, he recruited those who belonged to the same caste-group, or its subdivision, and were either related or known to each other. The other lines were similarly occupied caste-wise. The first block of lines on the upper division of Craigavon housed these communities. The same grouping was repeated in the other blocks and divisions.

The thickly-deitied faith of India's majority—Hinduism—was the faith of Craigavon's majority as well. Caste had shown a resilience in this foreign land, governing marriage and ritual. The caste headman of the old Tamil village had been replaced by the caste's head kangani on the estate.

But there was adaptation also. All the workers had been wrapped in the blanket of a single appellation—'Indian Tamils'—as distinct from the higher caste 'Ceylon Tamils' who had immigrated over a thousand years earlier. History, geography and class assigned to the Indian Tamils on the estates of Ceylon the role of workhorses. Their having been drawn from the lowest

Indian castes made the assignation easier. The following pages tell the story of some of these people.

Perumal and his wife Peramayi were the oldest residents of line number seven. They came from Marudampatti in the erstwhile Pudukkottai State of Madras Presidency near Trichinopoly. Perumal remembered having been told by his father that their ancestors had worked as labourers in the millet fields of the Raja of Pudukkottai. The Raja had kanganis to recruit labour for Ceylon. It relieved distress among his famine-ravaged subjects like Perumal's father. Perumal himself was born in Ceylon on an estate near Craigavon. But he had been to Pudukkottai twice with his father. They had crossed the Gulf of Mannar by steamer on tin-tickets, discs with two numbers punched on them, one showing the number allotted to the estate's checkroll and the other showing the number allotted to the estate in the island's register of estates. Perumal's father made those trips with the permission of his kangani and the estate in order to find brides for Perumal's elder brothers from among the same community in Marudampatti. There were girls from the same caste on the estate and on neighbouring estates but Perumal's father wanted his daughters-in-law to belong to the same kin-group from India. Peramayi had been found likewise in Marudampatti. But things were different now. Perumal's son, Kandan, for instance, had married a girl from another kin-group in Cork, the next estate. One did not cross the seas for such things any more.

Perumal, who had been a sweeper of the estate's roads and cleaner of the estate lavatories all his life, and Peramayi, had lived in the same lineroom for forty-three years.

Ennui assailed the old couple; chatter afforded some relief. But company being scarce when everyone was out at work, Peramayi (who was too weak to work herself) spent much of her time daydreaming and soliloquizing.

Their son Kandan lived in the lineroom next to theirs, with his two daughters, Valliamma and Theivanai. Other neighbours were old kangani Ramasami's grandson, Adaikkan and his young wife, Sinnathal; Arumugam, Sinnathal's bachelor brother; Velu, the conch-man. Their lives interlocked. They could not but. The proximity helped, at times. Often, it grated on their nerves.

Sinnathal, Adaikkan's wife, who lived in the lineroom on the other side of Peramayi's, was to be taken by bullock-cart to the Keselgoda hospital for her first confinement.

'Take care,' Peramayi cautioned her neighbour early that morning. 'Don't forget what happened to my daughter-in-law.' Adaikkan had not forgotten the fate of Amaravathi, Kandan's late wife, who had been dead some few years. He wished Peramayi had not made that inauspicious comment. Adaikkan had decided against having the baby delivered at the estate's dispensary. He did not want to take any chances. Having heard of the competence and *kayi rasi* of a new surgeon at Keselgoda's government hospital, he had arranged for his wife to be confined there. The couple was soon gone, and in good time.

Peramayi, still lost in recollections of her daughter-in-law, came out to her veranda space in search of conversational relief. Resting her old brown hands on the wall, she turned to see if her granddaughter Valli was anywhere around. Spotting the girl sweeping the veranda floor in front of Kandan's room, Peramayi called out: 'Valli, if only your father had heeded my advice and sent your mother a day or two earlier like Adaikkan has done now!'

'Hush, appayi,' Valli said. 'Don't you start all that over again.' The old woman sat herself down. She had learnt not to think of Valli as a child any more. Valli was not a child. She had grown into adulthood without fuss. She seemed to know the way ahead and entered each successive stage of her mental and metabolic development with quiet confidence. No surprises for that one, Peramayi thought. She was sure that Sinnathal had prepared Valli for the coming of age. Thank goodness for that. *She* couldn't have coped. Valli was fifteen now and had long since taken her father Kandan's affairs as well as the old couple's, in hand. And Theiva! Thirteen now, the little thing had even got herself registered as a worker. Valli had encouraged the younger girl, staying back at home twice a week in order that Theiva might go and work instead. Today was one of those days. Valli was at home, doing the chores in the room, helping her grandmother keep her equilibrium.

A little reassured after all this reflection, Peramayi stood up. Steadying herself against the wickerwall, she went into her room to fix herself a chew of betel. Thank goodness for Valli, she said to herself again. What a load of worries the girl had lifted from her old shoulders! Peramayi tucked the leaf-roll into her toothless mumble house and settled down on the floor. If only Valli didn't brood so much. Thought-beguiled that girl was. And no one could read her thoughts. Amaravathi had been a bit like that, too. Just a bit.

Peramayi folded a few slivers of tobacco into the betel which was now just as it should be, soft and warm and astringent. She was soon in the twilit world where sleep strokes wakefulness.

Valli had been able to divert the train of her grandmother's thoughts. But she found she was unable to control her own. She left the broom on the floor and looked out of the veranda. Everyone was out at work. Her father had gone out early, followed by Theiva. Others in the line had gone too. There were just her grandmother and herself.

Valli wished her grandmother had not brought up the subject of her mother. It was all so painful. She went up to the picture that hung on the wall inside their room. She brought it down from the crooked nail and took out a piece of paper that lay pressed between the picture and the back of its frame. It was much creased now. Smoothing it out, Valli took it to the door where the light was better and gazed at the print, not being able to read the English. Even if the text had been in Tamil she could not have made it out easily since, like most other estate children, she had not been beyond the second grade of the estate's five-grade school. Valli had been taken out of school in order to look after the younger sister during the long hours that her father was out tapping rubber. And, besides, it was reasoned: What would Valli do with five years of schooling?

Kandan had brought that piece of paper into their lineroom some ten years earlier. 'There, Valli, that's for remembering your mother.' Valli was just a child at the time but she had been able to perceive the profound change that had overtaken the family when her mother had died. She had gazed at the print which said:

Report of Death on an Estate Registration S 57
Death on the Craigavon Estate in the Medical
District of Maradeniya

1. Date and Place of Death	: 16-3-1956—Estate
2. Full name and age	: Amaravathi—Wife of Kandan—29 years
3. Sex and Race	: Female—Indian—Tamil
4. Class and Rank (whether Kangani or labourer or wife of such or child)	: Labourer's wife
5. Cause of death and if buried or cremated outside the estate, place of burial or cremation	: Obstetrical complication— cremated on estate cremation grounds

6. State whether seen by   : Treated by Estate Medical
   medical officer, estate   Assistant and Junior Medical
   dispenser, apothecary or   Assistant
   superintendent during last
   illness

7. If not treated by anyone : —
   give reasons

I, Sarath Abhaya Ranasinghe, do hereby declare the above to be a true and correct statement. Witness my hand at Craigavon estate this sixteenth day of March 1956. Signed S.A.R., Superintendent.

At the end of the page was a pattern in brown ink, like a tangle of wire. 'That is the periyadorai's signature,' Kandan had explained to Valli at the time. 'He has put down his name after the clerk-sir had tap-tapped the account of your mother's death on the writing machine.'

Valliamma's imagination sauntered from their lineroom and the similar barrack rooms of other workers to the wavy estate road which divided the rubber half of the plantation from the tea half and went up to that squat building enclosed in a prim garden—the estate office. She remembered one of her early visits there with her father, a couple of years after Amaravathi's death. She was barely seven years old then, or eight, and had been taken there by Kandan one day. Kandan wanted to get his daughter's birth registration cards from the office. He had applied for the cards some months earlier. All that was required was for one of the clerks in the office to refer to the register of births on the estate and to make an extract of the entries on a little card. But what was one birth on an estate for an office that had so much else to do?

Kandan had thought taking Valli would improve, by visual impact, the chances of his request for a birth card being heard. 'Wear your new frock' he had told the girl. And so, dressed in clothes she had acquired two Deepavalis earlier, Valli had gone clutching her father's fingers all the way. How large his fingers were! Her fist, she remembered, could not grip more than one of them at a time. Kandan had gone straight to the window behind which sat a short dark man in spectacles with great tufts of hair springing out of his ears. Sriskandanathar, the chief clerk at Craigavon, was used to workers coming up to his window. They could wait. Adjusting his glasses, he went on with his work, taking no notice of Kandan. Valli, he could not have even seen; her head barely reached the window sill.

Sriskandanathar was typing out an application for a house building loan. He had acquired a plot of land in Jaffna and was being prodded by his wife to start construction soon. What an irksome thing it was that workers came along asking for this or that just when he had settled down to typing that application! And this Perumal Kandan was a particularly sticky kind of labourer. Not easy to shake off.

Partly to draw the clerk's attention and partly to overcome a slight nervousness of his own, Kandan said to Valli loud enough to be heard through the window: 'Greet the clerk-sir, Valli,' and, as if to impress her, added 'He comes from Jaffna.' Valli had not obliged, wondering what Jaffna meant. A forest perhaps. Or a large hill where everyone including trees and animals wore spectacles?

Valli clasped her father's fingers tighter as the two men talked. How angrily Kandan had jerked his hand loose of her clasp in order to receive a paper that the clerk-sir stuck out through the window! Valli remembered, at that point, an enormous vehicle—'jeep' her father had called it—roaring up to the building. A very round man in tight shorts had emerged from the vehicle and entered a room that had been opened for him. 'The periyadorai,' Kandan said to Valli's ears. She noticed that the periyadorai's legs were thick and tree-like but tapered rather ridiculously into two very small black shoes. She instinctively turned round to see her father's legs and found them slender in contrast, ending in large unshod feet. Kandan brought his banana-comb palms together in salutation and crouched a little as the periyadorai passed them. The clerk had disappeared in the meantime, and Kandan's business had been interrupted. 'Let's go' he murmured to his daughter. 'We'll have to come back again.' That was ten years ago.

Valli now looked at the periyadorai's signature on the death certificate and wondered whether it was of the dorai with the thick legs (or another one's). It was all so long ago and two other periyadorais had come and gone since then. She folded up the paper and returned it to its lodging place. The photograph, taken before Theiva was born, had Kandan and Amaravathi and Valli (on her father's lap) and Kandan's parents, Perumal and Peramayi. It had been taken just outside the lines by an itinerant photographer who, Kandan said, had come with a great big camera on three legs that had to be kept covered by a big blanket 'to keep the picture warm.' That photograph and the death certificate were the only reminders of Amaravathi that were there now and Valli thought it right that they remain pressed together for her to see and feel whenever the mood caught her. Valli's eyes and thoughts turned now to the picture and to her mother in it: a slight figure, just about reaching Kandan's shoulders. The face very young, a surprised expression on it. The cameraman must have perplexed Amaravathi totally. Eyes wide, mouth parted, breath held, hair groomed, as always, in a long plait, the centre parting laid well and truly in the centre, directly above the ridge of her nose. Valli ran her finger over the image. That was how her mother looked every morning, when going out to work. Exactly like that. And that was how she had looked that calamitous morning too, hadn't she?

Amaravathi had told Valli and Theiva that they were to have a baby sister or brother very soon (Peramayi was sure it was going to be a brother). 'From here?' Valli had asked her mother, touching the rounded belly. 'Yes, from there,' Amaravathi had confirmed with a laugh and a gentle slap on the girl's cheek.

She had sweated unusually that morning. Valli was sure she saw her mother shrink in pain more than once and then look both surprised and grieved that she should be in such pain. A couple of times after this happened, Valli remembered her father rushing out, saying he would get the cart that Raman, the timber man, had promised to lend for the purpose of taking Amaravathi to the dispensary. Peramayi had been appealing to Kandan to shift Amaravathi to one of the lines near the dispensary so that she could go across to the dispensary easily when the pains started. 'I am sure Kamalam, cook Velayutham's wife, who lives on those lines will have Amara for a day or two.' Velayutham's father had been a cook in the periyadorai's house, before him. They were kallar, not regarded by tradition to be beyond touching. But Perumal had been a friend of Velayutham's father for long. As cleaner-out of the bungalow's lavatories and supplier of beef to the dorai's dogs—a task which only lower castes did—Perumal had got to know that kallar family well. 'I am sure Kamalam will oblige,' Peramayi had repeated. 'What rot, amma, this is not Amara's first child' Kandan told his mother off brusquely and then made the arrangement with Raman.

But Kandan returned half an hour later, justifying Peramayi's fears. The vein running from his shoulder blade to his neck throbbed fast as he spoke. One of the cartwheels had broken and would take some hours to set right. Could one wait? Amaravathi did not reply but her discomfort was manifest. Kandan then rushed out a second time saying he would meet the field supervisor and ask if the tractor-trailer that transported the latex from the collection centres to the rubber factory could be borrowed. He would pay for the use, he said as he went out. Amaravathi tried to look cheerful. But Peramayi was disconsolate, saying she should not have left it all to her son and should have fixed up a house-job woman for the confinement as in the old days. Perumal, reminding his wife that they were not living in the old days, asked her to be quiet.

'I'll be all right' Amaravathi said. But it was clear that she was worried. The gripes were more frequent now and longer-lasting. Kandan returned once again, in white heat. Maithripala, the field supervisor, was on leave and Jayasena, the assistant field supervisor, was not prepared to give the vehicle. 'I gave that ass a blow on the face,' Kandan said. Everyone was speechless. Kandan and Amaravathi finally set out around noon, on foot. The distance was about three miles. 'We will find some transport on the way, I am sure. There are always lorries and suchlike' said Kandan without convincing anyone. Valli remembered seeing her mother sit down on a culvert a little distance away from the lines. The sun was behind Amaravathi and she sat silhouetted against the blaze. She turned to look towards the lines, towards the children, and lifted her arm weakly in a reassuring goodbye. Valli saw the two resume their walk a little later and, turning at a bend in the road, disappear from view.

Twelve hours later, around midnight, Valli was wakened by the sound of Peramayi's wail. The two children had been made to sleep in their grandparents' room that night. Sitting up, the girl saw through her bleary eyes Amaravathi laid out on the ground in front of the lines. Under the dark sky. Kandan, Perumal and a large number of workers (who had all been away at work when Kandan took Amara out at noon) sat or stood around the body. Kandan looked wild, muttering away between convulsions of grief. 'I smote him, sent him flying into a latex drum. I should have killed him. No vehicle came our way . . . she couldn't walk, couldn't sit . . . I ran to the nearest lines, only children there . . . ran to the dispensary leaving her under a tree. Doctor not there . . . only the assistants. Jayasena had sent word not to help the Tamil swine who had hit him. I fell at their feet. They wanted to help. Especially the older assistant, Perera. He said

he didn't care about Jayasena's message. He asked his junior to
prepare a bag and both came . . . on cycles . . . I ran behind them
like a mad dog. Amara was insensible when he arrived. They tried
their best for two hours, they tried . . . some lads had gathered.
I sent them running. This is no joke, I said. Do you know what it
is to give birth, what it is to die? Two old women from cook
Velayutham's lines came. But Perera said they could not help. He
wanted a screen. Where was I to get a screen from? I took off
my shirt, my sarong, tied them to branches, to plants. They tried
some more then shook their heads. No use, Kandan, Perera said,
no use. Chord round the baby's neck, he said it was. Round the
neck and between the arms and round the baby's chest . . . and
before our eyes . . . under the tree . . . before our eyes . . .'

The half-door of their lineroom opened with a creak and
Theiva's voice, clear like a flute, interrupted the chain of Valli's
reminiscence. 'Akka, I am absolutely famished.' The girl had
returned from the plucking round for her midday meal.

Nimal Rupasinghe was one of the younger planters in the island.
Wheat-complexioned, of medium height and slim, he had a
good mind besides his good looks. Nimal had occasioned
a certain amount of envy when the Irish company owning the
group of Maradeniya estates had asked him to join Craigavon as
superintendent in 1966. Nimal's father, a Queen's Counsel, had
helped the company's principals in Belfast with some tricky legal
hassles in the Colombo courts. Old Edwin Rupasinghe liked
to 'keep his ears to the ground', as he called it. He had learnt in
the course of his transactions with the company (through such
intelligent genuflection) that the principals were looking out for
'a fresh and fresh-minded' superintendent to run Craigavon estate.
Would not his own son, Nimal, fill the bill? With more than
three years in Oxford behind him, unquestionably. Nimal got the
job. Nimal's years at University College, Oxford, had, if anything,

made him over-qualified for the job. 'An experiment,' is how the Board described the appointment, adding that it expected Nimal to improve the estate's working. 'We have felt things stagnating on our estates in Ceylon. That has to change. We have undertaken to seek a fortune for our stockholders in many parts of the world. We trust you will not fail us,' the company secretary wrote to Nimal. The superintendents on the other three estates in the same group—Cork, Limerick, Armagh—were older men. They made no secret of their resentment of Nimal's appointment but knew better than to make waves over it. They did not have his academic qualifications and the field experience of many years they boasted was precisely what the company was now viewing with scepticism.

'But more than all that, the guy has pull, man, pull,' said Dick Wimalawardene, superintendent of Cork, to his two colleagues, Tilakaratne, superintendent of Limerick, and Pieris, superintendent of Armagh, at the Keselgoda Club one evening. The three of them homed to the Club every evening like bats that congregate in a tree, crevasse or similar retreat. Like bats again, they wrangled for places in the perch and snapped at each other. Above all, they cackled ceaselessly. The Club itself was an interesting building. Red tiles capped its large white walls. Well-padded chairs, polished brass and fading but good paintings of the English countryside lent the Club an air of elegance. Tilakaratne and Pieris nodded in agreement with Wimalawardene's analysis. But since getting the better of one's neighbour was a habit, Tilakaratne could not resist making his own little hypothesis: 'Rupasinghe must have clinched the deal in England after a little something with the chairman's niece.' Dick Wimalawardene (who was often referred to by the others as 'Hic' Wimalawardene) conceded the subtle superiority of the point, as he called for another round of drinks.

'They aren't even interested in making a success of their estates,' Nimal complained to his father over dinner that evening.

'They are like the old tea bushes that need to be pulled out or the exhausted rubber trees that are due for slaughter-tapping.' Edwin Rupasinghe did not understand the technicality Nimal had in mind and, in fact, deep inside him felt his son was showing off newly acquired knowledge. But he mumbled agreement. Nimal is on the right track, he mused. No doubt about that. Just the right amount of superiority. He lifted a tiny quantity of the finely-powdered mint that the cook had brought round and spread it in a thin layer over the elaborate Russian salad consisting of eggs, greens, avocado seasoned with vinegar and olive oil. Just the right amount of competitiveness. The older Rupasinghe worshipped success and wanted his son to do likewise, only more ardently. As things stood, he was satisfied that his son's future was bright. Bright as the silver on the dining table. Only one little matter remained, the father thought to himself. A bride for the pucca sahib. Must be fixed up soon, he resolved. His salad plate was replaced by a warmed dinner plate, warmed just right. The plates, old Maradeniya property, bore a rather unexpected motif: the violation of Lucretia by the son of Tranquinius Superbus, her hair and limbs in desperate and vain tumult. Nimal had never spoken to him about his extracurricular time in Oxford, the old man thought to himself. But *he* would not have either, to *his* father. He had never spoken of such things at home. How long ago his own days at Lincoln's Inn seemed now! London in the thirties. Ah, well. His senior's chambers. The clean-up girl, Molly O' Flaherty. Edwin Rupasinghe fingered the still warm china. What were those lines of Pope's in *The Rape of the Lock*? 'If the nymph . . . Whether the nymph . . .' That's right. 'Whether the nymph shall break Diana's law, or some frail China jar receive a flaw . . .' He, Edwin Rupasinghe, was the cause for not a few of the chippings on that one. Molly O'Flirty, he had called her afterwards.

'Don't you agree, father?' Nimal interrupted his father's reverie. 'Yes, yes, absolutely,' the old man said with total dishonesty. He hadn't heard a word of the proposition to which he had just subscribed.

Nimal had decided to learn the working of every department on the estate. He did so by doing the work himself, howsoever trivial. He did not want anyone's superior knowledge of the work to get the better of him. He took about three months to get through this process. 'I want to demystify planting,' he wrote to the company secretary in his first field report. 'For too long has planting been regarded as shrineroom secret, known but to its priesthood. It is nothing of the kind. It calls for no more and no less of sound management than any business undertaking.' Supervision, he said, was the secret, if there be need of any secret, to effective management.

Valli busied herself as soon as Velu's conch sounded. She mixed the wheat-flour, kneaded it with her thin but supple fingers into dough for the rotti and ground a sambol of coconut and chillies. Kandan, Theiva and Valli sat down to their two-course meal well before seven. And at the second siren, the one for the prayt (the muster), they all got up and left, half-walking and half-running to their respective muster sheds. There could be no delay, for if one was late one could be left out of the day's assignation of work and thereby forgo an entire day's wage.

Perumal attended the prayt too, although his work— scavenging—was virtually unalterable. They specified the roads, and the lavatories which he should clean each day. He walked down slowly to the muster each morning, often reaching it just as the others were dispersing.

The new periyadorai came down himself these days and supervised the supervisors. He made workers show him their instruments. Tapping knives that had lost their edge, latex buckets that had holes in them, hoeing forks and rakes that had gone blunt, were all singled out by him and sent to the whetstone or the welding torch or, not unoften, to the estate's stores of rejects.

On one of his early visits to the muster, the dorai decided that some of the workers standing at muster were also too old to be effective. After a confabulation with Maithripala, the supervisor, and Jayasena, the assistant supervisor, the dorai asked half a dozen workers who had not quite reached retirement age yet, to report to the office accountant to finalize their pension papers. One man to be singled out thus was Perumal. 'I can work,' the old man remonstrated to Jayasena, 'for another two years at least.' This was translated into English by Jayasena (who, though Sinhala-speaking by birth, had picked up enough of the workers' language to supervise them) for the dorai. 'Tell him,' Nimal shot back, 'that I am not Emperor Ashoka palliating my conscience here by nursing the sick and the old. I am here to nurse the estate which is sicker and older than he is. Tell him also that I am going to give him a pension and am going to let him live on the lines.' Jayasena did not get the nuances nor did he have enough Tamil to translate all that for Perumal. He spoke a few words, the crux of which was that Perumal would not be assigned work any more. The old man hobbled slowly back to line number seven wondering, as he went, what it was the dorai had said about Ashoka trees. There was a whole row of those behind the dorai's bungalow. Perhaps he was going to be asked to water those, a lighter task?

The prayt dispersed soon thereafter. The middle-aged workers left the site with an additional bounce to their gaits so as not to attract the dorai's age-detecting eyes. The younger ones left feeling vaguely thankful at age being on their side. Kandan tarried. He was convinced Perumal's ouster was Jayasena's doing. He tarried long enough to catch Jayasena's eyes and then gave him a look which seemed to say, 'I will remember that.'

The skein of human relationships is infinite in its variety and caprice. The dorai noticed Kandan's unspoken skirmish with his assistant field supervisor. After the man had gone, he motioned to Jayasena to come up to him and asked, 'What is that man's

name?' For Jayasena, this question opened a vista of possibilities.
Weeks, nay, months of artful servility had not given him the chance
with the superintendent which Kandan had now unwittingly
provided him. Jayasena bent his head, looked around as if
to confirm no one was listening, smiled and then erasing his
smile, shuffled up to his boss. 'The name is Kandan, sir. A good
worker . . . but temperamental. He is capable of wild behaviour
also, sir. I know, no? As the field man, it is my duty to watch
and . . . to report, no? Mr Maithripala has so many things to
do. Besides, I also know Tamil, no? I control the kanganis and
sub-kanganis very well, sir. Very close. Necessary, sir. Don't
you know? Sir can always ask me . . .'

Jayasena had killed many birds with that one stone so deftly
spun and flung. He knew Kandan well, that had been made
clear. He could handle men like that one and could be relied
upon for inside information, that had been made clear. He knew
Tamil and, thereby, the cipher-key to the workers' thoughts,
that had been made clear. And Maithripala, that moon-faced
innocent! *His* ground had been cut so neatly.

What a smiling pick-thank Jayasena was, Nimal thought to
himself. What a classified slime. Nimal halted his thoughts
to address his supervisory assistant. 'I see,' Nimal said. 'Keep an
eye on him. I don't want malcontents creating any indiscipline
around here.' A spectator and an actor in the drama of this estate
I will be, Nimal thought to himself as he walked away.

Velu had just returned to his lineroom from the day's second-
siren-seismos one morning when sub-kangani Arumugam, his
neighbour and Sinnathal's brother, came up to him and with a
few swift gestures conveyed the message that the periyadorai
wanted him. The two men then sprinted to the muster where
the workers stood assembled. The dorai was at a little distance,
Jayasena by his side. As Velu approached them, the dorai asked:

'How long has he been using the conch?'

'He can't talk sir.'

'I did not ask about his biology. My question can be answered by you.'

'Ever since he was a small boy, sir. His father was the conch-blower on the estate before him. Same conch also, sir. Very old now. Its colour gone now. I know, sir.'

'The conch seems to me a particularly outdated organ for muster. Can he operate a mechanical siren?'

'Sir?'

The periyadorai, repeated the question. Jayasena, after an effort, understood it but did not know how to interpret his understanding into sign language. Velu watched the dorai, the assistant field supervisor and the sub-kangani with sphynxian detachment. The conch? Why is Jayasena palm-forming the conch? Could it have broken? A slight fear ruffled Velu's placid nerves now. He had replaced it all right, as usual, in the old steel box near the office clock. Had it been stolen? Velu's heart beat a little faster. And *now* what is Jayasena trying to say? Shaping something long . . . a pipe, a hose pipe. Is a tube missing? Are they asking me if I stole it? No! I have done nothing of the kind. But look, Jayasena smiles. He is not accusing me, he says. A tube, yes . . . a tube with holes in it. A flute? Is he asking me if I can play a flute? But his face does not ask that, only his hands do. Pressing? A button . . . switch . . . oh, ayya, what are you trying to convey? I can't hear you, don't understand you. Leave me alone, please. Let me go back to my room. Steady, Velu. Steady. Don't lose hold over yourself.

'Stop this pantomime,' Nimal spoke. 'It's no use asking him. We'll get a proper siren. The conch is about as ineffective a medium of communication as he is. Can't be heard beyond the first division. Can't have workers trudging up to muster as if to a picnic because they didn't hear the siren.'

Someone nudged Velu from behind. He could go back. He turned to do so. But why, he wondered, was everyone smiling so strangely. He could tell between smiles of friendliness and smiles of derision. He had seen both kinds. But this was different. It was a smile of . . . as if they were all saying, 'It's over for you, Velu, all over for you and for your conch.' Velu hurried his steps. I must sleep now, he said to himself. In sleep, I dream and I hear voices. My father's and my mother's. In my dreams, they tell me what is happening, what that meant and what the other.

Velu returned to his lineroom, did a few somersaults and then, unusually even for him, stood on his head. That form of exercise he did very rarely, when he wanted to feel a different set of sounds, beats. He closed his eyes. He heard. The throb of his arteries travelled from his breast to his neck, to behind his ears. His inverted head registered the beat of drums. Softly at first and then, close, strong, regular.

Nimal, in the meantime, was pleased with his decision about the mechanical siren. The Board would be interested in knowing that one! A conch, a ruddy sea-shell! Must get Walkers to fix up a decent siren with a multi-tonal valve connected to a network of speakers. But after a while, he found his thoughts straying, for some reason he could not straightaway comprehend, to his 1964 visit to Bonn, on vacation from Oxford. He had made a point of seeing the little house where Beethoven was born and where the piano with its keyboard worn by the Master's continual touch was preserved so devotedly. Odd, that I should think of that now, Nimal thought. He consciously directed his gaze and his attention to the muster.

'I am convinced of it,' said Dr Paul Baptist, surgeon and medical officer-in-charge at the Keselgoda hospital to his associate, Dr Lakshman Samarawickreme, washing his hands at the sink. He had just delivered Sinnathal's baby, a five-pounder boy. 'I am convinced that man's fascination for the sound of the drum, for percussion, is elemental. It is not like his attraction to the sounds of stringed or wind instruments, which he had acquired later. He has been born with the fascination for the drum. The foetus hears nothing except the thrum of its own and its mother's heartbeat. That is the first sound the baby has heard. Not just heard but felt in a fusion of sound and sensation.'

Dr Samarawickreme was not quite sure but was inclined to give his boss a respectful hearing. The conversation had started in the midst of the obstetrics. The mother's heart and pulse rate were faster than they need have been and the younger doctor had deliberated the application of anaesthesia. One thing had led to another and to Dr Baptist's sharing his views on the subject of the prenatal acquisition of a sense of the beat. The discussion continued right through the uneventful delivery and until wash-up. Dr Samarawickreme knew nothing of music and so heard the theory in silence. But as a fellow surgeon he knew and respected Dr Baptist's deftness at the operation table, the nimbleness and agility of his hands, the firmness of his muscular arms. The Tamil labourer's child had posed no problem. But yet, in Dr Baptist's hands, the birth had been such a perfect thing. 'She seems a bit hypertensive,' Dr Samarawickreme had said at the beginning. Dr Baptist neither agreed nor disagreed, perplexing his associate somewhat. But what an act of psychological insight the old man had showed when, seconds after birth, he put the newborn infant straight on to the mother's breast! She had beamed, forgetting in an instant all her pain and anxiety.

'And that is why, I think, every society, primitive or modern, has a percussionist tradition that is quite advanced even though other departments of its music might not be.' With that conclusion, Dr Baptist removed his surgeon's mask and surgical cloak. Paul Baptist was in his early fifties. He was big-built and had an appropriately large face. He wore rimless glasses that did not hide his big, curious eyes. If the face is an index of the mind, Paul Baptist's open and clean-cut face mirrored his mind. He had done his medicine at Colombo in the 1940s and then specialized in surgery in England. On returning, he had joined government service and sought hospital appointments in the interior.

The Baptists were Eurasian. Paul's parents, long-time residents of Colombo and ardent parishioners in the Anglican diocese of Colombo, were now no more. Both Paul and his wife Constance had liked the small towns he had been posted to: Kurunegala, Hatton, Bandarawela, Deniyaya and now, Keselgoda. Coincidentally, all the towns were in and around the island's estate sector. The postings had placed him, therefore, in the midst of estate workers, malnutritioned and anaemic in body and despondent in spirit. He answered the standard question about his specialization by saying he had studied morbidity in the estate sector, leaving his medical or non-medical questioner to interpret the answer as he liked.

Paul combined his interest in medicine and the health of plantation workers with a passion for Western classical music. Constance assisted her husband with enthusiasm in his work, continuing it on her part, with a keen interest in birdwatching. The two formed an unusual and gifted pair. Their arrival in Keselgoda was, therefore, an event of some local significance.

Within a month of their coming Paul was asked by Father Giovanni S.J., an Italian who was Keselgoda's parish priest, whether he could give a recital on the piano, which he played so well, to finance some repairs in a school building on Limerick estate. Father Gio, a statuesque man in a white beard that made him look older than his fifty-five years, told Paul that the schools in the estates around Keselgoda were worse than stables, made heaven knows when, in the image of the paradigmal stable at Bethlehem. The one at Limerick, he explained, was particularly bad, its zinc roofing having come apart in most places with rust and the corrosive attention of rain. It was, besides, no school 'building' but a single shed with half-walls, which was also used

as the estate's weighing shed for green tea leaf. The women brought
in their pluckings to this shed and after their collections had
been weighed, the still-wet leaf stacks were heaped on to the
floor. The children were generally packed off by the teacher who
rather liked this *coup de grâce*. The floor, as a result, was damp
and dumpy, a most unhealthy place for children to meet in. Father
Gio had asked Tilakaratne, superintendent of Limerick, if
something could not be done. The superintendent had said he
had no funds 'that year' and asked Father Gio to raise some if he
so liked! The padre had decided to take this rebuff as a minor
challenge and thus it was that he was making the recital proposal
to Paul. The priest was confident that superintendents from
neighbouring estates, private doctors, advocates and businessmen
would come to such a recital. Not out of love of education or of
estate children, but out of sheer boredom. 'They have nothing
to do with their time and money in Keselgoda,' Father Gio said,
with knowledge of the area's spare time. But he accepted Paul's
suggestion that notices for the recital should say 'For Charity
in the Parish', rather than specify Limerick and its school shed.
'You will put off fewer people that way, especially superintendents,'
Paul said, 'and prevent the wrong notion that you and I have
a racial bias towards the Tamils.'

Fareed, the local printer, undertook to print a dozen posters
for the occasion, free of charge. One of these was put up at the
Keselgoda Club, a couple at the hospital and other prominent
places. Paul had played for private audiences earlier, but this was
the first time someone had asked him to perform in public.

The chapel half at St John's where the recital took place,
was packed on the day of the recital with Keselgoda's elite, as
also several estate superintendents and their wives. They sat in
silent expectation until Paul began and listened with attentive
admiration. Paul played from the music of his favourites—
Beethoven, Bach and Liszt—his fingers moving on the keyboard
like antelopes in flight. A collection tray was passed round after

Liszt's Dante Symphony and while it was still going around Paul played, specially for Father Gio, a Requiem by Giuseppe Verdi. The priest closed his eyes in nostalgia. His mind travelled, over the Indian Ocean, across the Near East, to the Adriatic Coast, to Apulia, that fertile region in south-east Italy from where he (and the composer) hailed. His mind's eye hovered over Brindisi, his hometown, and he saw around the family dining table the faces of his old parents, his brothers and sisters, and on it wine, bread and the exquisite varieties of *dolce* his mother made. Nostalgia, he said to himself. Father Gio's thoughts turned then to something he had seen on his visit to the hospital to meet Dr Baptist. An estate worker, a woman and her infant. The child's head bloated. Hydrocephalus, Dr Baptist had explained. A genetic phenomenon. Little can be done about it. He had looked at them. His tranquillity, his faith, had trembled for a moment. Why should this bizarre tragedy have overtaken the hapless woman? She had enough troubles of her own already. The woman had staggered up to her feet on seeing the padre. He had seen her face, her eyes, almost guiltily. A vision, very brief, had crossed his mind. Mary and the Child. That unforgettable icon—Lady of Vladimir—with anxiety inscribed on Her face, an Asian face. And fear on the Child's. One foot encased in woven footwear, the other exposed. Had the one on the exposed foot come loose at His trembling prognosis of the future? Father Gio opened his eyes as the recital came to a close.

'*Grazie dottore!*' Father Gio went up to the organ and said to Paul. Others, including a few superintendents, walked towards where the padre and the pianist-doctor stood and congratulated them on the recital.

Some of the society women shook Constance Baptist's hands. 'He is so good, my heavens.' 'Wonderful, it was.' 'Such a change for us.' 'Do come and visit us up on the estate. We have an old but solid piano. It was tuned a long time ago, but it sounds promising. Maybe your husband could take a look at it.'

Constance heard all the comments through the rustle of silks and the vaguely unpleasant fragrance of imported perfume. But her eyes were trained at her husband throughout the handshakes and thank-yous. He had played well.

'*So* lucky you are, dear, to have a husband like Dr Baptist.' Constance turned round to see an oldish woman in a buffy white sari with black stripes and a very long golden yellow stole. 'My son is the superintendent of Limerick estate, very close to here. I was told the proceeds of this recital may be used for repairing the so-called school building on that estate. Very good idea, my dear, *very* good.' The lady's head moved up and down in twitchy spurts as she spoke. A golden-backed woodpecker, Constance thought to herself. 'Yes, I believe that is what Father Gio wants.' '*Good* for him that he does.' And then, lowering her voice, she continued, 'It's a *sin* the way they let the miserable children huddle up in that pigsty of a school. I have seen the place. It is just *appalling*. My son won't agree, though.' Constance was delighted to have met the old lady. She resolved to extend the acquaintance with Mrs Tilakaratne, Senior.

Nimal was there. Like Father Gio, he had heard most of the recital with his eyes closed. He had been moved, not having heard Western classical music live since he had returned from England. Must get to know that doctor, he told himself Does one just go across and introduce oneself? Don't want to be jostled by those around him. And that meddlesome priest is avoidable. Why not just stand outside the chapel building and wait for him to come out? Nimal did that and was rewarded. Paul and Constance Baptist emerged a few minutes later. Nimal addressed the man softly. 'Dr Baptist, I am Nimal Rupasinghe, superintendent of Craigavon. I wish to thank you for the music. It was very moving.'

Father Gio was not displeased with the collection, four hundred and twenty-seven rupees. There was a hundred-rupee note. He wondered who had put that in. Perhaps the new superintendent of Craigavon? He had meant to speak to him, but in the forest of departing handshakes, could not get to doing it. The most interesting thing about the collection, however, was a gleaming gold ring with a small emerald set in it. On the inside, behind the emerald, were inscribed the initials: S.T. Now who was that? A most valuable contribution. The estimates for ten new zinc sheets for the roofing and the red oxide for the floor of the school, had been estimated to cost about one thousand rupees. The cash collection at the recital by itself would not have sufficed. The ring, therefore, was most handy.

Constance Baptist, when told of the ring, had a hunch. She dialled the Limerick bungalow. 'Could I speak to Mrs Tilakaratne?' she inquired of the man's voice that had received her call.

'Er . . . which Mrs Tilakaratne?'

'Mrs Tilakaratne, Senior.

'Ah, my mother.'

And then the old lady had come to the line.

'Sujata Tilakaratne here.' Constance's hunch was confirmed.

'A *small* contribution, really, dear. Considering the cause and the music. Where does one hear such *authentic* music these days? I am a Buddhist, dear, but the atmosphere in the chapel was just *too* affecting that evening. The ring is not worth mentioning.'

'But it is.'

'Look, why do not you and your husband and Father Giovanni come up and *visit* me, one of these days? My son has been good enough to give me an annexe and he would not mind such a visit.' Constance imagined the lady's head jerking up and down with every accented word. She promised to visit Limerick very soon with or without her husband and the padre.

A week or so later, Nimal opened the drawer of his ornate writing table in the study and brought out his letterpad. 'Dear Dr Baptist,' he wrote, 'I will be delighted if you could join me for a drink at the Keselgoda Club coming Thursday. I am not sure if Mrs Baptist would enjoy visiting the Club which has

an unfortunate air of languidness about it and am, therefore,
resisting the temptation of inviting the two of you together.'

'You'd better walk up to the Club for your date with Rupasinghe,'
said Constance to her husband, early on Thursday morning. 'I
will take the car up to see Mrs Tilakaratne. And I must check if
Father Gio's mason has started work on the school.'

That Thursday was the sixteenth day of the babe's life and
Adaikkan and Sinnathal went with it to the estate temple in the
evening. The priest, a toothless old man with a squint, sent
unintelligible prayers up before the goddess. Sinnathal was sure
the prayers were in the right language. Mariamman, the idol, was
of plastered clay, with eyes painted black and the extended tongue,
scarlet. The priest had been in charge of the temple for many
years and practically lived in the tumbledown ill-ventilated
structure that was the local temple. He placed small square pieces
of camphor on a brass plate and lit them. Aromatic fumes filled
the distance between the goddess, the priest and the young parents.
The babe in her arms, Sinnathal stood motionless before the idol.
The priest lifted the plate with the shimmering camphor high
enough to light up the goddess's head. With the plate thus lifted,
he turned to face the young mother and began to rotate the plate.
Sinnathal's eyes moved with the plate. She saw the goddess's
eyes, the camphor, all rotating in one smoke-befogged swirl.

    Name him Mari, the priest told her. She will protect him
from the pox, from cholera and typhoid. But make sure you bring
ten rupees for the goddess, on the first Thursday of every month
for one entire year, he warned. Confident that the goddess's
benediction had been obtained for their child, Adaikkan and
Sinnathal returned to their lineroom with their precious Mari.
The first ten rupees tucked safely into the folds of his veshti and
a betel leaf into his mouth, the divine mediator sat down in one
corner of the temple to ruminate. Adaikkan was lucky in the

girl, he reflected. Very lucky. Soon there was more slaver inside the priest's cheeks than they could hold. Standing up, he sent a red emission flying down the way Sinnathal had passed.

'I was hypnotized by the music,' Nimal told the doctor. The two had selected a quiet corner, overlooking the Club garden.

A man trimmed the lawn's hedge with a pair of large shears and another, squatting in the middle of the lawn, cut the grass with a large curved knife. They wore white sarongs that were turned up at the knees but were bare chested. The fast snip, snip from the hedge and the slower swish, swish from the middle of the lawn were the only sounds they could hear. The Club regulars had not come in yet.

'Thank you for saying that,' Paul said. 'Music can have such an effect. It is not unlike light in that respect. Music can be used to focus attention, to take it away from whatever it is that was engaging one's mind minutes earlier. A musician who has gained a hold over the audience can be sure he is not functioning very differently from a hypnotist.'

The boy brought in two slender glasses on a tray. The clink of ice in a drink. Where did I read that? Nimal's mind strayed. Auden?

'In New York,' the doctor continued, 'there is an Institute for Research in Hypnosis, where some people are engaged in a study of the use of music for therapeutics.'

'You could not have had an audience with a lower hypnotic susceptibility than you did at the chapel that evening' said Nimal through a laugh. 'You know, superintendents and suchlike.'

'I can assure you I was not trying to be a hypnotherapist. I was playing for my own satisfaction, mainly. But good music has a way of seeping into a person's ego functions, consciousness.'

'Especially, if it is well played.'

'I am complimented again, thank you. But I am sure even if I had played Verdi indifferently, Father Gio would have liked it.

One of the better known effects of hypnosis, you know, is emotional catharsis through "age regression"—taking the subject to an earlier time. The padre told me he travelled to Brindisi and to his family in the space of that half an hour.'

'Do you use hypnosis in your medical work, doctor?'

'Not systematically. I am not trained for that. But I have used simple hypnotic techniques to alleviate pain and anxiety by masking the parent sensation so that the patient goes through a seizure or an abnormal heart rhythm, aches, childbirth and so on with reduced stress.'

The man on his haunches had completed most of the lawn. The uncut portion was a diminishing island of grasses taller than the rest of the smooth lawn. Nimal watched the doctor absently as he spoke.

'You will be surprised, though, at the extent of the unofficial practice of hypnotic techniques by amateurs and less innocuous agents like medicine men, vedarala, light-readers and so on. The abuse of hypnosis is endemic in our part of the world. It takes its place with the great oriental addictions—tobacco, opium and, generally, totemism.'

'We have a great amount of those on my estate. The tattooed spewer of red dribble is my idea of the typical estate worker.' Nimal looked out again towards the grass-cutter.

'Yes, the habit has persisted. I have tried hard to get my patients from the estates—and I see scores of them every day—to give up their betel leaf and tobacco. But it does not work. The tobacco smoke or chew is like a drug dependence. The Tamils have apparently known it for centuries. If "tabac" is Spanish, the word "cheroot" is from the Tamil "shuruttu" which means "roll". I dare say tobacco had a recognized place, like opium, in easing physical stress.'

'Really?' Nimal asked, more in genuine curiosity than in cynicism. Paul wondered whether his host was disbelieving. And so, to substantiate what he had said, continued.

'Opium was used in ancient Mesopotamia and Egypt medically, to relieve pain and induce sleep, and continued to be so used throughout Graeco-Roman times. Original Greek writings and their Syriac versions transmitted the medical properties of the opium poppy to early Islamic physicians. Likewise, the therapeutic use of cannabis is noted in early Chinese tracts on medicine and one is told of the Chinese "discovery" having travelled later to India and further afield. Tobacco, I am sure, has had a similar journey. But today these substances are being abused.

'I am not sure of the beginnings of the use of tobacco but its use by the estate population is now more harmful than otherwise,' the doctor continued.

'But is it anything other than harmful?'

'For their bodies, it can only be harmful. It definitely enhances the risk of oral cancer. But there is, I think, an extenuation that we must not overlook.'

'Oh?'

'You see—and here I speak non-prescriptively—the estate worker needs to benumb both hunger and exhaustion for long hours. Nothing can help him achieve this as effectively as a betel leaf with a little tobacco in it. So if you are to make them give that up, you would have to get more food into them.'

The light was failing now. The grass-cutter had reduced the uncut island to a small circle. He paused, wiped his brow on his forearm and looked around to see his accomplishment. He shifted from his crouch to a more commanding posture. Resting on his knees, he straightened up to his full height. The sunset glistened on his dark, taut limbs. He raised his right arm that held the scythe and with one decisive swoosh levelled the last tuft of overgrown grass to the sameness of the rest of the lawn.

Constance Baptist looked at herself in the mirror before setting out to Mrs Tilakaratne's that afternoon. She patted down her soft greying hair and wondered whether she should wear her pearl earrings. Must not arrive at a superintendent's bungalow looking too prosaic. But having tried them on, she decided they were rather formal for that time of the day and went just as she was. Her blue dress with a light printed pattern of white flowers looked fresh. Equipped with her old prism binoculars for birdluck on the way, Constance drove off in their tough black Volkswagen.

It whirred like a bumblebee through the undulating roads that led from Keselgoda to the estates surrounding it. What an enchantment lies around us, Constance thought as she drove.

A pair of black-headed orioles flitted across the road just ahead of the car, brilliantly yellow. Constance slowed down and parked the car under a huge rain tree. Must see if they are nesting, she resolved. Binoculars in hand, she walked to the tree into which the pair had dived with a limpid call. The afternoon sunlight was upon the tree and the spaces between the leaves looked like so many yellow lamps. How is one to beat this camouflage, she fretted. But Constance had been named by her parents with foresight. Her perseverance, head uplifted, paid. As she adjusted the focusing wheel of her binoculars to the greatest magnification they were capable of, the precise spot she wanted was captured by the oculars. A wonderfully woven cup of grass and fibres swung hammock-like from the fork of a thin branch. The female oriole resented her viewer and jerked up and down around her nest in nervous excitement. Constance was suddenly surprised by a slim and agile black drongo that came charging out of the same tree with a harsh scolding call. Hello, there must be a drongo nest up in the same tree too! Shifting her field of view, she could see another fork in the extremity of a branch right above the oriole's, holding another cup of twigs which doubtless housed the drongo eggs.

Constance remembered having read that the orioles and other similar mild-mannered birds build in the same tree as holds the nest of the black drongo, for protective help from that plucky bird against raiders. 'Good drongo,' Constance said softly, 'do your job well. I am going to be back in a few days to see the oriole's babes and yours.'

Pleased with her luck, Constance drove up to the Limerick bungalow with a feeling of friendliness towards all. 'It is *so* good to see you again, dear,' Mrs Tilakaratne said as she took Constance in to her part of the sprawling house. The annexe was, really, a complete residence by itself with a beautiful veranda in the shape of a hexagon. Behind this was a large drawing room furnished with few but very comfortable deep sofa chairs. A cool, fresh breeze blew into the room from the veranda which ran right round it and beyond, to a couple of rooms further on.

Constance was slightly surprised to see two others in the room. One, a frail white man in his seventies in the ochre robes of a Buddhist monk. The other, a gentle-looking young man, in his thirties. 'I would like you to meet Venerable Seevali, who is originally from Austria but has been in Sri Lanka for the last forty years.' The monk rose from his seat and nodded with what Constance thought was the most spontaneous and uncomplicated smile she had ever seen. She also noticed that he had stood up, which was unusual for a monk. She wondered whether this was because he was from the West and she, quite obviously, was half-Western.

'And this is Colin Samarasinghe, a very good friend of mine and Venerable Seevali's. Mrs Baptist, wife of the newly arrived surgeon at the Keselgoda hospital.'

Constance sat between the two men. Sujata Tilakaratne resumed her seat facing them. 'I have heard of your husband,' the monk told Constance. 'He combines surgery with music, nein? Like Schweitzer, nein?' Constance was surprised and pleased. 'I wanted to come to the recital but could not as I was away at Ratnapura for a *dané*' he told her.

Constance had been given to understand that Buddhist monks

stay away from all forms of entertainment. So she asked with some curiosity, 'Do you attend music recitals?'

'Laymen who have taken the ata sil or the Eight Precepts and the Buddhist clergy are required to abstain from nacca-gita-vadita-visuka-dassana, that is, from seeing dance, hearing music—both vocal and instrumental—and all shows. But I think the Buddha's essential teaching—"One is one's own refuge, who else could be the refuge?"—transcends the Vinaya, the monastic rules.' Venerable Seevali adjusted the folds of his robe and gazed through the room's very wide door, over the veranda, to the mountains lying beyond. He cleared his throat softly and continued. 'The Buddha once visited a small town, nein? Kesaputta, in the kingdom of Kosala. The inhabitants of the town asked him to remove their many doubts over the conflicting teachings of brahmins and recluses. The Buddha then gave them advice which is quite unusual in religious traditions. He said to them that they would not be able to leave their doubts behind them if they were led merely by the authority of religious texts or by mere logic or inference, or by considering appearances or by the idea: "This is our teacher." They would be able to go beyond their doubts only when they knew for themselves that certain things were good and wholesome.' Venerable Seevali turned to Constance and smiled his quite unique smile and added: 'The Buddha then went a step further, nein? He told them not to accept even that advice given by him merely because he, the Buddha, was giving it, but to examine it within themselves so that they might be fully convinced of it.'

Colin Samarasinghe almost imperceptibly got up from his seat and went to a built-in bookshelf behind where they were all seated and, picking up a volume, returned to his seat. Trained by years of birdwatching not to miss movement in the sidelines, Constance observed this. He seemed to know the book from an earlier reading of it and, going through the index, opened the page he was looking for.

The monk turned again to Constance and said, 'To answer your question, therefore, I think it is not the enjoyment of pleasurable things like Western classical music but the craving for it that is unwholesome. And so, even though others in the Sangha may not approve, I like listening to it when chance brings it my way.' Constance was stirred by what the monk had spoken. She had not intended her question about music recitals to receive such attention. Feeling silently grateful, she looked towards her neighbour with the book to ask whether he intended to read something from it. He gave her the book, pointing to a paragraph. Constance placed her hand on the page and turned the book over to see its title. Nehru's *The Discovery of India*, it was. She read:

Personality counts today, as ever, and a person who has impressed himself on the thought of mankind as the Buddha has, so that even today there is something living and vibrant about the thought of his, must have been a wonderful man—a man who was, as Barth says, the 'finished model of calm and sweet majesty, of infinite tenderness for all that breathes and compassion for all that suffers, of perfect moral freedom and exemption from every prejudice.'

Paul will like that sentence about prejudice, Constance thought. Must tell him about it.

'Is that the Nehru book, Colin?' Sujata intervened. '*Such* a *fine* book. I have his autobiography too. He describes his visit to Ceylon in that one. He says in it that he saw many bhikkus on the highways, looking peaceful and calm, strangely detached from the cares of the world. Life for the bhikkus was a smooth-flowing river, Nehru says, moving slowly into a great ocean. But Nehru himself did not covet such a life, for his lot, he says, was cast in storms and tempests. Such an *honest* man, he was.' Constance passed on the book to Venerable Seevali. 'Yes,' he said reading the passage. 'Nehru was an upasaka in the true sense of that term, nein?'

Sujata had laid out quite a spread for Constance. 'All of it is from my own kitchen in the annexe, dear,' she assured her visitor, imagining, not incorrectly, that the assurance would be welcome. There was tea served in shining silverware with muffins and sandwiches. The bungalow's second cook served the guests. 'Thank you, Ganesan,' Sujata said, when he had poured and served the tea to everyone. The man withdrew as quietly as he had come in. Constance noticed there was a certain contentment on the man's face that came apparently from being treated a bit differently by the senior *nonna*. Treated, that is, as if he mattered.

The monk did not have tea or any of the dainties. He adhered to the one-meal-a-day principle of monks. A few questions revealed to Constance that Venerable Seevali lived in a monastery just outside Ratnapura town and wrote extensively for specialized Buddhist journals in Ceylon and abroad. He was regarded as an authority on the Abhidhamma Pitaka, the systematization of Buddhist psychology. Colin Samarasinghe was in charge of the monastery which housed six other monks and students of Buddhist meditation. He also functioned as Venerable Seevali's unofficial secretary. The two had been invited by Sujata for their midday meal and had stayed on, at her suggestion, to meet Constance.

'Coming back to Nehru,' Colin asked Sujata, 'do you recall his reference in the autobiography, to estate workers in Nuwara Eliya?'

'Yes, indeed, I do.'

And then, for Constance's benefit, she gave details. Nehru's month-long holiday with his family in Ceylon in 1931 included a spell in the hills. Groups of estate workers, having heard of his being there, would come daily to the house they were staying in, bringing what Nehru called 'gracious gifts' with them—wild flowers, vegetables, home-made butter—to be given to him

Refuge 37

out of their poverty. 'And he says, dear,' Sujata continued, 'so touchingly, that not knowing Tamil they could not converse and so he and the workers merely looked at each other and smiled. What a *difference* that would have made to them, dear!' 'I am sure it would have' Constance said. 'How many even bother to observe them, now?'

'You are *right*, you know, quite right. When I showed that passage to my son, do you know what he did? He just said "humph." Imagine, "humph"!'

Colin Samarasinghe, who had hardly spoken all this while, said somewhat hesitatingly to Constance: 'I wanted to show that passage, Mrs Baptist, because I heard from Mrs Tilakaratne of the interest you and your husband have taken in the condition of estate workers and because I suspect you must have wondered why it is that the Buddhist majority in this country has not shown even a fraction of the same interest.'

Constance did not quite know how to respond to this. The man had spoken her mind. She and Paul had often wondered why and had lamented the absence of care. But it was difficult to say so in as many words to one who was so clearly a devout Buddhist. And yet, it seemed to Constance, the three Buddhists she was with—a monk, a layman and Sujata—were untypical, were 'exempt from every prejudice'. So she said, quite simply, 'Yes, Mr Samarasinghe, some of us have wondered.'

'Well, I hope you can see that the Buddha's own position is not always reflected by those who speak in his name. The picture might have been different if we had followed the advice given by Max Müller to Anagarika Dharmapala.'

'What was the advice?'

'Max Müller wrote to the Anagarika when he represented Buddhism at the World Parliament of Religions in Chicago, somewhere in 1883, that he should endeavour to do for Buddhism what the more enlightened students of Christianity have long been doing in many countries; he should free Buddhism from its later excrescences and bring it back to its earliest, simplest and purest form as taught by the Buddha and his immediate disciples.'

Kandan had not been himself for some days.

The night before Thursday, the day when Sinnathal's son was named, Kandan had woken up in a cold sweat. The arrival of the child in the lines had stirred memories. The dreaded sequence of Amaravathi's death had ticked through his dreaming head. He sat up in a daze, his heart pounding against his ribs. His two daughters lay sleeping huddled together in the other corner of the room. The moonlight seeping in through a long vent above their door lay across them like a sash. A nasty dream, he told himself. Must get it out of my system. Kandan got up and stepped unsurely into the night outside. Under the big canopy of the tamarind tree, he fancied that the uric pale yellow which flowed from him sparkled with silver flecks, turned orange and finally a bizarre purple. The pool he formed became an effervescent mirror with a dancing frame. He saw his head outlined on the mirror. The moon, borrowed by the puddle, bobbed up and down behind his reflected head. Seconds later, the mirror's silver edges slowed their dance and to his horror became a scaly serpentine chord which began to close in upon the reflection, blanking out the moon, closing in tighter and tighter into an intolerable constriction. There must be a demon above that tree, he said. Kandan looked up. Nothing. The fluid snakiness at his feet had moulted and now writhed towards him. Kandan ran panting back towards the lineroom, stumbled into the open drain and collapsed on his mat.

Valli decided not to wake her father that Thursday morning. He had been out of sorts for the last few days and he might as well stay in that day. She would go, instead, with Theiva. She made the rottis and left them inside a covered aluminium plate for him beside the oven. Into an earthen bowl she put the sambol he liked—red chillies and coconut—and placed it beside his eating plate. She did not want him to miss anything.

The new siren had blared twice already. She went quickly out, Theiva following her, to make it to the muster in time.

Kandan's head spun with a heavy, painful rhythm when he woke. He could not get the night's phantasm out of his head. He wandered out of the room, ignoring his mother's suggestion that he eat. A couple of workers hurrying to their allotted chores saw him, a piece of straw in his mouth, walking aimlessly. 'Are you not working today?' someone asked. 'I have two daughters working: is not that enough labour for a family?' To Maithripala, the field supervisor, Kandan offered an elaborate greeting and said he was not well enough to work. But seeing Jayasena at the collection centre, he glowered.

'Not working today, are you?' the assistant field supervisor asked with a wry smile on his face.

'No, not tomorrow either. Nor the day after.'

'You must be a rich man, then.'

'In memories, as well as in money.'

'Get along, man. We have things to do.'

'So do I. I have things that are yet to be done, too.'

'You cur, if you think you can play around with me you will be in trouble, deep trouble. The dorai himself knows about your doings.'

Jayasena climbed onto the latex bowser and asked Rafeeq the driver to take him on to the rubber factory. Rafeeq looked at Kandan with an expression that seemed to say that he, Rafeeq, did not endorse what Jayasena had said but could not help obeying orders. The bowser drove out. Kandan kept standing where he was, the straw between his teeth, a gob. Cur, he called me, Kandan ruminated. And then, spitting the stuff out, shouted behind the receding diesel fumes, 'Cur, am I? Maybe. But, Jayasena, have you heard of rabies?'

Returning home that evening, Valli and Theiva wondered what
had become of their father. Their grandparents had no idea of
where he had gone. Another resident of line number seven,
Selladorai, on coming back from work, said he had seen Kandan
going towards the toddy tavern earlier in the evening. That was
not unusual for Kandan, as for most men on the estate. But at
the end of the month could they afford it? Valli calculated that
her father would have bought and drunk a full bottle of toddy at
the very least. Her wage for the day had, therefore, been spent
even as it was being earned.

Kandan was the only customer at the tavern to start with.
Mendis, the grey-haired tavern keeper, dressed as usual in a bright
sarong and vest, was delighted to see his first quarry. He started
to mine it at once. Three others trickled in and joined Kandan
on a long bench which was Mendis's equivalent of bar stools.
They were from the same estate, but different lines. Always, in
taverns, the customer who has been there the longest and has, as
a result, imbibed the most, holds the stage. The others, full of
sanity, view him with objective mirth. But the soloist's magic
begins, in slow degrees, to spread like an invisible net over the
entire company until every one of them is inside it. Miner, one
may call him, or a fisher of men. Mendis knew when his day
was made. Not that his bibblers paid any attention to the faded
sign which said 'Terms Strictly Cash' in English, Sinhala and
Tamil. Mendis had put that one up for the trilingual status it
gave him and for the offchance that some non-estate worker might
come that way too. With Kandan and his like, Mendis had a
standardized credit account. On pay day, Mendis sent his
assistant, Sumathipala, to the bend in the road just outside the
shed where the pay-table was installed. As each worker emerged
from the shed, cash in hand, Sumathipala would name the sum
due from him and collect it on the spot. By an established
understanding, tavern sales on pay day were rebated. Sumathipala
would inform the workers of the extent of that pay-day's rebate.

Mendis and his assistant would then have a busy time, totalling their receipts, and catering to the specially discounted and, therefore, large sale that evening.

Kandan was about to leave when he noticed Raman, the timber man whose shed was close to the tavern, dragging a load of sawn wood. 'How are things with you, Raman?' he asked. 'Ayyo, my cartwheels again. I am tired of repairing them. But who can afford new ones now? The new dorai has put various checks on felling, besides.' Raman went on to describe these checks but was not heard by Kandan for, by then, the cartwheels of Kandan's mind had begun to turn. They turned at first with the same momentum of any cartwheel, but were soon turning fast, very fast, faster, until they became a rotating firework. Kandan saw and felt its pivot extend towards him, seize him, draw him into its revolution.

Raman watched Kandan go pale and turn suddenly in the direction of the estate and then run. 'Hey, Kandan!' he called out to the running figure. But Kandan heard nothing.

Kandan felt propelled, painfully, inescapably. And soon, he found himself under the tree. *That tree.* The sun was about to set, just as on that day ten years ago. Quick, quick, a voice said to him. Put a screen. Kandan stripped. From that branch, yes, from that peg there. Tie it fast. Now draw the other end of the cloth. Over here. That is how. Bring it now over here, here, to this plant. A little higher. That will do. That will keep the wind out. There, there you are . . . that should be better . . . better . . .

Kandan did not feel the soft earth on which his toddy-logged head dropped.

The sun set over Craigavon that Thursday evening in some embarrassment and much pain.

Nimal was not quite pleased about the turn their conversation had taken. The nutrition levels of his workforce gave him a sense of uneasiness. He wished Dr Baptist had been an art-for-art's-sake man. But, nevertheless, his guest of the evening had given him a badly-needed change from planting and planters.

'We must remain in touch,' he said to the doctor. 'You must visit us at our home here,' Paul responded. 'We can listen to some music together.'

Sujata suggested that Constance, the monk and Colin go to the school shed and see the work on repairing it. 'You should be able to give Father Gio ideas.'

It was a very unusual spectacle, the four of them, with Ganesan the second cook as their guide, getting out of Constance's car in front of the school building. One half of the work was over. The flooring was still wet where it had been freshly laid. The new plaster on the walls looked firm, the new rafters and zinc sheets, tough. The unrepaired half was a study in contrast, derelict and totally unsuitable for occupation by people and, much less, children. Ganesan, whose six-year-old son went to the school, explained in broken English that its five classes were not taught simultaneously for the space was not adequate. Three grades commenced at eight in the morning and ended at eleven, while the other two were from eleven to one in the afternoon. There were two teachers, he said, who conducted the sessions between them. Two boards which had long ceased to be black and two desks and two chairs for the teachers, made up all the furniture the shed could call its own.

'Quite typical' Constance said. 'Paul and I have lost count of the number of schools like this one on the estates we have been through.' Colin said he remembered reading somewhere that a Chairman of the Planters' Association had stated in 1904 or 1905 that too rapid a spread of education among the coolie class might cause a shortage of labour and that the coolie should, therefore, be taught nothing beyond the three R's.

'The three R's in three hours,' Sujata said. 'And all so that the children are kept occupied while the parents are at work.' Ganesan, in the meantime, had gone to the nearest lines and told the inmates of the visitors to the school. Whether at his suggestion or of their own, a dozen or so of them came up to where they were. Two of the men carried handfuls of tomatoes and drumsticks from the vegetable gardens adjoining their lines. They knelt before the monk and placed their gifts at his feet. Venerable Seevali was moved. He looked at the workers, at Sujata, Constance and Colin, and smiled. Ganesan picked up the offerings and placed them in the car.

'What do I tell them, Sujata?' the monk asked. 'I cannot get myself to say to them: May the blessings of the Three Refuges— the Buddha, the Dharma, the Sangha—be upon you. Their set of the three R's is different, nein?'

And then, after a little thought, he asked Colin and Ganesan to tell them that the Buddha was born in the land of their ancestors, India, that he was born a prince who lived in a great bungalow which he renounced after he saw the suffering of people around him. 'Tell them also, please, that the Buddha taught the way out of that suffering to king and farmer, brahmin and outcaste, alike. They should know that.'

As the words were being interpreted, Constance noticed that the faces of the workers lit up in recognition, in appreciation, of the message. Several pairs of hands and palms came together in a respectful goodbye as the four of them left in Constance's car.

'Yes of course,' Constance said when Sujata suggested that she give the monk and Colin a lift from Limerick upto the Keselgoda bus stand from where they would be going on to Ratnapura.

Driving past some rice fields in the twilight Constance told her companions to look out for the paddy-bird. 'You would not be able to see it until it begins to fly, for it is coloured streaky-brown, like a clod of earth, and sits motionless until surprised.' Almost immediately, a paddy-bird rose from the middle of the

field and flew away from the road with a harsh croak. Edgar
Hamilton Aitken, an Indian Civil Servant (she told the monk)
who had written numerous books on nature and wildlife, had
said of the paddy-bird that 'it suddenly produces a pair of snowy
wings from its pockets and flaps away!'

'Very interesting,' said Venerable Seevali. 'I had never noticed
that before.' And a moment later, added: 'One does not expect
a bird that lives in the slime of the earth to be capable of such
whiteness, nein?'

At Craigavon, Valli stayed up until after nine that night. 'It's no
use, child,' Peramayi told her from the next room, 'no use waiting
any longer. He has probably drunk himself to sleep somewhere.'
Perhaps, Valli said to herself But there was anxiety in the breath
with which she blew their lamp out.

'Quite a find, those two,' Constance told her husband the
following morning. She wiped the surface of her binocular lenses
with cotton wool dipped lightly in cleaning fluid, as she spoke.
'Let us have them home one evening, and Sujata.'

'I have invited Rupasinghe. So maybe we could get them all
together and Father Gio. A monk, a planter and a padre.'

Putting the instrument into a desiccator, Constance suggested
the following Thursday. But that was not to be.

Sevugan, an estate worker from Cork, came panting into Paul's
room in the hospital an hour later, just as Paul was due to go
in for the day's first surgery. There was an outbreak of cholera,
he said, on Cork. It had started three days earlier on a particular
line with the very young and the very old, seven of them dying
in those three days.

One of Paul's juniors, Dr Jamal, a young Muslim who was
equally fluent in Sinhala, Tamil and English, interpreted the
informant's words as they tumbled out. The medical assistants

at Cork had, at first, shown no interest. But after two fatalities, had taken fright.

Answering Paul's searching questions, Sevugan said two of the affected lines had been ordered to be cordoned off. Kanganis had passed on the instructions that no one was to enter or leave those lines. He himself had been able to leave because he knew the sub-kangani well. Nothing was being done by the estate to admit its incapacity to handle a situation like this and to refer the patients to the Keselgoda hospital. Sevugan said he had asked the medical assistant for a chit referring his old father and two-year-old daughter to the hospital but he had been waved away. He said he had heard the medical assistants did not want to refer any case to the Keselgoda hospital because that would affect the image of the estate's medical service. His father had been seized by the attack the previous night, and his daughter early that morning. The fingers and toes of the child, Sevugan said, had become blue and wrinkled and her tongue was white and tremulous. She was crying for water. But could he, sirs, give her any more of the same contaminated water?

'Scandalous!' Paul shouted rising from his chair, 'scandalous.' Dr Jamal stepped back to give way, as it were, for a storm to pass. Dr Lakshman Samarawickreme, who was already in the operating theatre, came out, mask, gloves and all, to see what had made the boss raise his voice so.

Within seconds, Paul Baptist was transformed into an engine of restless activity. 'Get the jeep, Jamal, and go in it with this man straight to Cork. Take chlorodyne and antispasmodics with you. Meet the superintendent and tell him that the Keselgoda hospital not only can but must treat the patients and that he is duty-bound to send them in lorries, jeeps, tractor-trailers or what-have-you to the hospital at once. Bring at least two patients back with you in the jeep. Make sure they are recumbent throughout the journey. Sister, get me the Director of Health Services on the phone, please. Lakshman, the goitre can wait. He has been anaesthetized? Never mind. He can come back later. There is no time to lose. Please have all the non-infectives moved out from the wards to the empty quarters of the matron. The choleras will outnumber the normals. Both wards, Sister, one to become the cholera ward. Get my wife down, will you, please, to help. Oh, is that the DHS on the line? This is Paul Baptist from Keselgoda, sir. There is cholera in Cork estate, near here. I have had word sent to the superintendent that the patients must be shifted here. I am mobilizing as many people and agencies as possible to handle the situation as far as Cork is concerned. Is that all right? Thank you. But please send a team of immunizers with all the staff and a sturdy four-wheeled vehicle to comb the estates in the neighbourhood. We must contain the epidemic, sir. Thank you. Ah, there you are Constance. You have heard. Can you please do two things? Go to Father Gio and get his mason to install a large firewood furnace in the courtyard at the rear. We will need that to keep the linen and patients' clothes boiling all the time. And, Constance, can you tell the mason to make a smaller chamber in the same fireplace? He will need that to cook the mustard poultice. He will also have to put up an incinerator at the far end for the mop cloths. The second task? Oh, yes. Go to the manager of the Eros Cinema. Remind him that I had done his appendectomy last month. Ask him to lend the giant water cooler installed in his theatre to the hospital for a couple of weeks. You know how the choleras need iced water. Thank you, dear. Lakshman, how many glucose and saline drip-sets do we have today? Twenty-five? Won't do. Get me the DHS again, please. Sister, can I have all the sanitary workers come in, please. Matron, can you have large quantities of the following antispasmodic made at once. Dosage: strong tincture of ginger, drachm one; aromatic spirit of ammonia, drachm one; spirits of nitrous ether, drachm one. And we will need some brandy, one ounce per dose. Where does one get the brandy from? Please get me Charles Singho of the Bar Deluxe on the phone. After I have spoken to the DHS.

Is that the DHS? Baptist again. Sir, I urgently need twenty-five intravenous drip-sets. Could you have them rushed? Yes, tomorrow will do, thank you. Ah, the sanitary workers. Listen, boys. We are going to have fifty to a hundred cholera patients coming in today and tomorrow. Important for the hospital, important for you. You will soak up the patient's body discharges with rags which *will then be burnt*. I am having a special incinerator built in the vacant plot at the rear. You will all be required to wash your hands in carbolic acid solution every time you touch a patient or his clothing. Right? Utensils used by them will have to be similarly immersed in disinfecting fluid every time they are used by patients. Right? Ah, Mr Singho. Sorry to trouble you with this. But can you spare about four bottles of brandy? We need the stuff as medicine, not liquor. Very good of you. No problems now with your wife's eczema? Good. Thank you.'

By four that afternoon, twenty-two patients from Cork had come in. Paul, Jamal and Lakshman Samarawickreme had them put in beds, given intravenous drips, antispasmodics, poultices. Keep them warm, keep them quiet, Paul said every now and then. Check their thirst by a tablespoonful of brandy in a tumbler of water. But if they want water, give it to them ad limitum.

The water cooler had come and the *baas* had almost completed his work. By the next day the oven and incinerator should be ready. Paul placed Constance in the section where thirteen children and infants had been warded. She administered green tea in teaspoonful doses to the children, with numbered drops of aromatic spirits of ammonia. Most of them revived rapidly. She was responsible also for preparing the mustard poultices which, guarded by muslin, were applied over the children's bowels, and she prepared special diets. That whole night, Paul and Constance kept vigil.

Within the next week, they had a hundred and seven patients. The hospital's capacity was seventy-five. They included six from Limerick, eleven from Armagh and nineteen from Craigavon.

Father Gio had helped. He brought with him six nuns trained in nursing and, noticing the shortage of mattresses and linen, he had twenty-five sets transferred from the Keselgoda convent.

Some of the patients who came were delirious, near death. Many came in good time. A few, very mild cases, who need not have been hospitalized at all, were accepted too. Paul had organized and was orchestrating an intricate opera. 'Thank you,' Paul said to Jamal and Lakshman when they used the analogy of a musical drama to describe the exercise Paul had engaged them in.

'Well, sir, Jamal and I must admit that when you started the exercise we thought you were being a bit of a martinet,' Lakshman volunteered. 'But that very evening when the first lorry arrived carrying the patients in that condition, we knew that without all those steps we couldn't have coped.'

Work on the cholera epidemic was not, however, all harmony.

On the fifth day, Sevugan, who had brought the information about the epidemic, came to Paul again. His message this time left Paul aghast. One of the medical assistants on Cork had leagued up with Sabhapati the clerk handling admissions in the hospital and, by a mutually beneficial arrangement, Sabhapati had begun a charade with the patients. When a cholera patient or his representative came up to the Keselgoda hospital admissions' counter, the clerk would ask for a letter from the estate to the effect that the man was being referred to the hospital by the estate medical assistant. This procedure had been wholly circumvented by Paul who wanted speed in admissions, in treatment. But how were the patients to know? Nonplussed at first, they pleaded with the clerk. With a simper, Sabhapati then wrote out on a slip the amount of money he wanted. He was paid at once.

'Is this true?'

'Yes, doctor.'

Paul's blood boiled. He strode out of his room, through the first ward, then the second, down the open passageway which linked the wards to the entrance hall. Nurses, ward-boys, sanitary workers, patients and their relatives, shrank back to let him pass. Fists clenched, mouth pressed tight, eyes ablaze, Paul burst into the hall where Sabhapati sat behind his counter. Paul grabbed the admission register from his desk. Half a dozen slips fell out. Each had a sum written on it. Twenty, Thirty, Fifty. Some people, relatives of patients, stood around. Paul raised the register in the air and brought it down on Sabhapati's head. The man covered his head with his hands. Paul brought it down on him again and yet again. 'You swine! Thought you could make a fast buck, did you? Wanted to squeeze some money out of their fear of death, did you?' And then, grabbing the man by the back of his collar, Paul hurled him to the ground. He turned then towards the people in the hall. 'Look, this man has been taking bribes from you and your kind to get you admitted. Get him, before my eyes, to return the sums.' No one moved. Sabhapati was half-sitting on the ground, clutching his head. 'Come on, tell me, who among you has paid him?'

An old woman came forward. Her married daughter with her baby had been admitted. They had paid ten rupees. 'Return it,' Paul commanded. Sabhapati staggered up. He sidled to his desk and opened a drawer. There was a small heap of notes inside it. He brought them all out and placed them on top of the desk. Paul was surprised to see the debris of the crime. How is one to have all that cash returned?

Jamal and Lakshman, who had come into the hall in the meantime, then came up to Paul. 'We will handle this, sir,' Jamal whispered to the boss. 'The money will be returned to all those who paid it. We'll get the names.'

'You'd better return to the room, sir,' Lakshman said, touching Paul's elbow.

Paul turned to do so but before he had gone halfway, he stopped again and, looking witheringly at Sabhapati, shouted 'You, just get out!'

'And an Indian Tamil at that!' was Constance's first remark on the subject when Paul returned home that night. She had heard of the episode earlier, when Matron had rushed to the house, which was in the same compound as the hospital, and given her a gist of the incident. ('But don't tell Doctor I told you, madam!')

'What does language or ethnic origin have to do with integrity? You are making the same common mistake, Constance,' he corrected her. 'I know it doesn't. But one would expect a person not to be so vile with his own people. I mean, he could have seen himself on their faces . . .'

'Ah, that way, perhaps, you have a point!'

Constance was making a meat broth for one of the cholera patients, a very old man, who hovered between revival and collapse. She and Paul were both in the kitchen. She stopped stirring the pot after a while and said, thoughtfully, 'But, you know, in a way I am glad he was Tamil. If he had been Sinhala, your hitting him would have acquired a different complexion altogether.' 'Yes, you never know,' Paul agreed. 'Perhaps the staff— the majority are Sinhala—would then have been alienated from the Tamil patients, and from me. That wouldn't have been good.'

The broth was ready. Constance put the vessel directly under their dining room fan for it to cool. When it had, she transferred the whole of it into a lidded dish and gave it to a ward-boy along with a long-handled spoon with a big curve at the neck that facilitated liquid food being taken to a patient's lips. 'Don't mislay that spoon,' Constance warned the boy. 'It's been with me over thirty years.' Paul lifted his spectacles from his nose and put them aside. Taking his shoes off he stretched himself on their drawing room sofa, a cushion under his head. Constance's mention of thirty years opened a book of compressed memories. They sprang up like cardboard cut-outs in a nursery book. He closed his eyes to see the images better. Their meeting twenty-three years earlier, at the wedding of a mutual family friend at St Paul's church in Kandy. Paul had gone there with his parents from Colombo and she, with hers, from Nuwara Eliya where her father taught in a missionary school. Would you care for a walk around the lake, he had asked Constance. Their parents had exchanged glances of satisfaction mingled with hope, when the two set out. They had not talked very much during the walk but a bond had been established. Along the lake were a great variety of trees. One gaunt rain tree drooped towards the lake. Paul, having preceded Constance through the natural arch formed by the tree, held his hand out for her to hold as she came through. Constance had hesitated for a second but then grasped it with a smile. For Paul, that smile was the one thing he remembered clearly of that visit to Kandy for a long time. His trips to Nuwara Eliya, thereafter, had been frequent. A year later at the gardens in Hakgala, near Nuwara Eliya, in a cool dense fernery, he had proposed to her. They had leaned against a tall pine after she said she could marry no one else, and kissed. Their marriage took place by their wish at St Paul's in Kandy the year after. Sunlight had set its stained glass panes ablaze. Music played from an enormous organ at the rear of the church had filled the chapel as the two of them walked the aisle. Paul's mind travelled through their first small home in Nawinna, just outside Colombo, their painful separation when he had to be away in England for his specialization and through their many homes all over the island since his joining the medical service of the government. Their life had been uniformly and often ecstatically happy in those homes.

A thought, a fraction of a thought, crossed his mind like a familiar but unwelcome backyard cat. There were no children. 'Rubbish! What difference has that made?' Constance had told him recently when he brought the subject up. 'In fact,' she'd said, 'I think it's just as well, we are left with more time this way to handle all that you have taken upon yourself.'

All that he had taken upon himself. Paul sat up, replaced his spectacles on his nose and slid his feet into the shoes. Time to go round the wards again.

'It is not that a guy in my hospital has been corrupt that surprises me' he said to Constance. 'I have seen corruption earlier. But it is the damned cynicism in its timing. Now, of all times, when we are engaged in a life-and-death situation, for someone to make those wretches pay up! That is what got my goat!'

Sujata Tilakaratne and her son breakfasted together every morning. 'If you have got to have a meal with her every day, you might as well make it breakfast. Less trouble for all,' his wife had told him. And breakfast it had been, on the annexe veranda, every day at eight. Upali Tilakaratne liked that bit of mothering. It made him feel strangely clean every morning. Clean and fresh. He deluded himself over each breakfast that he could start life from a clean slate over again. As clean as the fresh table napkin his mother handed him each morning.

On one such morning, shortly after the Sabhapati episode, he told his mother that her doctor friend had offended a few people.

'Oh, and how?'

'First he bashes up a poor clerk in front of all those labourers with cholera because some labourer accused the clerk of taking bribes from them. And then he writes to the four Maradeniya superintendents to find out if any of our clerks has teamed up with the chap he had beaten.'

'And did you find out?'

'Don't be silly, mum. I have better things to do.'

'Such as spending all your evenings and much of what you earn at the Keselgoda Club.'

'Don't insult me, mum.'

'Listen, son. I know Dr Baptist. If he thinks there has been some foul play, he would have good reason to do so.'

'No reasons, mum. Bias. Plain bias. He and that padre have no sense of . . .' the superintendent sought the right word.

'Perspective, you want to say. Well, if anyone does, they do.'

'And do you know what the doctor has written to Dick Wimalawardene? He has written that Dick is guilty of criminal negligence in not having contained the epidemic on the very first day and in not informing the health authorities himself. He has also accused the medical assistants on Cork of having colluded with the hospital clerk.'

Upali Tilakaratne bit a crescent into the thickly buttered piece of toast. His jawbones moved in waves as he munched. Another bite. The waves moved faster. Must check quietly, he decided, if any of those cholera labourers have been blabbing.

Sujata watched her son with sadness. How totally insensitive he was, she thought to herself. How unlike his father who had been a planter too. Ashoka Tilakaratne would have gone to the hospital the very day his workers were taken there. It had not even occurred to Upali to do so. But sadness gave way, within minutes, to anxiety. Her son had fallen very silent. It was not his usual silence, the silence of boredom. It was different.

'Buzz!' The bell above Sriskandanathar's head at the Craigavon estate office called. The boss had summoned him thrice that morning. What could it be this time? And just when that little message about the Keselgoda hospital was being conveyed to him, being opened before him, like a gift-wrapped present. Buzz! Buzz! Most annoying! Sriskandanathar motioned to Nandasena, the young maintenance assistant, to come back later. The maintenance assistant, even though Sinhalese, was such a blessing, Sriskandanathar said to himself. Nandasena was in charge of repairs, renovations and the like. Every 'estimate' had a cushion tucked somewhere inside it where only Nandasena's nimble fingers could reach. And reach they did.

'Buzzzz!'

The superintendent's back was towards the door. He had had his desk swivel chair turned to face the window away from the door. He waited for whoever came in to start the conversation with a polite clearing of the throat, or a 'Sir . . .' And even after that preliminary, he was capable of conducting a whole conversation without turning or lifting his head to look at the clerk.

'What is this hanky-panky in the Keselgoda hospital?' Sriskandanathar blanched. How did the superintendent know? Had he and Nandasena been overheard? Impossible. The blood evacuated his head and flooded his lungs, his heart, and there began a series of acrobatics over which he had no control.

'Ssah?'

'Dr Baptist has written to ask if any member of our staff has colluded with one of the clerks in the hospital in taking bribes from the cholera victims.'

'No, sir. We don't do all that kind of thing here, sir.'

'I certainly hope you don't. For if there is anyone here who does, he will be . . .' Nimal swung his chair round to face the clerk, 'chewed up.'

Nimal handed him the doctor's letter. 'Get me the facts behind this.'

If one were to say that Sriskandanathar reeled back to his seat under the buzzer, one would be only being factual.

The facts behind this. The facts. Nimal's words circled inside Sriskandanathar's head. How much did the superintendent know? And how much the doctor? He caught Nandasena's eye. That greenhorn in the routine of an estate office was, however, an adept in the psychology and modality of crime. Nandasena knew instinctively that the buzz had something to do with their plan, that it had misfired. 'Come home at lunch time' was all that Sriskandanathar could tell his assistant.

Sitting in a cane chair in the veranda after his lunch and mopping his face with an increasingly damp handkerchief, Sriskandanathar asked Nandasena to tell him what exactly the plan was. Six days ago, Nandasena said, he had got word from his friend, the estate medical assistant at Cork, about prospects of good money from the Keselgoda hospital. Sabhapati, the admission clerk, had offered a fifty-fifty deal on every cholera case admitted, to be shared equally between him and the estate contact. Already about one hundred rupees waited to be so divided. If patients were coming in from Craigavon, would not he like to . . .? Nandasena had, therefore, gone across and met Sabhapati. Did Sriskandanathar remember that Nandasena had been absent for three days last week? Seventy-five rupees against the Craigavon admissions had been handed over to Nandasena on the spot.

The man is lying, something told Sriskandanathar. Lying. He must have got a hundred at the very least. And why did Nandasena not tell him at once? Had he, Sriskandanathar, not shown promptness in dividing that lovely little payoff from the sub-contractor who installed the new siren? Well, Nandasena gulped quickly. When does one come across a bonus like that seventy-five? He had, do you not know, gone to the Bar Deluxe at Keselgoda and had a couple. Why did he not come the next day? Well, do you not know, after the Bar he had sought a small diversion . . .

Sriskandanathar looked through the door that led to his three-roomed quarters to see if his wife was eavesdropping. Money was her end and heaven knew she was not fastidious about means. But on the subject of sex, Thaiyalnayaki Sriskandanathar would have done Savonarola proud. She was nowhere around.

A diversion he had sought, had he? And that is why he did not turn up for three days. Sriskandanathar's sense of equity told him that one half of the estate's share from Sabhapati's collection should justly be his. After all, Nandasena's absence had been left unrecorded by him. Three days of French leave, he, Sriskandanathar, had given to Nandasena. The man idles the money away and ambles in with the plan after the damned lid has been blown. And even the epidemic may subside. Ayyo.

Sriskandanathar snorted, ayyo. Pouting and pursing his lips in turn, the chief clerk of Craigavon looked like a spaniel. One that has had a chiken leg snatched from its very mouth. 'Don't worry too much if this chance has gone. In our work, another will come soon enough,' Nandasena comforted his senior.

'Listen,' Sriskandanathar pulled Nandasena's forearm towards himself. There, Nandasena thought to himself, there the bloodsucking starts again. 'It is not just a question of losing the chance, *no*. Now it is also a question of losing our jobs.' Sriskandanathar then told Nandasena that the flower he had whiffed at was now blighted, ruined, laid in the dust. Sabhapati had been caught and all superintendents alerted by the doctor. The doctor, he said, and that superintendent were 'close', and he feared, greatly feared, that that wretched son of a coolie, Sabhapati, might give out their names.

Nandasena thought of the possibility. Was there a logical need for Sabhapati to mention their names? Sabhapati had been caught taking bribes. Would the fact that he shared the booty with others reduce his guilt? But there was the letter from that doctor. That constituted a danger. If the doctor grilled Sabhapati for more information of estate contacts, the man might talk. What is one to do? Nandasena looked into the valley beyond where they were sitting, for ideas.

And then, like a comet in the sky, an idea formed on the iridescent canvas of Nandasena's imagination. Leaning forward, he spoke into the fuzz of the older man's ears. Sriskandanathar listened, rapt. Slowly, his mouth opened and his cheeks tingled at the wonder of discovery.

At Cork, Dick Wimalawardene stalked his room, a caged tiger. Clutching Paul's letter and gesticulating, he tried to dictate a reply or 'rejoinder', as he had described his imminent literary effort to Tilakaratne and Pieris when they met at the Club the previous evening.

Priyani Perera, his steno, doodled.

'Dear Dr Baptist . . . no, say Dear Sir. Just Dear Sir. Dear Sir . . . no, cut that out. Plain Sir. Sir. Reference your letter regarding the cholera epidemic . . . no, not epidemic. Cases. Regarding the cholera cases on my estate . . . On Cork stroke Armagh stroke Limerick stroke Craigavon estates. I reject your charge stroke contention . . . cut out reject. I cannot accept your charge stroke contention . . . no, just contention, that there was dereliction of duty on our part . . . on the part of some members of my staff . . . of the staff at Cork . . .' Any steno would have been at her wits' end. But Priyani liked to indulge her boss. Indulgence, she knew, was a two-way street. Did not her perfume prove that?

She wished the superintendent would leave such difficult letters to the chief clerk. The cholera affair was really too much. She remembered having shut the window on that Sevugan chap's face. Catch her catching something. She had gone quietly to her boss's seat where the poor thing was dozing. He did so every couple of hours for a few minutes each time. His mind wandered then to where he heard the music of the spheres. He did not mind silent dreams either. Just spheres. Dick Wimalawardene was seeing one such silent film on the silver screen of his mind when Priyani had gone up to where he was seated. She stood directly in front of his eyes, the symmetrical quintessence of femininity. She had informed him of the cholera gently, giving him time, giving him time . . . 'We . . . no, the staff rose to the occasion although there was a small delay . . . no, an unavoidable delay of two stroke three deaths . . . or, days. I stroke my staff. Priyani! What's so funny?'

'Well, where were we?' Priyani told him where they had been. Wimalawardene recalled the lines and forgot the subject. Softly biting her lips, Priyani suggested that Ambalavaner, the chief clerk, be asked to put up a draft to the superintendent. 'He has gone into the subject with the kanganis,' she informed her boss.

Ambalavaner was a cousin of Sriskandanathar, but a couple of years younger. 'Smart Amby,' they called him.

'We need not reply to him, sir. We can write to the DHS and mark him a copy.'

'Yes, yes. That is what I was going to suggest myself,' said the superintendent.

Was what *he* was going to suggest, Ambalavaner thought. When he does not even know the correct expansion of DHS. How can he? With that Perera girl occupying him before five and that Club, after five.

Tippy-tap, he went. Tippity, tappity, tap, dhuk, dhuk, tap, dhuk, dhrook. Amby rolled out a neatly typed sheet from his machine and sent it into the boss's room. Wimalawardene read it with satisfaction and signed it with a flourish. Better than a rejoinder, a counter-complaint! Must tell the others at the Club this evening.

The letter informed the Director of Health Services that the management had acted 'effectively and in good time' to isolate the cholera cases in the two lines where they occurred. 'But for that timely measure, the incidence would have been unimaginably greater,' it assured the DHS. The estate medical assistants had done everything in their power and were themselves going to refer the cases to the hospital when a 'disgruntled' worker went and made malicious complaints to the medical officer in charge. As to the 'most regrettable' deaths, the letter stated that the traditionally low sense of hygiene among the labourers was the sole cause. Had they cared to seek advice or diagnosis when the disease 'first manifested itself', they would not have had to lose so many 'precious' lives.

The letter ended with a request to the DHS to advise the medical officer in charge of the Keselgoda hospital to continue the treatment of the patients 'still not quite out of their sorry pass' rather than 'hurl baseless accusations against a management and personnel who have done their duty as they best understand it.'

Ambalavaner had marked copies of the letter not only to the doctor but also to the other superintendents. One copy, not officially so marked, was sent by him to the district's association of clerks in governmental organizations, and one other, to the all-island association of subordinate medical attendants.

Tilakaratne and Pieris greeted Wimalawardene at the Club the following evening as their natural leader.

'Good show, Dick!' Tilakaratne waxed.

Pieris held Wimalawardene's hand in silent admiration.

'We have to tell the doctor where he gets off,' Wimalawardene explained. 'We have not been planting since yesterday, have we?' Tilakaratne and Pieris shook their heads in grey agreement. 'Podiyan!' the superintendent of Cork shouted. 'A round and make it stiff.'

Nimal had been disturbed by the Wimalawardene letter. It seemed to make surface sense. Had Dr Baptist been a trifle hasty after all? He called for the doctor's letter and reread it. There was sense in that too and he liked, subconsciously, its tone of righteous indignation. He admired the hauteur. But, finally, having placed both the letters on the scale of his professional discrimination, he fancied Wimalawardene's weighed with him more. Surely the doctor had trespassed into the superintendent's jurisdiction in making all those allegations. Nimal remembered his own sense of unease when Dr Baptist had spoken at length that evening at the Club, about estate labour. He had somehow felt encroached upon, although he allowed neither words nor expression to convey this to his guest. He had also imagined, that evening, the presence by proxy of that priest, Father Gio. He was certainly an interfering type, that Italian.

Not happy about being in two minds, Nimal decided to drive down to the Club where the others were bound to be and discuss the matter.

He showered and changed into cool white clothes. Slipping on a buff-coloured cravat and a soft brown sports jacket over his shirt, Nimal looked at himself in the mirror. Approving the reflection, he reminded himself of what his fellow student Mustafa Pirzada had told him some two years earlier at Oxford. He, Pirzada and Ronald Manners were dressing in his digs for an evening at the theatre. Ronald chafed him about his devotion to smartness and Mustafa came up with an original contribution. 'You do not look Byronic, my friend. People here can think of no other example. You have the looks of a camel boy somewhere in the deserts of Arabia: supple limbs, clean sharp features. Ready for the exhausting sameness of miles and miles of sand. And ready too for the surprise of enemy bullets.' Mustafa gesticulated to describe the expanse of the desert. Coming to the bullets, he narrowed his lips, closed an eye, and pulled an imaginary machine-gun trigger to the sound of ballistics from between his teeth. Nimal responded by feigning instant death and slumping on his bed. 'It looks like we need not go very far for theatre,' Ronald had said, prompting them to get to the show on time. It was Eliot's *Murder in the Cathedral.*

Revving his cold jeep, Nimal kept hearing two lines from that play:

Where is Becket, the traitor to the King?
Where is Becket, the meddling priest?

He stepped on the accelerator hard. It was good to feel the motor coming on like that. Within minutes Nimal was turning into the Club driveway.

'Ah, Rupasinghe! Join us!' Wimalawardene greeted him patronizingly. The others shifted chairs to fit an extra one into the circle. Podiyan rushed to relieve the dorais of the strain involved in that operation. Wincing ever so slightly at the proximity to his colleagues, Nimal sat down and crossed his legs. Doing so, he noticed how poorly the socks and shoes of the others

compared with his matt-finished browns. 'We were discussing
Dr Baptist's letter and Dick's counter to it,' Tilakaratne informed
Nimal. 'That, in fact, is what I wanted to discuss myself.' 'Look,'
Wimalawardene exclaimed, moving up to the edge of his chair
so that his legs had to be furled under it. 'That man has no
business to ask us the things he has. He should look after
the cases that come to him and not worry about the wide
world outside.' Wimalawardene looked around and waited for
approval. 'My suggestion is that Dick has done what needed
to be done and as for the rest of us, we should keep quiet about
it all,' Tilakaratne said.

Pieris grunted consensus. Six eyes turned to Nimal to seek his
stand. Bats, he said to himself. Bats. I could send them scurrying
out. But Baptist has equated me with them by writing to me in
the same vein. Can't ignore that, can I?

'Well, gentlemen, I would like to view Dr Baptist's
communication at two levels. One, the medical, where his
suggestions for immunization and supervision of estate
dispensaries need to be attended to. We can't have a sick
workforce. Two, the administrative. Now as far as this second
level is concerned, I think I am in agreement with you that the
medical officer in charge of the Keselgoda hospital is not required
to have an extraterritorial concern over the integrity of our staffers.
If his clerk were to come up with any tangible evidence that
implicates any of my men, then, certainly, I would like to be told
about it. But a general hurl of suspicions and accusations gets
one nowhere and, frankly, is professionally unacceptable.' Nimal's
three-man audience listened to him wide-eyed and almost open-
mouthed. They missed the nuances completely but got the general
idea. The Craigavon guy was with them.

'Hear, hear!' Wimalawardene said and would have perhaps
managed to sound sarcastic had he not risen simultaneously and
continued. 'Nimal,' he said. 'Nimal, if I may call you that, and if
I may move on to a more interesting subject, it is our unanimous

wish that you be President of the Club when I relinquish office this year after six years of unbroken stewardship.'

Tilakaratne and Pieris had no conception of this plan but were too overawed by the suddenness and grandeur of Wimalawardene's gesture to dissent. And so they smiled and held their smiles like garlands in the hands of a waiting oriental host.

Among prisoners of circumstances can be found the most independent of persons. Being President of the Keselgoda Club meant nothing, either in terms of authority or prestige. Who knew or cared about it? Reflecting, as he drove out of the Club, on the weightlessness of the crown that had been placed on his head, Nimal tried to define his response. Embarrassment there was. He had been embarrassed into accepting. But there was something else. A sense of discomfort. Nimal was uncomfortable at the compact which their offer and his acceptance represented. A compact, a pact. Had he, Nimal Rupasinghe, joined the company of the bats? He shuddered at the thought.

It was dark and the street lights had come on. At the main thoroughfare in Keselgoda, from a distance of about two hundred yards, he caught a glimpse of Paul and Constance Baptist walking past a row of shops. He saw a few people, Tamils, stopping to greet the couple respectfully. Nimal's first impulse was to move his vehicle to the kerb and to go up to them. But impulses arising from the heart can be checked by amber and red signals beamed from the head. And so he braked and turned into a by-lane instead. He was unfamiliar with the interior of the town and had to thread his way out of that deviation with some difficulty. Going in and out of potholes, Nimal cursed his timidity. Why did he want to avoid a couple whose company he had sought only the other day?

The question was rhetorical. He knew the answer. In the chaturanga of a planter's world you were either on the black or the white side. A sentient chessman might dislike his assignation but had no choice. He was a prisoner of the ground rules which were precharted for him, rigid, unalterable. Nimal had to proceed on the step-moves laid down for him by unalterable laws. The Baptists were in the opposite camp, as was Father Gio and all the labourers they had identified themselves with. Nimal Rupasinghe was not expected to meet them except in order to confront them, to transmit and to receive rays of tension, intertwined with challenge. He was to watch his move, proceed, withdraw, or sidestep to the extent his allotted versatility permitted him. For the present, the equestrian knight had lifted its forelegs and done the sidestep and onward trot that was required of it when faced with an adversary.

On seeing his cousin's retort (he knew it could not be the superintendent) Sriskandanathar summoned Nandasena to his desk. 'Read this, da,' he said, squeezing the assistant's arm in unconcealed glee. 'At our level, your wonderful plan. At their level, this letter. Read it, da.' Sriskandanathar stuck his tongue between his teeth and winked.

'Our' level was underground. It had been reached the previous evening. Sriskandanathar, Nandasena, Mohotty the medical assistant from Cork, and Sabhapati had met in the cellar of Charlis's Bar. A poor cousin of Bar Deluxe, this one was operated by Charlis, a dismissed employee of Singho of the Bar Deluxe. The man had kept his links with the parent bar alive through one of Singho's attendant boys. This brat kept Charlis supplied with a not infrequent stolen bottle and, more significantly, with scandal about Singho's customers. This latter supply had proved lucrative for Charlis who had used it on at least half a dozen occasions for fraud and blackmail. A plywood partition divided the Charlis bar room from the cellar. Ranaweera, the boy, had only to sidle up to the partition within the cellar and he could hear very clearly the conversation at two tables adjoining the partition. And he could hear without being seen. The last such case had given Charlis

aesthetic satisfaction as a job well done, apart from the money
it brought in. The soft-footed boy had heard Daud, a visitor,
tell his companion:

'Of the nine packs, two are yours.'

'No use. Nothing but three.'

'Leech! You know I cannot but satisfy the accomplice.'

'Tomorrow then, at ten in the morning. Near the clock tower.
Bring the packs inside a coconut-oil can.'

Ranaweera had gone panting to Charlis and told him of the
plan, the identity of the persons. Charlis knew Daud's house. He
thought for a while and then sent the boy with a note (which was
sealed so that the boy would not read it) to be slid under Daud's
door. The note changed the rendezvous. It told Daud that the
clock tower was suddenly unsafe and that the three packs
should be placed inside a basket of avocados and kept among
half a dozen such which Daud would find on the luggage carried
at the top of the 7 a.m. bus bound for Galle the next day. Daud
was also advised not to tarry at the bus stand but to go away as
soon as the basket had been loaded.

Charlis arranged for six avocado baskets to be placed on the
carrier of the bus and himself travelled in it like an innocuous
passenger. He looked away when he saw Daud turn up with a
basket of avocados and have it loaded on to the bus. Charlis got
off two stops away, had all seven baskets offloaded and brought
them home. Chemical narcotics the packs contained. He was in
big, anonymous, luck. He chuckled when he heard three days
later that Daud had been arrested by the police on a tip-off from
a disappointed accomplice turned approver.

Such was Charlis, host for Sriskandanathar, Nandasena,
Mohotty and Sabhapati. The fivesome went into the cellar.
Sriskandanathar was quite uncomfortable. The dark atmosphere
of that arrack-hole nauseated him. For the others the place was
not all that unfamiliar and, besides, the business was pressing.
They sat down at a dealwood table on stools. A naked dust-covered

bulb shone over their heads. For about ten minutes Charlis queried the others on what had happened. And then, holding a pen in his left hand, wrote:

Most Honered Diructur Health Servis

Your Doctor Baptis mischief makin. Sayin helpin labrers realy helpin himsulf. Chek and you knowin. Bar Deluxe givin brandy botls to doctor in name of cholra labrers. Where goin brandy botls? Chek and you knowin. Hittin poore Clarc for old anger no mistek Clarc. Doctor askin Mason job hospital even realy for hot water for his bath and askin Ero Cinema michif frend to giv koolr for kool water all for bunglow in name of cholra and hospital. Chek and you knowin. Lot other mischif doin bad name hospital bringin. Your honer wantin knowin more we tellin. Your honer please interdic Baptis.

'Ayyo, the spellings!' Sriskandanathar exclaimed from the depths of his excitement. 'Good that the spellings are all wrong. No one will think we have written it,' analysed Nandasena.

When the company crept out of Charlis's cellar room, it found the gentle breeze outside too strong, the open faces and assured gaits of the average man in the street too alien, and the absence of a pollutive darkness altogether too much to take in one exposure. The men slunk away in different directions, Nandasena carrying the letter in a nondescript brown envelope to be posted.

Bryan de Silva, the Director of Health Services, generally had his mail opened for him by peons, reserving for his own thumb and forefinger only those letters which were addressed to him by name. By the form of the address on this cover, therefore, the Keselgoda letter came to be opened for him. It was part of a stack of letters and might have been missed were it not for PURSONEL written shakily across its top. Bryan de Silva was not unused to receiving anonymous letters. But whenever he did, he suffered palpitations. At his age and health (he was fifty-four and had 'heart') he could not afford to be provoked. He feared, every time he saw such a letter, that it would contain an accusation against himself. His retirement, his pension, was at stake. And whenever, by a quick vertical glance at the text, he found other names, not his, a wave of relief passed over him, smoothing the ruffled nerves. That is what happened with de Silva that morning. Noting that the letter was for and not about him, he crossed himself and lit a cigarette. It was not time yet for his first smoke but the circumstances justified it.

Sending dragon-like fume jets out of his nose, he wondered about Paul. No smoke without fire. The letters, one from the superintendent of one of those Irish-owned estates and then this. How was one to ignore them?

'Chi, chi,' Ambalavaner said to his cousin in contempt. 'You should not have joined these low characters. We can get the doctor put in his place without soiling our hands.'

Having asserted this attitudinal edge over his cousin, Ambalavaner made a mental note of Mohotty's involvement and of what could be done strictly between him and the medical assistant—back at Cork. There was that divergence he had noticed last month between the dispensary stocks and the inventory.

Sriskandanathar was abashed. He had asked Ambalavaner home to Craigavon for lunch and, in a moment of weakness, told him of the meeting in the cellar and the nameless petition to the DHS. He regretted having mentioned it to Ambalavaner. The man wants to act superior, he noted. But Sriskandanathar was not going to be unduly worried. Blood, even at one remove, was thicker than water.

Paul had just returned to his house from the day's sixth round of the isolation ward. He had noted, with some satisfaction, that of the cholera victims admitted, only one—a very old man—had succumbed. Paul calculated that within a fortnight the last patient would have been treated and discharged.

He was surprised to see a cover waiting for him. It had the rubber stamp of the superintendent of Cork gleaming at one end of it. He has replied promptly, Paul thought, and opening it, wondered what its contents were like.

It has been said that man is not merely a flask of amino acids. Paul, for one, was a great many things besides. And yet, on seeing his copy of the Wimalawardene letter, it was as if into the acids of his personality a pill of contrary effervescence had been dropped. A column of bubbling rage rose from somewhere inside his being and tore its way up to his brain.

'Constance!' he called, reddening. 'Look at this.'

She went through it slowly and fell silent. Placing her hand on his, she interlocked their fingers. So they sat for several seconds. What would I have done without her? Paul thought. And then, resting his gaze on their clasped hands, he imagined she was transfusing his blood system with a stream of tranquillizing fluids.

A few minutes later their doorbell rang. Constance saw an ochreous gleam at the clefts in the door. 'Oh, the Venerable Seevali, I am sure,' she said and hurried to open the door. Paul rose to wait for the monk's entry.

'I have heard much of you, sir,' Paul said to him, bowing deeply. 'And I, of you,' replied Venerable Seevali. He introduced Colin, who had also come. Sitting down, the monk continued 'We had come to Keselgoda for a *dané* and met there a Tamil schoolteacher from one of the nearby estates. He told me that his sister and her two children had been stricken by cholera and that you, your wife and your staff restored them to life. We thought we would visit you and tell you this before returning to Ratnapura.'

'Very kind of you, sir.'

'But there has been some unpleasantness also, nein?'

'Yes, sir. There has been unpleasantness.'

'If you can for a while reflect on what has happened, you might be able to understand the episode better. By understanding it you might be able to overcome the feeling of unpleasantness.'

'I am not sure I would know how to go about it, sir.'

'May I suggest a few steps?'

'Please.'

'You could begin by draining your mind of all its thoughts on the subject. Like you would an abscess, after it has been lanced. And, thereafter, you could consider the bare facts of the episode. Consider the facts, attend to them, without interpreting or evaluating them. You may find that you have so far seen but fragments of the episode. Seen in all its totality, the factual condition, the episode, may not even seem unpleasant. You may find, then, that your responses are under your discipline and not the other way about.'

'A physician is being physicked,' Paul said and won from Venerable Seevali the smile that Constance had described. 'Buddhism, in fact, uses the analogy of medicine to exemplify mental discipline. A surgeon cannot afford to become agitated by the condition of his patient. He must, if he is to help his patient, hold his knife in steady hands.'

Colin asked Constance and Paul if they had ever been told of the etymology of *thero*, the honorific suffix that is applied to names of Buddhist monks in Sri Lanka, Thailand and Burma. He explained that the word is derived from the Sanskrit *sthavira* and incorporates a range of adjectives—untrembling, unwavering, resolute, steadfast. Theravada, the Buddhist system which obtains in Sri Lanka, Colin said, meant 'the School of the Steadfast'.

'It is interesting and rewarding to go into the origins of words, nein? By studying the origins of words one can see their full scope. The etymon, the primary word, is the true core of the word.' And then, with a twinkle, the monk said, 'I have often wondered whether *thero* is not, in remote ancestry, connected with the Greek *therapeuo* meaning "to wait on, to cure" from which "therapy" is derived.'

The monk and Colin left after a while. Paul felt a sense of almost physical wholesomeness after that discussion.

Later that day, in his office room, Paul closed his eyes. A procession of patients passed through his mind. Numb and dry, they all were. They needed warmth, care, and medicines. He had provided those. But someone who viewed patients without sympathy, without care, someone who probably had pressing problems of his own which precluded thought for others, had decided to exploit those patients. Facts. Bare facts. Paul had learnt of this someone and—exploded. Fact. Bare fact. He could, instead, have gone up to Sabhapati and told him in cool and measured tones that he had learnt of what Sabhapati had been doing. He could have got him to return the money to the individuals and could have asked Sabhapati, thereafter, to ponder the act and, if Sabhapati thought it fit, to resign in expiation. To the superintendents, instead of writing the kind of letter he had, he could have shared his information with them, explained his fears to them. Nimal Rupasinghe would have arranged a meeting with all of them.

But what of the future? What of this letter from Cork?

A few, very few, bubbles of anger started to rise inside Paul again. But midway up, drew back and settled down.

I will just let that letter be. My intentions, my actions, are known to me. I know them to be guiltless. They cannot be affected by others' interpretations. The etymon, the core word, is unaffected by later additions to the word. The letter from Cork is immaterial. It does not touch my action. I will go on with my work. If others, my patients, my colleagues, wish to speak on it, they could. I will be steadfast.

Ten days later, after all but three of the cholera cases had been discharged, two letters were delivered at the hospital. They were both from the office of the DHS. One was for Sabhapati, interdicting him on the basis of Paul's report to the DHS. The other, marked 'confidential', was for Paul. It asked Paul to meet the DHS at Colombo for an urgent discussion.

Bryan de Silva couldn't look Paul in the face. Smoking nervously, with his face turned to the wall behind Paul, he told him that an inquiry into certain complaints pertaining to his handling of the cholera ward had been instituted and that, in the interests of an effective inquiry and in order to save Paul embarrassment, could Paul take three months' leave? Dr Lakshman Samarawickreme would hold temporary charge of the hospital.

Whether because of Venerable Seevali or for some other reason, Paul was unaffected by this development. He would go on leave at once, he said. But for six, not three, months. He had 'accumulated' that much leave, never having needed it earlier. He would, under rules, be paid a part of his full salary during the leave. And that was going to help.

Emerging from the office building, Paul wondered where they were to go!

Constance suggested a tour by road of places in the island they had not seen or had not seen properly. She wanted a tight itinerary for the first few days.

'Can't let Paul brood over what has happened,' she wrote to Sujata. 'It could affect him irreparably.'

Leaving their heavier possessions in a hired godown in Keselgoda, the Baptists drove out of their hospital residence the following Saturday morning. Their first stopover was to be within the town, at Father Gio's. They had been invited by the priest to spend at least a fortnight with him. '*Dottore*, would Verdi forgive me if I did not do this? Would your patients, the estate workers?' he said when Paul apologized for the inconvenience.

It was evening. Kandan walked slowly towards the lines.

'Oh, there you are, Kandan,' Peramayi called to her son. 'I was wondering where you'd gone.' Perumal, who was chopping firewood outside the lines was also relieved to see his son back. Kandan had got into the habit of disappearing for the entire day and returning late in the evening. But masculine egoism made him correct his old woman.

'He's past the age when you should worry about where he has gone.'

'So he is. But it is a mother's nature to worry,' Peramayi sighed. 'What do you men know of our worries? Have you or Kandan even *begun* to worry about Valli? She is no girl now. It is time you men thought of a groom for her.'

This was the first time the subject of Valli's marriage had come to be mentioned. Valli and Theiva were in their room but could hear the old woman. Valli started at her grandmother's words. For one thing, Sinnathal, who had first spoken to Valli about it all, had been rather vivid in her descriptions. Valli had been greatly troubled by this and had put on a very brave face the day 'it' happened. For another, coming of age, marriage and childbearing were—like two leaves and a bud—all of a piece, a piece that lay with her mother in the dust of death. And they invoked memories, not of life but of death, of Amara.

Peramayi lost no time in reeling off names. Velu's was the first to be mentioned, to Theiva's great delight. 'He'll ask you for his food by blowing the conch!' she told her sister. 'And you'll have to learn to say, in sign language, that it isn't ready!'

Sinnathal's brother, Arumugam, the sub-kangani, was the second to be named. Sinna came out of her room, child in hand, and smiled at the suggestion approvingly. Arumugam had been a worker in the tea factory. He had studied up to grade four and could read and write. 'There is only that thing about his fingers,' Peramayi said. Arumugam had got the index finger of his left hand caught in the leaf-roller in the factory. This machine rolled out partially dried green leaf into convenient twists before it was further processed. The leaf bunches had to be pushed into the machine by one hand while the other turned the iron rollers. Arumugam had been a second too late to withdraw his left hand and the roller had pinned his finger down. It was permanently twisted now, useless for joint action with the thumb. But Arumugam's good record of work had been taken into account and he had, after a time, been promoted to the supervisory position of sub-kangani.

'But the finger does not matter very much,' Peramayi continued while Sinna nodded vigorously in approval. 'And Sinna has always wanted Valli to marry her brother.'

Before Peramayi could come up with a third name, Valli came out of her room and intervened. 'Appayi, you tell us how many suitors you rejected before marrying grandfather.' Everyone was delighted at the turn Valli had given to the conversation. Peramayi became very coy. The years dropped from her face as she spoke. 'Well, if you really want to know . . .'

'We do, we do,' Theiva screamed and the two girls came up and sat down in front of their grandmother. Kandan, who had been sitting in a corner of his room all this while also came out to the veranda and stood at his door to hear his mother. Perumal stopped chopping and looked up to listen, a smile hovering over his lips. Assured of three generations of audience, Peramayi touched up her hair, stroked the old ornaments and earrings she wore. The vertical tattoo mark on her foreheard seemed to brighten as she began.

'Let me see. There was Sengottuvan from the next estate. A bit cross-eyed, he was. My father said I should marry him because the boy's father and he were from our old village—Marudampatti—in Pudukkottai. But as soon as the match was fixed, a fat woman, Sundari she called herself, came to our lines and said Sengottuvan belonged to her and had been living with her. Prove it, my father challenged her. I will, Sundari said turning to go and returned a moment later with a baby on her hip, cross-eyed exactly like Sengottuvan! And that was that.'

When the hilarity raised by this account had subsided, Perumal said to his old woman. 'Tell them about Murugan also.' 'Oh, Murugan. Well, that story is a bit sad,' Peramayi breathed heavily and nostalgically. 'Murugan was not fixed for me by my father. He belonged to a different caste. It was I who had thought Murugan would be a good husband. Really good-looking, he was. Tall and lithe.'

Something stirred inside Valli's consciousness. It stirred under her skin, within her bones. 'He could carry big piles of firewood on his two shoulders as lightly as if they were two babies. And when he lifted the load the muscles on his arms and shoulders would firm up. Like this.' Peramayi made swift rounded gestures above her shoulders. 'This Murugan was always called in at festivals to help with the drums and the crackers for he was as brave as he was tough. There was to be a temple festival at that time. Murugan got down a roll of one hundred crackers to be set off at the start of the festivities.' Peramayi choreographed the one hundred by shaking her forefinger to signify the number so vigorously that her *koppu* trembled. 'The roll had one hundred wicks to it but Murugan couldn't somehow get them to spark. And so he took the roll under the tamarind tree where the drum was being warmed and showed it to the fire in order to get the damp out. But, my lord, no sooner had he sat down to do this than the entire thing—all the one hundred—exploded in his hands. What a blast there was! Three of his fingers were blown off as well as most of his palm up to the wrist. Oh, that poor man.'

Peramayi's audience fell very silent at this account. Theiva had great trouble in suppressing a question that nagged her: but why didn't she marry him? Theiva felt her grandfather, who had now resumed chopping, might not like the question. Peramayi supplied the answer herself. 'The festival couldn't take place that year as a result and I was told that what had happened was a bad omen, that I should not have thought of marrying outside my caste and that because he was also keen about it, a demon above that tamarind tree had blasted our plan. They all said I should put Murugan out of my mind.'

Everyone had forgotten, by this time, that it was the subject of Valli's future marriage that had started the discussion. But Valli did not forget.

Twice a week, on Tuesdays and Fridays, the thought of marriage, of man and woman, would come pounding back to her. For Tuesdays and Fridays were the days when the old fish vendor from near Keselgoda and his son came selling fish in the estate. And, unknown to others, for a couple of months now, Valli looked out for them, for the son.

She had seen him earlier. But it was only after her coming of age that she began to notice him. Passing the father and son one afternoon about a year ago, she had suddenly felt a strange sensation inside her. He was short, light-skinned and muscular. Bare-chested, he wore a red sarong that was turned up at the knees. He walked briskly carrying a yoke-pole across his right shoulder. Two shallow wicker baskets were suspended from the pole at its two ends, loaded with fish. The young man's right hand rested on the pole keeping it horizontal. A thin silver chain lay around his neck, clinging to his skin. The father, wearing a cloth round his head, a shirt held together by safety pins and a white sarong, walked ahead of the son. He carried on his covered head a wooden block on which the fish were to be chopped, and a knife. He gave, every few seconds as they walked, their vendor's call: *maalooo-ohmalu-malu-maaloooh*.

Father and son would go first to the superintendent's bungalow where the best fish were bought, then to the supervisory and clerical staff quarters. Rarely, if ever, did they stop at the lines for there was virtually no one in those who could afford fish. Besides, they were always in a hurry to return to Keselgoda.

Only Valli knew that it was with the fishermen's passing

through in mind that she had chosen those two days of the week for staying back.

Only she knew. Dare she let another know? The young man was Sinhalese, she Tamil. They belonged to two different worlds. No one intended them to come together. Could oil mix with water?

And yet, Valli had persisted in her fool's indulgence. For several weeks now, at the sound of the older man's call, Valli would come out to the veranda and see the men pass. Last Friday, for the first time, the son looked up. Their eyes met. She noticed for the first time that his lips were full and, she thought, relaxed in a half-smile. Did he intend a message in that smile? Or was it her imagination? The blood pounded in her heart and in her ears at that moment. She noticed, after the two men had passed, that the earthen floor where she stood was damp from the sweat she had broken into.

Father Gio was deeply affected by the details of the hospital episode that Paul gave him. 'You are a good Christian, *dottore*. Your work for the cholera victims was very important. It was spontaneous, powerful. It was the result of what we Italians call *sympatica*. The impetus came from within you, from your nature, your temperament, and actuated you. Like water moving a turbine.'

Paul told him of the advice Venerable Seevali had given. The padre was unimpressed. 'With due respect to the scholar-monk, I must say it is not natural to expect you, an impassioned man, to become so coldly calculated in your actions. You are propelled by the vita activa, not the vita contemplativa. I know it, *dottore*.

Constance asked Father Gio what he thought of Paul's having struck Sabhapati. 'Ah, that. Yes. There perhaps your husband could have restrained himself. That was a spilling over of the emotions. But you know, do you not, that when in Jerusalem, Christ saw money changers and people who sold captured doves inside the Temple, he drove them all out with a whip and cast their tables out behind them, shouting: "My Father's house is a house of prayer, but ye have made it a den of thieves." You know that, do you not? No, signora, the entire hospital episode is of a piece. It has what logicians call internal consistency.'

Father Gio then gave his guests his perception of the nature of the support that estate labourers need. He opened the palm of his left hand, each digit held wide apart. And he ticked, as he spoke, a point on each. 'The first task is to give them spiritual or, if you wish to sound secular, emotional support. They must realize that they are part of humanity, that they matter. Second, professional support. They must be backed up in their legitimate demands as employees for else they will continue to be regarded as pairs of hands and legs that are to be used by the estates like machines. Third, social support. If it is established that like everybody else they are mobile, they can travel and seek jobs outside their community, they will not be so easy to push around. Fourth, educational support. They must realize that education is their human right and can enable them to transcend their present occupational shackles. Why should they be tappers and pluckers forever? They should be able to become doctors, engineers, lawyers. Fifth, political support. They must have franchise, nationality.

'Their disfranchisement,' Father Gio said, 'is unbelievable. It is indefensible. This country won its freedom in 1947 and, within two years, denied that very freedom to almost a tenth of its population. Hundreds of thousands were made stateless and they are asked to go to India. To India! Why not to Timbuctoo? What is India to them? A distant memory of grandparents. *Dottore*, you tell me, are there many instances of such all-round deprivation among peoples?'

Paul's well-informed mind thought of a few parallels. But he chose not to mention them. The musician in him did not permit discordance at such moments. And besides, he argued, the fact that there is injustice elsewhere is no excuse for letting an injustice in one's immediate environment go unchallenged. Gadflies were needed in all societies. Father Gio was the gadfly here.

A couple of days after they had moved to Father Gio's, Constance made a trip to Limerick to see Sujata. Paul had no engagements in Keselgoda and could have gone. But he was not sure how the dorai would like that and so decided to stay back and read.

On the way, Constance stopped at the tree where she had seen the oriole nest. But there was no nest this time, only its remains. A raptor had been through it, leaving it in shreds. A coucal, she thought. Or just crows. Constance could not look for the disturbed birds or the predator. She did not want to leave Paul. How snug the nest had looked last time!

Sujata was unwell and in bed. Her grey-white hair was spread out on the pillow, like a halo round her head. She asked Constance to sit beside her and had tea served. 'You *can't* imagine how sad I am about it all. And I was so sure we would be able to meet often.' Constance told her they would do so yet, Sabhapati notwithstanding. Sujata was not sure. She had become very depressed, she said, after reading a poem in the Sunday papers. It was by a tourist. She had it brought and shown to Constance.

Black crows against leaden skies
Two monks walk by the Kandy lake
Nothing lasts, they say to me
Nothing
Not even memory.
That, they say,
Goes in an instant
At the moment of death

'Strange,' Constance told Sujata, 'crows were very much on my mind as I drove up.' She explained her happy discovery of the nests the last time she was coming up and the disappointment now. 'Oh dear,' Sujata said and sank further into her pillow.

But a moment later, she remembered something and revived from her dumps. 'Constance, I have checked on the possibility you mentioned of the cholera outbreak being linked to some festival or the other. Your hunch was absolutely right.'

Constance was most interested. She had written to Sujata of her hunch, as Sujata called it, and had asked Sujata to try and find out if any festival had been organized at Cork to which the story could be traced.

'A meeting took place at Cork just about the time of the outbreak there, of the trade union's temple sub-committee. They decided that the worship of Mariamman this year should be a grand affair and the temple sub-committees on the other three Maradeniya estates should also get together and organize a big joint celebration. Well, some men from Cork visited Limerick here, and Armagh and Craigavon in that connection. They stayed on those estates for a few days and were *sick* themselves. So you can see how the microbe travelled.'

Constance reflected on this information for a while. Wanting to propitiate the goddess and seek her security, these men had unwittingly acted as conveyors of disease.

'So is the grand temple festival to take place?' she asked Sujata. 'That's the thing, dear. They are determined to go ahead with the plan. Most ill advised it will be. We *must* get them to postpone it.' Constance agreed. But a sense of helplessness crept over her. What was she to do? Paul held no official position now. And what could she do by herself?

Back at Father Gio's she mentioned the problem to him. 'It must be postponed,' the padre said.

Paul cautioned him. 'Your suggesting the postponement of a Hindu festival can be misunderstood, Father.' 'But I am suggesting postponement, not a cancellation. I would put off any programme of the church in the same circumstances.'

'I am sure you would, Father. But not everyone is objective in matters such as this.'

'I see you have taken Venerable Seevali very seriously,' Father Gio said with a mischievous twinkle. 'Don't you worry. I will go about this very circumspectly.' He pronounced the last word with great deliberation.

Later that evening, he met two Tamil residents of Keselgoda, Sellamuthu and Rajaratnam. Of Indian origin, these gentlemen were trading partners in a small business concern. Rajaratnam was the young, energetic local correspondent for *Samudayam*, a Tamil daily published from Colombo. Father Gio put it to Sellamuthu, who happened to be President of the Keselgoda Indian Tamil Association, whether it would not be appropriate if the Association expressed its appreciation of Dr Baptist's work for the cholera victims.

Sellamuthu, a cheerful, rotund man in his late forties, received the suggestion enthusiastically. He and his fellow members of the Association were well-to-do men. They had education, and some clout. They belonged to castes higher than those of the kinsmen of the estates. Sellamuthu belonged to the pillai community of Hindus. The pillai, like the mudaliar and the chettiar, formed part of a non-estate immigration to Ceylon in the last decade of the nineteenth century. They were members of the mercantile castes back in India and had shrewdly calculated that the thousands of estate Tamils would need retail ends of an Indian hue and fragrance. They also anticipated, very rightly, that the estate Tamils would have problems in liquidity. Nothing would inspire confidence among them as an urban Tamil pawnbroker. They came, therefore, on the trail of the estate immigrants, settling down in towns like Keselgoda that were close to estates. They maintained links with south India through frequent journeys, and supplies. And they maintained a cultural identity through social and cultural associations. They took care to see that they did not offend the Sinhala majority or the authorities. Business prudence suggested harmony. Their difference from the estate Tamils was of degree only. There could be occasions when the more enlightened among the urban Indian Tamils saw the condition of the estate workers and reacted as they should. This was one such occasion.

Sellamuthu had heard of the entire episode and had been confirmed in his long-held dim view of Sabhapati. 'The man has never paid his subscription for the Association,' Sellamuthu told Father Gio. 'Nor does he pay his *Samudayam* delivery bills in time,' Rajaratnam complained. 'I have stopped supplying the paper to him.'

The two men undertook to have a resolution passed at the next meeting of the General Body, expressing appreciation of the good doctor's work.

'There is one other little matter,' Father Gio said. 'I understand there is a plan to hold a big temple festival one of these days. As I know, such functions are held to propitiate deities, to ward off evil, to seek protection. Now as far as the present time is concerned, the disease is already upon us although Dr Baptist has, to a large extent, checked it. I think you should advise the temple sub-committees to postpone the celebration by at least a month and then to celebrate it even more grandly as a thanks-giving service in my chapel before the Blessed Mary while the estate priest does so before the Goddess Mari.'

Sellamuthu and Rajaratnam were in total agreement.

The following week, when the General Body met at the hall attached to the local temple, Sellamuthu produced a draft resolution on the subject of Dr Baptist's work. He read it out to the gathering. A couple of members stood up and objected.

'The doctor hit one of our members. It is amazing that you want us to pass a resolution praising him.'

'The motive behind the idea is not clear.'

But many others stood up in support of the resolution.

'Our estate brothers and sisters—scores of them—were saved by the doctor.'

'The resolution is necessary, good.'

'Yes, it is good.'

The draft was amended, after a discussion, by Rajaratnam. A reference to the misfortune of the doctor's transfer was deleted. Similarly, in the mention of 'the doctor's devotion to duty and integrity,' the second attribute was dropped. The resolution was carried by 34 votes to 2, the dissenters being a cousin of Sabhapati's and the member who had raised the objection at the beginning.

Rajaratnam arranged to have almost the entire text printed in his paper two days later. He cycled across to Father Gio's with a copy. Seeing Paul there, he gave it to him with a slight bow. Paul thanked Rajaratnam and, after being given an oral gist of the report, asked Rajaratnam to convey his thanks to the Association. 'I am pleasantly surprised by this and very grateful,' he said with a faint blush on his face. And then anxious to take the conversation away from himself and from his work, he asked Rajaratnam, 'I have often wanted to ask someone what the meaning of your paper's name is.' Rajaratnam explained that *Samudayam*, when pronounced correctly, with the 'a' in the middle elongated to an 'aa', meant 'society'. But pronounced as it is spelt in English, without the elongated 'aa' in the middle, the name still had an accidentally appropriate meaning: 'Equal Dawn'. So one could choose the pronunciation, Rajaratnam said, and not displease the newspaper.

But Constance was not happy about the press report. 'It will rekindle animosities, Paul' she said. 'I think we'd better leave Keselgoda while the going is good!' Calpurnian, Paul called her foreboding. Constance, looking unusually grim, said, 'I suppose every married woman has something of Caesar's wife in her.'

But it was not Paul who was to attract violence.

Father Gio stopped by at Sellamuthu's later that day and, in a totally open manner, declaimed, 'Good resolution, my friend. Good press report. I hope those who manipulated the doctor's transfer will recall it and feel ashamed and afraid to repeat such an act.'

Even Sellamuthu was a bit taken aback by the effusive nonchalance of the padre. He looked around to see who the people were who had heard Father Gio. There were some dozen people. Anyone of them could be a friend of Sabhapati's, Sellamuthu thought. The Father should not have said that bit about ashamed and afraid.

'I hope the festival matter is also taken care of,' Father Gio continued. 'Yes Father,' Sellamuthu said a little irritably. 'We discussed that also. Your suggestion has been accepted. The temple sub-committee is going to be advised to postpone.'

'Very good, very good,' Father Gio said as he waved goodbye.

Can't the man be a bit discreet? Sellamuthu wondered. He had seen three or four of his customers melt away behind the padre. Any of them could have misunderstood him, Sellamuthu thought. Or me.

One evening, a couple of days later, Father Gio went to a small chapel at Imbulwatte, a village three furlongs out of Keselgoda, to conduct a service. A family of estate workers had requested it. A child had been born in the family after many years of miscarriages, infant deaths. The service was in Tamil. Father Gio enunciated each word fully, correctly. The congregation, a handful of families, was seated on half a dozen benches. The pulpit was the entire trunk of a jack tree, sawn chest-high. Two rows of candles burned softly on either side of a cross painted simply on the wall as Father Gio read out, prayed, spoke. He was unaffected by the occasional wails of some children, the racking cough of Samivel from Armagh, an old parishioner, whom Father Gio had christened Samuel.

The service over, Father Gio walked back towards Keselgoda in long brisk strides. The white of his clerk's habit made the surrounding darkness darker. When he had covered almost two-thirds of the distance he could see the lights of the town a furlong

away. Father Gio was still on the very rural highway when he
heard, suddenly, a footfall behind him. Fearless though he was,
Father Gio was not a naive man. Something told him the sound
he heard was not innocuous. He stopped and turned round. No
one. Only the empty road and bushes. He resumed his walk,
heartbeat and gait slightly faster than before. Footfalls again.
Turning round abruptly, he shouted 'Who's there?' Two men,
like shadows, leaped on him. They carried iron rods. One came
down on his head. Father Gio felt the hot blood as it came down
over his forehead. And then the pain. His spectacles fell. He could
not see. Anticipation of further blows paralysed him. The second
blow was on his left forearm, intense pain and then numbness.
He dropped to the ground. He was convinced they were going to
finish him. Father Gio felt the rosary plucked from his neck. The
men mumbled something and then took to their heels. They had,
apparently, decided to hit, to steal, and then to run. *Dio Mio*,
he breathed. Wanting to lift his hands to his head he found his
left hand would not move. He picked it up with his good right
arm. Indescribable pain. What was he to do? He got on to his
feet, very slowly. Blood, sweat and tears, he said to himself, are
blinding me. Father Gio asked Jesus why he had forsaken him.
O Gesu, perche mi hai abbandonato? He wiped his eyes with the
right-hand sleeve of his habit. His spectacles lay on the ground,
their arms pointing upwards pathetically. He stooped to pick them
up. But how could he? His right arm was supporting his broken
left one. It could not be disengaged. He squatted, resting the
broken arm gently on his lap. Again, indescribable pain. Then,
with the right arm freed for the moment, he lifted and put on his
spectacles. Fortunately, the lenses, made of good Milan glass,
were intact. The lights of Keselgoda seemed miles away.

Some minutes later, Father Gio was walking slowly, very
slowly, towards the town. *Himself He could not save.* The
words kept coming to him. *Himself He could not save.* Shame!
Gio scolded his ego. To think of His suffering and mine in the

same breath! To confound this miserable experience of mine with His. Shame.

At the entrance to the town, the headlights of a passing vehicle captured his bleeding, bruised frame. The vehicle stopped.

Father Gio must have had a total blackout at that point for the next thing he knew was seeing, dimly, Paul's elegant head bent over him. He was in hospital. Paul, no longer in charge, was in ordinary clothes. Dr Lakshman Samarawickreme, masked and cloaked was ministering to him.

'He's coming to, Lakshman,' Paul was saying. 'Another shot, I think.' A not unpleasant jab, and Father Gio slept.

Soma was the eldest of five, all the others being girls. And so his parents called him *ranputha*, meaning golden child, or *malputha*, meaning child-flower. Fish vendor's children, like those of estate labourers, are not automatic school material. Soma, therefore, had not been to school, learning whatever he knew about the world by observation. Of his ancestral calling, of course, he knew everything that could be known. Did not his genes ensure that? Of the karawa or fisher caste, his hand had been dealt for him.

Since the age of seven he had joined his father on vending rounds. Soma carried the chopping block and knife then and gave the fish call in his shrill-sweet voice, his father following him with the basket-pole. The father was ageing now and Soma was a young man. Their vending order had therefore been reversed.

Seelawathi, his mother, was one of the gentlest of persons. Reed-thin, one could scarcely believe she was the mother of five. She cooked their simple but ample meals of rice and curry, scrubbed, ran their two-roomed house and attended to the myriad needs of her growing children with complete self-possession. She was unlettered too but held her own in simple arithmetic. This she had learnt of necessity because in the late afternoons (the only time she was not preoccupied with the house) she sold fish herself. The smaller type. She had a spot at the Keselgoda market roadside which other fish vendors, by mutual agreement, did not violate. She would spread out her merchandise on two pieces of gunny, one for the dried, the other for the fresh fish. Into a tiny pouch fastened to her wrap she tucked the cash earned. Seelawathi made sure to be back home before dark and before her husband and son returned from their vending round. She heated up the dinner for the family then, and served it individually. For Soma, her most precious possession, she reserved the best portions of whatever was going. The others did not mind. Indeed, they scarcely noticed the discrimination. Soma was their corporate hero.

And yet, the young man was unspoilt. The credit for that went to the father. Stern-faced and of few words, Finando wanted his son to know no comfort that lay beyond their aspirations.

'Karawa we are, for this birth, karawa we will remain. Our kamma has ordained it. Nothing can change it.' He had advised Soma, ten years earlier, not to be absurd when the boy had asked if he could join some others of his age to toddy-climb.

Soma was now nineteen.

There was, however, one exotic indulgence which Finando permitted his son: callisthenics.

'Captain' Sando, as that sixty-one-year-old ex-soldier with a handlebar moustache from Keselgoda called himself, ran a very basic gymnasium in the backyard of his house. The apparatus, in its entirety, consisted of two pairs of parallel bars, one low and the other high, two sets of weights and a pit, eight feet by four, of very soft reddish brown earth from the Kalunganga river bed. Sando's real name was Sandasiri. That most people knew. But there was vagueness about other details of his past. He claimed he had joined the Royal Navy as an Ordinary Seaman in 1933. The Recruiting Officer had taken him on after just one glance, he said, at his splendid eighteen-year-old physique. Of the action seen by him in many theatres of war, Sando related epic sequences. The high point of his narrative was reached when he described how on 5 April 1942 he saw two cruisers, the *Dorsetshire* and the *Cornwall*, sink under Japanese bombing just outside Colombo harbour. How Sando came to be on the HMS *Enterprise* as it rescued hundreds of persons aboard the sinking ships, no one quite knew. But there it was, Sando's graphic account of his strong-armed battles with the waves as he helped men up the flanks of that well-named vessel. 'I went back to the waters thirty-nine times,' Sando would say, 'and each time I brought up two men to safety.'

It was rumoured that Sando's wife, married to him when she was just sixteen, had despaired of his returning from the sea and from the war, and had gone away to Batticaloa to live with a merchant. Sando never referred to her. Ever since his retirement and return on a pension to Keselgoda, he had resolved to compensate his own debilitation by a programme of toughening up the youth of his hometown. Irrespective of creed or race, he made it a point to emphasize. The eclectic tradition of the British Navy had done that for 'Captain' Sando.

He got a stone statue installed of the monkey god Hanuman, patron deity of Hindu wrestlers, near the sandpit along with clay images of the Buddha and Jesus Christ. He insisted that his pupils begin their exercises with a cry of Allah-o-Akbar, to be followed by a silent genuflection before the sandpit Trinity. 'Good for the lungs, that cry. Opens up the muscles, that worship,' he once explained to a sceptical bureaucrat from the department of physical instruction who had come to give Sando's gymnasium a grant-in-aid. Soma was one of Sando's favourite pupils. 'Remember how soft your baby muscles were when you first came?' he often asked Soma. And then, with an air of supreme satisfaction, would say, 'They ripple now, my lad, like the sails of a wind-blown ship.'

Soma went to the pit at daybreak every alternate day. He would do about an hour's gymnastics under the teacher's gaze. Seated on a high stone slab beside the pit, Sando delivered instructions, reprimands, compliments, as a dozen or so of his pupils sweated themselves into fitness. The sand in the pit acting as cushion and talc, Soma would be oblivious of the world for that one hour.

Khatm! Sando shouted at time-up, keeping alive his war acquired knowledge of Urdu. The boys would file out then and shower under a pipe Sando had fixed at one end of his sloping roof.

The exercise kept Soma fit as well as happy. His father did not mind his son's diversion at all, especially since Sando had said he wanted no fees from that family. Some fish, when they could spare them, would do. Soma saw to it there always was some to spare for his teacher. Small payment for the favour that had been done to him, for the change that had been brought to his life. Were it not for this hobby—passion, it could be called—Soma's round of fish vending would have been intolerably dull.

'But don't you mix with those boys from the durava and salagama outside the pit,' his father had warned his son. He feared the boy would lose interest in their ancestral trade. To lose that interest would be to get cut off and to drift. 'The fish that swims against the current has to be a big fish, son. Else it will flounder and be caught.'

To warn against something is, often, to put that very something in mind. Conformity to caste and avocation had been so dinned into Soma that deviation at some point in the future was like a crossroads which he was bound to reach. He was neither drawn to that crossroads nor frightened by it. He did not even know what options it would offer him. But he anticipated it, nevertheless, in a matter-of-fact way.

For some months now, he had been distracted by the behaviour of his body. Fish seemed to be astir under his skin. They would not let him be. The callisthenics kept them down. But the aftershower brought them to the surface again. He knew he was of the age when this sort of thing happened. He knew it was not unnatural that he should be drawn so irresistibly to the female paradigm. And yet the reaction held a mystery for him.

The other day, a car bearing a woman in wonderful fabrics had passed him. He was on his way out of the town, bearing the basket-pole on his shoulders. The driver had to slow down where he was. The woman had looked at him with an expression that made him feel very nearly naked. He must have blushed, he thought later. He was not quite himself for the rest of that day.

During one such phase, when he was doing a round of Craigavon estate, Soma noticed a Tamil girl in one of the lines look at him with the same searching, seeking expression of the woman in the car. He felt the girl's gaze upon him and looked at her with some shyness. She almost froze when their eyes met. Soma had felt very guilty: The next time he went to Craigavon, she was there at the same spot. But a smile of acknowledgement had lit up her face, to Soma's great relief. This happened regularly thereafter. A rhythm was established. The girl would rush out at his father's first call and wait for the two to pass. Soma would look up and they would communicate silently. He could not go to Craigavon or to any of the other estates for a couple of months at a stretch when his father was ill. He had confined the hawking to the town, being needed at home to help his mother look after the old man. The Craigavon girl had been in his thoughts very often during that interregnum. And when they resumed the round, she came prancing out, joy written on her face. Soma had raised his left hand up, much higher than he generally did for balance, and waved. She waved back now, every time. Something leaped inside him whenever this happened. Once or twice, he had slowed down in front of those lines and had gone out of step with his father. The old man turned round the last time and asked what was wrong. 'Nothing. Just a thorn,' he had improvised.

But happiness gave place soon to a nagging worry. That girl, slender, doe-eyed, burgeoning with youth, was yet a Tamil. Not even a durava or salagama but altogether outside the pale. A Tamil.

Soma could not get himself to see her merely as a girl. If he could she would have interested, not affected him. His difficulty was that he saw her as a person. He was made that way. This was perhaps due to the fact that in the Keselgoda sandpit, body and person came to be kneaded together. The Tamil girl became slowly but surely a part of Soma's daily consciousness and of his dreams.

'No, officer. I cannot possibly identify the men. It was too dark and, besides, I am not really interested in pursuing the matter any further.' Father Gio was talking to a young police inspector, Yusouf, of the Ratnapura crime range.

'I can see that, Father. I would like to know whether you are satisfied that the motive was robbery.'

'I can't be sure. My rosary was taken. The cross is white metal with an image of Christ incised in it. Whoever took that will not get much money on it. But for me, it was a priceless possession. My mother had given it to me. And my watch was taken too, as I realized later. I did not feel them removing it because my left hand was numb at the time.'

'The pattern is familiar enough. Rogues are known to hit the head in order to stun, and then the arms and legs to make the victim immobile.'

'So let us leave it at that, officer.'

'I would like to, Father. But there is an unfortunate complication.'

'Oh.'

Inspector Yusouf then showed Father Gio a letter. It had been received at the police station three days after the assault. 'Sir,' it ran, 'We Hindu merchants of Keselgoda town have been perturbed by a report that the imminent joint temple festival at the four estates of the Maradeniya group is being sought to be postponed by some interested parties. We have learnt reliably that certain members of another religious denomination (not Buddhist or Muslim) wish to impede this Hindu articulation. We are also given to understand that this move is not unconnected with the recent transfer of a medical officer belonging to the same denomination after a disagreement with a Hindu subordinate. We request the authorities to ensure that no quarter is given to this move. We say this not because our business interests are involved (we have already placed orders for hundreds of rupees worth of holy ingredients for puja, besides crackers, flowers, pandals etc.). We are making this request out of a deep devotion to the concept of religious tolerance.'

Father Gio, wearing a heavy plaster on his arm and his forehead covered with several layers of medicated gauze, winced when he came to the last sentence.

He did not know how to respond to the letter.

'It is very well drafted, isn't it, officer?'

'Yes, Father, it is. We only wish the merchants had signed the letter. That would have made our task much easier. We could have arranged a meeting between you and them and . . .'

'And what, officer?' Father Gio interrupted Inspector Yusouf. 'I would not have attended any such meeting. It would have been none of my business. But for reasons which the writer of the letter either does not or does not want to understand. My sole interest was that it should not inflame the cholera again. And I can assure you cholera is no respecter of religions. It would have attacked the estate workers, ninety-five per cent of whom are Hindus. And that makes no difference to me. I believe I should step in to thwart anything that is palpably injurious to estate workers whom I am privileged to serve. I was aware, I can assure you, of the likelihood of my being misunderstood even when I made the suggestion. But I know I have not been misunderstood by the majority of the people. I have been misunderstood perhaps—or misinterpreted—by some nameless few, some nameless but articulate few.'

The inspector was quiet for a while. He had not expected this strength of mind and lung in one so badly injured. 'Do you think the assault and this letter are connected?'

Father Gio was perplexed. He really could not say. 'I do not know, officer. But since robbery has been so clearly established, I am inclined to think there is no connection.'

'But robbery could have been a cover, Father. Or it could have been a side business.'

'I see. Perhaps.' Father Gio tried to reconstruct the sequence of events in his mind. A glaze came over his eyes. But then, suddenly, he said, 'No, officer. I am convinced there is no connection. The men who hit me were definitely not Hindu.'

'How can you be sure of that, Father?'

With a slightly unsure voice, a voice with an untypical tremor in it, Father Gio said, 'I heard one of them say to the other in Sinhala as they ran, "*aethi aethi, api duvamu*" or words to that effect. Those were the words of small thieves who had done their job and wanted to run. There was nothing sinister in the attack, officer. You can take that from me.'

Inspector Yusouf was greatly relieved to hear this detail. Saved him a lot of bother. He would pass the case on to the constable handling that area for further routine investigation as assault with a view to rob. There was no complainant and so the matter could languish. As for the letter from the nameless merchants, he would let his merchant friend know that the padre is not making a fuss about it, that they can go ahead.

He stood up to leave. His hand went half-way up, through habit, to salute. He arrested it there and bowed instead. 'Good bye, Father. Wish you a quick recovery.'

'God bless you, officer.'

But as the door of his hospital room closed behind the policeman, Father Gio was in deep distress. 'Lord, forgive me,' he said. 'I have stepped beyond fact. I had heard the men mumble something and my subconscious told me it was in Sinhala but I cannot swear by it. And I have told the officer that I am sure I heard them. Forgive me, my Lord. And may it be, my Lord, that I was not wrong in so imagining it.' Father Gio closed his eyes. His bandaged head rested on his chest. Strains of Paul's music went through his mind, lifting up fallen leaves of memory...

A little boy accompanies his mother, veiled for prayer, to church. 'And what is the bambino going to confess?' a large padre asks him. The boy clings to his mother's dress. 'You have nothing to confess, do you, son? You have not told a lie, spoken ill of others, have you?' the mother asks. The boy thinks hard. His mind is a clean slate. One slight smear, scarcely noticeable, lies at one edge of the slate. At school, Alberto, his friend, and he have a passion for stamps. They ask Maria, a girl in the same class, to bring her collection to school. Alberto purloins three brightly coloured ones. Maria notices the shortfall minutes later, cries. Their teacher asks him, Gio, if he knows how the stamps are missing. He knows but does not tell. Could there have been a mistake in Maria's count? Gio nods. Alberto's face is like one of the faces in the Giudizio finale in the Sistine. 'No confession?' the padre asks again smiling. 'Si,' Gio answers. The padre is delighted. He takes the boy into the recess. The stained glass of the chapel directs its glow on the boy's small presence as he kneels. All the eyes on its panels of winged figures turn to catch what he says in baby whispers, seeking the Lord's forgiveness. The colours, red, blue, yellow and white, fuse into a golden caress of his nape ...

Father Gio felt a suffocation. He must confess. He must confess in church. But he was forbidden to leave the hospital. He must speak to some individual then. But to whom? The Bishop was in Galle. Other priests were bound to come to visit. But Father Gio thought of each one of them and did not feel inspired to speak to any of them on the subject. Besides, they would get worried quite unnecessarily over the complaint made by the Hindu merchants.

'Paul! Yes. I will speak to Paul about this,' Father Gio resolved. 'The next time he comes—alone.'

But Paul did not come alone. He brought with him a most unexpected visitor.

The Venerable Seevali had not met Father Gio before, although they had shared the same platform once at a memorial meeting held for an ex-Mayor of Keselgoda, a devoted Buddhist who had, however, studied in the local Catholic school and been a pillar of strength to the institution later.

'Man is a bag of bones, nein?' the monk said when Father Gio explained that the X-ray picture had shown both the radius and the ulna slit in the middle, like two bamboos. These were to be fixed more thoroughly the following week by a renowned orthopaedic surgeon in Kandy, a friend of Paul's, who had been contacted.

'And what does that involve?'

'I am told it involves opening the arm, bringing the four pieces of bone together and fastening them with pins, and screws. Internal fixation, they call it.'

'Curious name, nein? Internal fixation. Almost metaphysical.'

The three laughed. Sunlight from the high window in the hospital room came down in a beam over the monk's robes. Millions of dust particles swam in the ray which, touching the robe, filled the room with a yellow-red luminosity.

This is the moment, Father Gio thought. A god-given moment. I will lighten my burden at the monk's side. And so, without sounding formally serious, almost conversationally, Father Gio told the Austrian disciple of the Buddha what had happened, the letter which the police inspector had shown him, the hypothesis of a denominational conspiracy.

'I am not sure if I have been entirely truthful.' Venerable Seevali looked up at the sunbeam and thought for a few moments.

'Truth is not verisimilitude. The intention is important. It is paramount, in fact. If in a forest you see a deer run in a direction, followed by a hunter who asks you which way the deer has gone, you might speak the truth and have the deer slain. Or you may refrain from the factual answer and save its life.'

A weight, like an enormous boulder, rolled away from Father Gio's shoulders. 'Wonderful,' he said, 'a wonderful analogy.' As word spread in the estates around Keselgoda of Father Gio's having been assaulted, streams of workers issued out of the tea slopes and headed towards the town. They came continuously, men and women and children, regardless of creed or age.

'Ayyo *sami!*' the women exclaimed as they saw his bandaged head and plastered arm. Many of them wept unreservedly and would not leave until nudged by others behind them to move on, make way. The hospital authorities had a time of it.

Dr Lakshman Samarawickreme sought Paul's advice on crowd control. 'I would leave them alone, Lakshman,' Paul advised. 'But you must decide for yourself.' The acting medical officer was not sure but deferred to his ex-boss.

Many of the workers brought with them fruit, fresh vegetables, packets of tea. Constance was reminded of what Nehru had said in his autobiography about the gifts estate workers had given him. She told Father Gio about it.

'And Nehru made over the labourers' gifts to the hospital and orphanage in Nuwara Eliya, did he? Well, Constance, will you help me find an appropriate institution in the town?' Father Gio asked.

Constance spoke to Sujata. 'There is a lovely School for the Deaf and Dumb two miles away from the town. They'd be so grateful for the gift.' And so, every evening, for the five days that the gifts kept coming in, Constance drove up in Paul's Volks to the School, the rear seat and boot filled with fruit, vegetables, tea. She was surrounded, each time, by the eager faces of the children who transmitted friendship and gratitude to her in a way words could never have. The first day that she went there she explained with the help of the principal that the gifts had come from estate workers. In an instant gesture of recognition, the children showed with their arms the pluck and fill motion of basket-carrying tea gatherers. One of the boys, a youth of seventeen, asked Constance if the estate workers she referred to included rubber tappers. He did so by holding his left forearm straight up, rigid like a tree and cutting a wavy line on its 'trunk' by the forefinger of his right hand. What a perfect simulation, Constance told the principal. Yes, she informed her questioner, there were some who had come from rubber estates too. The same youth then asked her to spell the patient's name. Constance drew on her palm Father Gio's name in block letters. Wait, the boy motioned to her and gave her the sign equivalent of each letter in the name. She became his student for many minutes, repeating every sign over and over again until she had learnt it. One of the children asked how Father Gio had got hurt. She pantomimed the assault. The children's faces were a study in consternation, grief.

The last day that she went to the School, the children asked her through the principal if they could all visit Father Gio to thank him for the gifts. 'I am sure he would be delighted,' she informed them. 'But you will have to come tomorrow morning, for he leaves hospital in the afternoon.' The principal said he would bring them all in the morning.

The next day, Father Gio's last in the Keselgoda hospital, was busy. He was going to be driven by the Baptists to Kandy that afternoon for the surgery. Lakshman Samarawickreme was visibly relieved at the prospect of the priest's departure. Not that he had been a difficult patient. On the contrary. But the visitors were proving too much for the hospital administration. He walked into Father Gio's room early in the morning. Father Gio had got his typewriter down and, seated at a small table, was typing away. 'Arrears of parish correspondence, doctor,' Father Gio explained.

'You are doing very well, Father. Are you typing on the touch system?'

'No, doctor. On the biblical system.'

'Biblical? What is that?'

'Seek and ye shall find! I do not know the touch system at all. If I did, I probably would not have been able to type with one hand now.'

'Yes. Disabilities can carry unexpected compensations.'

There was a patter of many small feet outside Father Gio's room, followed by a knock at the door. The principal of the institution which Constance had told Father Gio about peeped in and asked if he could bring the children in. Father Gio stood up. About thirty children crowded into the room and brought their palms together in a respectful greeting. Father Gio touched the heads of the smaller children. One of them pointed excitedly to the typewriter. An older boy turned to the principal and, with intricate signwork, said something beseechingly to him.

'He wants to know if he can type a message for you, Father.'

'Oh, he knows how to type, does he? Yes, of course. Please.'

The boy gently removed the sheet that was on the machine, inserted a blank one and began typing in the system Dr Lakshman Samarawickreme had described as 'touch'. But this was not touch. It was a very light touch, very gentle, but very fast. It was as if the boy was dusting the keyboard. When he had finished, he gave the page to Father Gio.

'Dear Father,' it said. 'We like to thank you for sending so many nice things. We sorry you hurt. We hope you better soon. Please visit us in school.'

Later that evening, as Father Gio and Constance and Paul were driving up to Kandy, Father Gio told them of his visitors. 'I could never have imagined one of them had overcome his defect so thoroughly as to convert typewriting into an aesthetic exercise.'

They passed through miles of rubber trees, coconut orchards.

'And, very strangely, for the first time since I have come to this island, I did not see my visitors through an ethnic prism. I am always asking myself whether so and so is Tamil or Sinhalese. Those deaf and dumb boys were neither. They were just themselves.'

'Never having heard a language, how could they think of linguistic differences?' Paul added.

'They have left, Gio and Baptist,' Mohotty came up to Ambalavaner in the Cork office and divulged the news with glee.

Ambalavaner was pleased. He knew his draft to the police, unsigned though it was, would work. When Sabhapati had sent word to him through Mohotty about the resolution passed by the Association and the doctor's plan to work for a postponement of the temple festival, Ambalavaner's mind had begun to work.

His interests, Mohotty–Sabhapati's, Sriskandanathar's, were related and were yet distinct. Petty financial gain did not appeal to him. Large nettings, yes. But he squirmed at the thought of wringing a few tenners off labourers. In the proposed postponement of the festival he did not see the financial stakes of merchants (Sabhapati had asked Mohotty to stress this point as being of importance). He had also waved away with contempt Mohotty's suggestion that a recrudescence of cholera would revive flagging business at the hospital admission counter. Ambalavaner's larger vision saw what a postponement could mean to Cork. It could amount to admitting the seriousness of what had happened a few weeks ago. It could mean trouble for Dick Wimalawardene. Ambalavaner had learnt with dismay from Sriskandanathar that the superintendent of Craigavon had written to Belfast about the whole episode, hinting at maladministration and neglect in Cork, where the attack first manifested itself. The Company heard Rupasinghe with respect. Ambalavaner knew that they might ask Wimalawardene for an explanation. And you know

these superintendents. In order to save his own skin he will throw
the blame on his subordinates. And now that he, Ambalavaner,
had compromised with Mohotty on the inventory (a tidy
sum *that* had brought in!) Mohotty would not accept the sack
quietly. He would fling mud on a whole lot of people. He,
Ambalavaner, would receive a dollop . . .

'So you want the festival, do you?'

'Yes, we all do.'

'Right. Leave it to me.'

Ambalavaner had then shot off the letter to Yusouf. He had
chuckled at the clever description of the villain of the piece as
belonging to a denomination other than Buddhist or Muslim.
Yusouf will like that, he had calculated.

But Ambalavaner was alarmed by the news of the assault on
Father Gio. 'Ayyo, chi!' he had slapped his head. 'I hope our
rascals are not behind this. This can spoil everything, everything.'
He had gone and checked with his cousin at Craigavon.
Sriskandanathar knew nothing about the assault and broke into
a sweat at the news. But Mohotty had dissembled, when queried.
Ambalavaner couldn't make out whether Mohotty was acting or
whether there was, in fact, a connection. He and Sabhapati could
easily have got that execration in the Keselgoda bar to do this
dirty deed. But he would never know.

On the way back from their rounds one sultry day, Finando felt
his mouth parch and his vision go hazy. Concentric circles of
light seemed to come out of the sun overhead, the spires narrowing
down upon him. He held his spinning head and sat down.

'What is it, father?' Soma asked, helping him sit down.

The old man told him what had happened. 'It's the sun,
the heat.'

Soma ran towards a streamlet nearby and brought two
palmfuls of cool water to sprinkle on his father's face. This
revived Finando. They resumed the walk after a while, but the

old man decided that he must respect the warning. 'I am too old now, son. Too old for all that climbing. I will do the vending on the plains. You better do the estate rounds.'

Great as his anxiety for his father was, Soma was elated at the prospect of going to Craigavon unsupervised.

There was an extra verve in his callisthenics the following morning, so much so that he twice drew applause from Sando.

On the first day of his solo rounds, Soma tried out his new posture. He jammed his father's chopping knife into the block so that it stuck to the knife-tip and could be held up like a tent peg on the point of a lance. Soma carried the chopping kit, thus, in his left hand and his basket-pole heaved on to his right shoulder. As he approached Craigavon's lines and called out *fish, maalu, maalu*, Valli was puzzled. The intonation was the old man's but the voice was young! She ran out to see for herself. Soma looked up and laughed under his breath. He was wearing his new role like a new shirt, happily but also self-consciously.

The cook, Velayutham, asked him what the matter was with his father. So did Thaiyalnayaki Sriskandanathar. 'Too old, now,' Soma told them all. 'Gets tired.'

On his way back, he went past Valli's lines again although there was another route out of the estate. Soma wanted to exercise the discretions that came with his new role. With the familiar sensation of fish swimming under his skin, he slowed down as he neared the lines. There she was, surprised at his return. Soma put the basket down. Lifting two fistfuls of fish he went up to Peramayi, as Valli stared in astonishment. She had never been so close to the young man. Soma placed the fish on the floor near where the old woman was sitting.

'What's this? I can't buy any fish!'

'No need to buy. They are a present.'

Soma had understood Peramayi's Tamil exclamation. But she did not make out Soma's words and so his action seemed even stranger. Soma then turned round and walked on.

'He likes you, appayi!' Valli told her grandmother. But Peramayi was intrigued. 'I don't understand. The boy must be mad. I wonder what his father would have so say.' She gave the fish to Valli to cook. As Valli took them in her hands, she felt as if she had touched Soma's bare shoulders. She shivered.

Soma did not repeat his extravagant gesture for fear of being thought mad. But he conceived of variations that could bring him closer to the girl. Luck favoured him in an unexpected way.

Ever since he had been replaced by a mechanical siren, Velu had had nothing to do. They tried him out at the factory but found he could not cope. Sriskandanathar then had a bright idea. He would employ Velu as a domestic servant at his house. The boy's deafness can be so convenient! The last servant boy was always eavesdropping. Dumbness, too, can help. The last servant boy was always gossiping with the next-door brats, always grumbling about overwork. The superintendent, when asked, said he had no objection as long as the estate did not have to pay him. And so Velu joined the employ of the Sriskandanathars. He swept their quarters, fetched their firewood, washed dishes, clothes. He also did the marketing. One day, soon after Velu had started working for the Sriskandanathars, Soma came there with the fish. He was surprised to see this young servant of almost exactly his own age and build, standing eyes closed, in a corner of the veranda, on his head. Soma was even more surprised to see him continue in this stance when the lady of the house came out to buy the fish. She noticed Soma's surprise and, on seeing its cause, said, 'Oh, that. He is our new servant boy. He goes and stands on his head now and then!' She then went up to Velu and prodded him on the legs. Velu opened his eyes and somersaulted back to his feet again. His face still very flushed, he looked blankly at Soma, at the fish.

Soma, after he had finished with Thaiyalnayaki Sriskandanathar, motioned to Velu to come with him. A few yards away, on soft ground, he showed Velu some callisthenic exercises and 'holds' he had learnt at Sando's gym. For Velu, the interest shown in him by this young man was a totally novel experience. In gestures, he told Soma that he lived on line number seven. Soma almost jumped when he learnt this. Line number seven was where *she* lived!

A week later, by arrangement, Soma came to Craigavon later than usual and accompanied Velu to the lines in order to learn the headstand. And, with a little bit of luck, to see the girl.

She wasn't there. Out in the fields, perhaps, Soma thought. But the grandmother was in.

'I hope your father didn't berate you over those fish,' she asked.

'No, not at all. I gave you just one or two.'

And then, seeing Velu with him, she continued.

'You know Velu, do you? Poor boy. Absolutely deaf. But he has a heart of gold.'

Soma placed his fish baskets just outside Velu's room and stepped in. He was most agreeably surprised to see, pasted on the wall, a large Hanuman print. He wished he knew enough sign language to be able to tell Velu that he worshipped the monkey god himself, at the gymnasium.

Velu got Soma to begin the lessons at once. First, tie your sarong short and tight. Velu pointed to the picture on the wall for an object lesson in how tight a tight sarong can be. And then, crouch. Like this. Put your head to the ground. Like this. And up!

Soma's training literally 'stood' him in good stead. It was quite wonderful seeing the world turned upside down. The door leading to Velu's room was a rectangle of light. The trees outside swung like inverted bouquets. The birds flitting past them seemed to swim, not fly on the surface of blue waters. And then, suddenly, in the rectangle of light the girl stood framed. The girl, followed by her younger sister. Soma tumbled back to how the homo erectus were expected to be and normalized his sarong. 'Crows,' Valli told him hesitatingly, 'they are pecking at your fish.'

Soma ran out to shoo the birds away, Valli, Theiva and Velu
assisting. Half a dozen or so of the fish had been lifted.

'No matter,' Soma said. 'Only the smaller ones.' And then
taking their collective leave, he began his journey back home. He
knew her better now, Soma told himself. And he knew her name.
Valli, the younger girl had called her. Valli.

Father Gio had been convalescing at the magnificent old seminary
set amidst woods outside Kandy. He went out for walks in those,
with the Baptists whenever they could come or with seminarians.
An enforced retreat, he called it. The retreat-convalescence was
coming to an end soon, and although Father Gio had liked it, he
was looking forward to a return to Keselgoda.

As he was emerging from the evening service in the seminary
chapel one day, the Vicar General from Kandy came up to him.
He had a message, he said. From the Bishop. Father Gio had to
go at once to Kandewatte near Nuwara Eliya and take over the
parish there. The priest in charge, Father Perera, had died.

'There is so much half-done at Keselgoda,' Father Gio told
the Vicar General. But subjective emotions are no part of the
Jesuit Order. He was sorry about the short notice, the Vicar
General told Father Gio, very sorry. But there was no way out.
The Bishop would send his own vehicle the following morning
to carry Father Gio to Kandewatte.

His left arm still under heavy plaster (snowman's arm, he
called it), Father Gio packed his bag the following morning.

He had sent word to the Baptists, who were staying with friends
in Kandy and they drove up to the seminary to say goodbye. 'Be
in touch,' Paul told him. 'In touch, yes. But it should not, as you
say in English, be touch-and-go! It has been like that, has it not,
dottore? Touch-and-go!'

'It won't in the future, Father' Paul assured him.

'Touch wood, for that!' Constance added. There was sadness
in their laughter.

'You know the origin of that phrase, don't you?' Father Gio asked the couple. 'It is Greek. You propitiate Nemesis, the goddess of retribution, immediately after boasting in order to immunize yourself against her pursuit. Nemesis apparently likes wood.'

'Paul, maybe you should have done that during the epidemic. Nemesis would have protected and not overtaken you!' Constance suggested.

'Perhaps. We seem to have offended both Nemesis and Man.'

Getting into the waiting car, Father Gio waved out with his right hand. '*Arriverderci, dottore.*' '*Arriverderci, signora.*' '*Arriverderla*, Father!'

The Baptists stayed on in Kandy for a fortnight thereafter. Paul's unofficial help and advice was sought by surgeons at the government hospital in the town and by doctors in charge of private nursing homes.

At a gathering of doctors, Paul was introduced to Dr William Paine of the World Health Organization who had come to do a study of health services in the villages and estates of central Ceylon. His work was part of a larger study of such services among tribal and non-tribal residents of hilly terrains in South Asia. He had travelled widely in Pakistan, north and south India, and north-west Burma. His Ceylon itinerary was the final.

'Also the most decisive,' he told Paul. 'The position here seems to be the classical South Asian position. Not as depressing as it is in Burma and not as satisfactory as it can be in parts of India, but typical.'

Paul asked Paine how the position on the estates in the Madras and Kerala provinces in India compared with those in the highlands of Ceylon.

'Well,' Dr Paine started. 'This might become a mini-lecture. But let me go ahead anyway. The estate health apparatus is not better or worse here than it is on south Indian estates. The buildings, if anything, and some of the older equipment, are in a better state of maintenance in this country. But in the matter of records Ceylon's estates have slipped. I have not found it so difficult to get data on morbidity, mortality and related matters in south Indian estates. There has been a considerable amount of bureaucratic hesitation in India. But the data is there. It is there and it is complete.'

'What about the health standards of the people concerned?' Paul asked. 'There again, I have found that malnutrition— identifiable most easily by the incidence of angular stomatitis— occurs in the same degree in both places. But whenever it is necessary the health machinery swings into action much faster in India. I suppose that has something to do with the fact that the estates in India are not an island within an island as they are here.'

Paul then narrated (remembering Nemesis) the cholera outbreak at Keselgoda. Paine was most interested. A day or two later, he asked if Paul would like to spend a year working at a small hospital for immigrants in Southall. The doctor in charge of that hospital was coming out to Ceylon to work here for Paine's project for a year. His place needed to be filled. Paul could act as a substitute. 'And besides, we could be in touch with you about our findings and seek your assistance in sending them through analytical methods in England.' 'Paul, this is great. Please accept it,' Constance advised. Paul accepted, subject to his being able to take Constance with him.

'Of course, Dr Baptist,' Paine said. 'That goes without saying.'

Leaving their car with friends in Kandy, the Baptists went to Colombo shortly thereafter. Paul called on the Director of Health Services. 'A good break, good break,' Bryan de Silva kept repeating. He left his prospective address in Southall with de Silva 'in case you have to write to me about the inquiry in Keselgoda.'

Constance bought a pair of second-hand overcoats for herself and for Paul, and within a week was able to tell her husband that she was quite ready for England.

Walking over the tarmac towards their aeroplane, she said, 'I think we have to thank Sabhapati for this.'

The noise from crackers deafened Nimal's ears. Appu Velayutham was helping his master dress for the festival.

'Must festivals be that noisy?' he asked Velayutham. 'Yes, master. Always noisy. Gods sleeping, no? Waking time now, master.' 'And for a lot of people who are not gods, as well,' Nimal said brusquely. He had been reluctant to join the festivities at the temple. But his accountant and clerk had persuaded him. 'An old tradition, sir,' the accountant had told him. 'Quite harmless also, sir,' Sriskandanathar had chipped in. 'And this year, it is very special, sir. The festival is going to start at Craigavon and then the procession is to go on for the next two days from here to Limerick, Armagh and is going to end at Cork. Sir, your presence at the inauguration will be very greatly appreciated. It will all be over in a few minutes.' Like hell it will, Nimal thought. It will take hours. But one will have to go. Thank goodness this takes place only once a year.

Appu Velayutham suggested he wear sandals instead of shoes. 'Master to take them off at temple.' Drat! Nimal cursed his loss of freedom.

The noise was becoming louder, more insistent. Drums had begun to beat and various conch-like sounds came up every now and then. Loud laughter punctuated the cacophony. Nimal stepped out of the bungalow as warily as he would to meet an adversary. Face grim, limbs stiff, he walked to a clearing near the temple. A series of crackers went off ratt-a-ratt-a-ratt, machine-gun-like. An old woman came up to him and daubed his forehead with sandalwood paste and smudges of various other colours. His mind recoiled at the touch. Very wet flower garlands descended on his shoulders. More crackers. Applause. He was asked to proceed to the temple. Labourers, hundreds of them, pressed round him. He could only inch his way forward. The air thickened with body odours, arrack and cracker fumes and laughter. They are taking it out on me, Nimal concluded. They have me in their power today. Bear it, Nimal Rupasinghe. Bear it. He removed his sandals at the entrance to the temple. The grit on the floor tickled his soles. A toothless priest came out and mumbled a speech of welcome. His words sprayed betel spittle. Execration! But Nimal stood like a statue. He was led further in, towards the sanctum, the idol. Bells rang out, lamps glowed. Nimal could hardly breathe. He swayed slightly. Someone came up to him and said, 'Sir, now they want you to make a speech.'

Speech! He had not been warned. 'One word will do.' It was no use protesting now. He cleared his throat. 'I thank you for having invited me to this function. My best wishes for its successful completion.' Applause. More crackers.

With the Baptists and Father Gio gone from Keselgoda, the Maradeniya estates returned to customary rhythms. After the festival, there was a not unexpected flare-up of cholera. Some two hundred cases were reported of which six ended fatally. But the hospital attended to the incidence with calm. There was no indication of crisis. The deaths were put down to a spectrum of secondary causes, malnutrition among them.

Like bad monsoons, malnutrition was something to be sorry about. But nothing positive was done about it. The main thing was that the estates were 'doing very well,' cholera and malnutrition notwithstanding. They were churning out endless quantities of tea and rubber.

A year passed. A year of productivity.

Valli was seventeen in 1973. Soma was twenty-one.

Soma's trips to Velu's room were almost as many as his rounds of the estate. He liked Velu for himself too. He had taken him to Keselgoda, introduced him to 'Captain' Sando and to his parents. The tutor had been greatly affected by the fact that Velu was deaf and dumb. 'See,' he had told the others at the gym. 'This young man cannot hear, he cannot speak. And yet, by himself, in his loneliness, he has pursued the goal of physical fitness. Learn from him.' Soma had felt greatly pleased with himself for having brought Velu to the gym and had basked in the sunshine of praise that bounced from Velu to him. Velu had been asked to give demonstrations of the headstand to the others and had been offered an invitation to use the gym whenever he liked. They would watch a variation of rugger being played at that town's vast grounds, gawk at shop windows, eat large meals of godambe rotti.

At the Keselgoda marketplace one day where Velu had gone to do some vegetable marketing for the Sriskandanathars, he asked Soma to explain the mystery of the lottery. Velu could not understand why there was such a demand for a piece of paper. Were those tickets for the cinema? Soma tried as best he could to explain what the sweeps meant, but could not make himself quite understood. He then asked Velu to buy a ticket. Velu indicated he did not have any money on him, except for the amount his employer's wife had given for the vegetables. Soma took one rupee from that, bought a ticket and stuffed it into Velu's shirt pocket. 'This has cost one rupee, right? Just keep the ticket with you. If you are lucky, you will understand what it all means.' Soma noted that he must return that rupee to Velu before they parted that day. But, curiously, he forgot. Luckily, the lady did not notice the short-change.

Soma's visits to Velu's room were, of course, largely to see Valli. The timings were such that Valli was almost always alone, except for the grandparents. And they were unsuspecting. Very recently Velu was asleep when Soma had come to his room, and so were Perumal and Peramayi. Valli followed Soma to Velu's room and, in the world of their friend's silence, primeval emotions surged within their veins simultaneously. Valli clung to Soma like a creeper. 'Take me with you, Soma,' she said to him. 'Take me away.' Soma and Valli had known the affection of relatives. But in the daily recurrences of their lives there was a tedium, a monotony which they sought to overcome in each other's company. Each was an oasis in the other's desert. They had never felt another body as they did each other's that day. Valli trembled in his clasp. Soma breathed heavily. Were it not for the precariousness of the moment—Velu sleeping with his back to them and the possibility that someone might pass that way— nature might have drawn them to a longer journey. But it had other plans for them.

The north-east monsoon set in shortly thereafter. One day, as Soma was nearing the Craigavon lines, the heavens came down in sheets of rain. He ran, baskets dancing, to Velu's room. Velu was not there, nor were any of the others. Valli made him a glass of tea, which he drank gratefully. She gave him a piece of dry cloth. He wiped his arms, shoulders and chest. When he returned the cloth to her, she asked if he would not wipe his back. He grinned and turned his back to her. Valli looked nervously out of the door in Velu's room to see if there was anyone who might see them. Finding no one, she ran the cloth over Soma's smooth, muscular back. There was a silence between them, stemming from their experience in Velu's room the other day. And there was a silence, generally. The only sound was of the rain on the tree-leaves and on the ground. Like the scent of dry earth on getting the first showers, something moved within him, softly at first, but then powerfully. It suffused his being. 'Can we not go somewhere,' he asked Valli. She was silent, thoughtful. Soma remembered the collection centre in the rubber section had a few unoccupied sheds at the rear. He passed that way every day. 'Follow me,' he told Valli. 'At a distance.'

They were soon at the place Soma had in mind. The rain poured even heavier. Rainwater washed the ground, coming down in great spurting gushes wherever the ground sloped. The shed where Soma and Valli found themselves, meant to house latex drums, was the last of about seven or eight such. It had drums stacked on its floor. Rainwater flowed over part of the sloping floor. It came down through vents in the zinc roofing and poured into the drums, heightening the din. From the open side of the shed one could see only pale green veils of rain against rubber trees. A breeze moved them occasionally, revealing only more rain, more veils. Soma was wet through and Valli's clothes were drenched. With the utmost seriousness, he loosened and removed their garments. Valli was absolutely silent. Their limbs, wet and yet warm under the wetness, locked. There was pain. They verged on failure. But the rain, which seemed to intensify every minute, carried them on. It carried them, like a storm-tossed boat moving through currents, to their destination.

With the aid and inspiration of the monsoon, Soma and Valli repeated their journey on three occasions. But on the last one, fate overtook nature.

Soma emerged from the shed to return to Velu's room when the inevitable happened. He was seen. 'Greetings!' a voice said behind him. Soma turned abruptly to see who had spoken. Sarcasm etched on his face, there stood Jayasena. He was leaning on a latex drum, picking his teeth with a grassroot. This was the collection centre for latex, his attitude seemed to convey. And he was in charge. Nothing happened there without his knowledge.

Soma could not find a response. He stood, fixed to where he was. Before he could say or signal a warning, Valli emerged behind him. 'Greetings,' Jayasena repeated with heightened sarcasm. Soma and Valli were like speared fish. The logic of the situation required the spearer, not the fish, to make the next move.

'No harm done. Don't worry. I know and I do not know, I have seen and have not seen,' Jayasena dissembled, with a wink thrown at Soma.

The spear had been withdrawn, leaving the fish limp, struggling for its last gasp. Valli darted, like a gazelle running from a predator, to Soma and clutched his arm. The two moved on. As they crossed the edge of Jayasena's territory, a laugh like that of the crimson-backed woodpecker on a coconut tree— loud, harsh, chattering—came from Jayasena, tearing the thin curtain of drizzle.

The weather had told on Nimal. He disliked staying indoors and being unable to do his field inspections. The jeep did not take him as far as he would like to go. One round in the morning he made invariably, rain-coated and gum-booted. But, for the rest of the day, he was obliged to stay in.

Nimal was also concerned about the estate's production graph. True, the estate had continued to make a profit. But he had hoped for an even more spectacular profit that year. Being as good as last year was not good enough. A letter had come to him from the Board hoping the Maradeniya group would do 'even better' in the coming year. He had taken this to mean that he must improve production on all the four estates. 'But,' he explained in his reply to the Secretary to the Board, 'there are factors totally beyond our control which will tell adversely on our performance. The average price of Ceylon tea has not been maintained in recent years. The rapid expansion of East African teas—under British blessings— has depressed our prices. Take little Malawi, for instance. That country used to give a "filler" tea of low quality. But today Malawi tea is in demand for its own sake and the whole of its crop is exported. Here a powerful ring of twelve buyers has the entire process of production and marketing of Ceylon teas in its vice-like grip. Our efforts on Maradeniya to earn profits for the company will have to be redoubled. We will have to expand even more in the coming year to ensure regular fertilizer, weed and pest control programmes. But, having done this, we may still find our efforts stalled by the external forces that have been described.' Nimal urged his company to enter the Colombo auctions as an agent for British blenders and also enter the London auctions as a retailer buyer. 'In other words, I would urge the Board to reconsider the adequacy, in these days of competition, of being a long-distance producer company. The free market determination of price through competition does not hold now because the buyers and sellers are, in most cases, the same. The company must consider joining the auctions and influencing prices.'

Nimal knew that the recommendations he was making were not merely for intrinsic reasons. They had something of an alibi for the future built into them. He could tell the company later that he had warned of the pitfalls ahead. Pitfalls of the kind which he, Nimal Rupasinghe, could never hope to fill. And behind the alibi, hidden inside it, was something even more critical: a forewarning, a faint and distant bell that served to inform the company that he, Nimal Rupasinghe, could not be taken for granted. He might reach a point when he would have to call it a day.

Nimal gained in reputation, gained in weight. Shortly after he had taken over as President of the Club, he received a communication from Belfast to the effect that the Board had decided he be designated superintendent of Craigavon and Resident Director of the Maradeniya Group as a whole. This meant that the superintendents of Cork, Limerick and Armagh were to be accountable to him.

If his colleagues resented this development they did not show it. 'Hand it to him, man, he has done a good job at Craigavon,' Dick Wimalawardene pronounced at the Club one evening. Tilakaratne reminded Wimalawardene that he had predicted Rupasinghe would change. 'Yes, of course, I said that,' Wimalawardene admitted. 'But this is exactly what I

meant! I had said he would change. He has, has he not?'
Tilakaratne and Pieris were not quite sure what their senior
colleague meant. 'Let me explain,' Wimalawardene continued.
'Does he sneer at us any more? Does he keep judging us, making
mental or oral comments on us any more? Is he not one of
us in his reactions to things. To labour matters, for instance?'
The clarification was revelatory to the others. They agreed with
Wimalawardene unreservedly.

'And hand it to him also that he maintains the best
superintendent's bungalow in the whole district,' Wimalawardene
went on. '*That* without a wife!' Tilakaratne amplified. Taking
no notice of the interruption, Wimalawardene asked, 'Is there
another bungalow with the hedges—of pure tea—kept in so
perfect a trim? Or the floor in so constant a shine? Or a swimming
pool so completely free of moss?'

No, no, the others replied like members of inchoate and
mindless mobs. 'And so it is, I say, that his directorship should
not affect us, much less trouble us. We should feel complimented,
in fact, that the best of us—*the best of our type*—has been selected
to lead us, to guide us.'

Nimal's ears would have turned green had he heard the
typification. But he would have also liked the abjectness of their
surrender. He had, for instance, enjoyed the nervous trepidation
of his colleagues during the late abortive insurgency after two
young extremists had been found in the quarters of the
schoolteacher at Craigavon. Nimal had asked the Army to search
every line, every quarter, and had let the teacher be beaten up
mercilessly—on suspicion—and be marched off. The others had
marvelled at the decisiveness he had shown.

Nimal wrote to his father about his new responsibility, taking
care to remove any trace of elation in his letter. He made it seem
that the logical, the inevitable, had taken place.

But somewhere in his consciousness there was a distinct sense
of guilt. Had he not risen by a lowering of something? In his

gains were not some losses embedded? The feeling seized him suddenly, and was a trouble while it lasted.

A week earlier, for instance, when some superintendents had come to his bungalow to congratulate him on the 'promotion', he had smarted at a comment of Tilakaratne's.

A marble replica of the supine L'Aurora, from Michelangelo's Tomb of the Medici group in Florence, lay on the liquor cabinet. As Nimal poured out a drink for Tilakaratne, the guest pawed the work of art. 'I prefer the real stuff,' the man had said.

Nimal had just finished breakfast and was preparing to go to the office one morning when Velayutham brought in the silver salver containing the day's private mail. He was expecting a letter from his father. But this cover bore another equally familiar handwriting. It was from his Oxford friend Ronald Manners. He opened it with mixed feelings. There was a pang of nostalgia for Oxford, for Ronald's company. And there was, again, that familiar sense of guilt. He read:

6-2-1973

N,

I was rummaging my papers the other day for an address when your very first letter from Craigavon fell out of the box. 'I wonder if I can survive' you've said in it. I bet you have and pretty well too, considering you haven't written for almost two years. Has the Keselgoda Club beer lined your arteries so thick you can't put your old indignations to work? I must end this rush note for I've a pile of home assignments of boys in my class that I've got to wade through. Write!

R

P.S.
Incidentally, I find the Asian boys uniformly way ahead of the whites and the blacks. I only wonder if they'll ever return to their countries and put their brains to some account.

Nimal was quiet for a long time after reading the letter. Nimal had a monogrammed letter pad of his own. But he could not get himself to reply to Ronald Manners in one of those. He tore off the printed top from one and wrote on the decapitated page:

21-3-1973

R,

Forgive my not writing often enough. You are right about the beer, you know. I find I am not indignant about things as I used to be. Do you remember how hot under the collar I'd got when someone had done you-know-what to the Shelley statue in College? Well, I was driving home the other day and saw on the estate grounds one of my Tamil workers—Kandan, I think his name is—lying across the road exactly in the manner of Shelley in that statue. I honked loud and long but the chap would not budge. So I asked my driver who was sitting at the rear of the jeep to get down and move him out of the way. When the driver went up to the prone figure he found the man was not drunk as we had suspected but unconscious and burning hot. Well, you'd like to know what I did, wouldn't you? I just had him moved to a side and drove on. You'd like to know why, wouldn't you? Some superintendents were expected home for a drink and I didn't want to be late! So that's the scene here, R. I bet you are not going to write for some time now!

N

P.S.

I'm sorry if this has sounded like a confessional but you asked for it.

Kandan had practically stopped working on the estate. His daughters worked on alternate days and Kandan thought that was enough. Moreover, he had stumbled into a new line of work.

Daud, the narcotics man in Keselgoda, pursued a flourishing business in illegal gemming in the Ratnapura district. The area abounded in gems of all kinds, ranging from very precious to semi-precious. They lay mixed up with humbler stones in the soil. The government had tried to restrict indiscriminate gemming by making it a strictly licensed trade. But how much could a handful of officials do in so vast a tract? And, besides, officials were also human beings. Daud knew that a modest wad of currency notes, or a small gem-find, would make officials look the other way. No, it was not officials that posed obstacles to his trade. By its very nature, gemming involved more than one man. A pit had to be dug, sometimes nearly a hundred feet deep, and the water in the pit bailed out with a diesel water pump. Daud's problem was getting reliable men to do the digging for him. Reliable men who would not advertise the venture, would charge but a reasonable wage for their labours, and not help themselves to the finds.

The gempits were all over the place but, for some strange reason, were particularly rewarding when they fringed streams. Daud's pursuit of gems took him to many of the nearby estates for water streams and for labour. At Craigavon, he was advised by Mendis, the tavern keeper, that an idle and slightly moonstruck but otherwise good worker came frequently to the tavern. Daud could consider employing him. Mendis asked for but a small fee if Kandan was found suitable. He was. Almost at once. Daud took him one morning to a gempit near Armagh and got him to work there for several days as an apprentice. But before a full week had gone by, Kandan was easily the hardest working and most regular of the diggers. Daud was very happy. More than any other factor, Kandan's total ignorance of the difference between precious, semi-precious and worthless stones was his greatest asset. He brought up everything from the muddy sieve and laid it on the floor for Daud's nephew and dig-supervisor Falil to inspect. Daud was also superstitious. The very first collection after Kandan joined brought in an irregular object of the size of a small cherry. Falil recognized the sapphire at once. 'Allah be praised!' Daud exclaimed when shown the find and at once gave a hundred-rupee note to Kandan as reward. Kandan was overwhelmed by the generosity of his employer.

Covered by the slime of the pit, Kandan would bob in and out of it like a gopher. There were five other diggers under Daud's pay and Falil's control. For them, Kandan was alternately a figure of envy and of fun. Envy, because by his extreme regularity he enjoyed the mudali's trust (and could claim a disproportionate share of rewards) and fun, because he was not quite 'there'. They told Kandan one day that the real gems lay deep down and that the stones now being brought up and given to Falil were only 'poor relatives' of those that lay further down. Kandan believed them. He imagined that the real gems, when they came to his view, would glint as they do in pictures or in the shop windows of Ratnapura. They also told Kandan that if he went to the pit on a moonlit night he could, if he was lucky, see many a sparkling gem and one that was like fragments of the moon. And Kandan believed them.

'What do we do about Kandan?' Peramayi complained, one rainy afternoon. She was really more worried about what Kandan's long absences would mean to her granddaughters than about Kandan as such. 'We don't know where he goes away and what he does with his time.' Perumal had heard about his son's gempit work but decided not to tell his wife about it. She was bound to begin worrying about what her son did with the money he earned. So he went on chopping the firewood he had brought in that morning, in silence. Just then, a boy came up and said he had a message for inmates of Perumal Kandan's lineroom. Valli appeared at the door and asked him what the message was. The boy said he had been asked to tell Valli that she was wanted at the collection centre where 'they' wanted to ask about Kandan's not having reported for work.

'But at this time?' asked Peramayi. The boy, a footloose brat from another line, had disappeared. Asking Theiva to keep an eye on the rice pot being cooked over the veranda fire, Valli went out. The rain had abated but she covered her head with a piece of cloth. There was no one at the centre. She went into the complex of sheds to see if the people concerned were in any of those. Nobody. Then, behind her, she heard a man cough. Turning round, she saw Jayasena. The rain had revived. A couple of mynahs had entered the nearest shed for shelter and were making raucous noises.

After a few moments of silence, Jayasena spoke. 'Your father has stopped coming to work.' Valli stood quietly, head bowed. 'Has he told you why?' Valli shook her head. 'Well, I will tell you. He is doing illegal things. Things that can land him in jail.' Valli's heart beat fast, painfully. 'I am not reporting against him, because of sympathy for his two daughters.' Valli's toes dug into the earth. 'I can report him to the dorai on two counts. One, absence from work. Two, illegal gemming.' 'Gemming?' Valli made her first remark. It escaped her, like an exclamation. 'Yes, gemming. There are gems under the soil around here which no one is allowed to touch without permission. Kandan is digging those.'

'Ayyo!'

'But . . .' Jayasena looked around at their surroundings. There was no one in sight. 'Let's not stand in the rain. Come into the shed here.' Valli hesitated. Jayasena took the lead. He went into the nearest shed and stood. Valli moved slowly towards it, through the rain. 'Fool, don't get wet. Come in.' Her woman's instinct told her what Jayasena's intentions were. And yet she felt powerless in the situation. The rain had helped her and Soma on the first occasion. It was now aiding Jayasena. She came into the shed.

'I also want to gem.' Jayasena said moving closer to her, his tone suddenly different. Valli could not comprehend the man.

'There are gems above the soil too. Like you.' He then lunged forward and brought Valli down on the floor. She tried to push him back. 'You wretched girl. If a fish vendor can have you, so

can I.' 'Soma!' she cried bitterly, softly. 'Soa-maa!' Jayasena
repeated with derision.

Soma came to Craigavon the following day and went, as usual,
straight to Velu's room in line seven. Velu could not understand
why Valli, who rushed in after Soma, was speaking through tears.
Velu knew of their feelings for each other. But be knew nothing
of the recent dimensions these had acquired. Neither had told
him. They would not have known how to. Velu could see an
anger, a hatred of something or someone, well up inside the man.
He saw Soma free himself of Valli, almost pushing her down,
and then turn to Velu and signal him to follow. Velu did as he
was told. He saw Soma pick up the basket-pole, chopper, and
walk out. He followed. They didn't stop anywhere until they
reached a house which Velu recognized as Jayasena's. He saw
Soma put down the basket and call out. An old woman-servant
came out first. And then Jayasena. Velu saw the two men speak,
Jayasena leering. He saw them gesticulate, Jayasena raising his
arm and lifting his forefinger in warning. Having done that,
Velu saw Jayasena turn to go back into the house. Soma then
bent to pick up the chopper from the basket. The man was
climbing the two front steps of his quarters when the blow fell.
He stood petrified for a second in that position. One leg on
the step, the other about to be raised. And then a great gush of
blood flowed out from under his nape and cascaded down his
back. Jayasena crumpled on the steps.

Years of baton-swinging in the streets of crime had inured
Inspector Yusouf to things like murder. But he had cultivated a
by-lane, so to say, to the theory and practice of murder which
kept some of its wonderment alive for him. Else, homicide
would have palled. Yusouf had made so close a study of Injury
by Metallic Objects as to be able to say, by a mere glance at the
wound, whether the instrument used was an ordinary knife, a

scythe, an axe, an alavangoe, or some other weapon, whether it had been wielded by a right-handed or left-handed person, a man or a woman, an adept or a novice. While weak-livered colleagues and subordinates of Yusouf's preferred to move on to the circumstantial and jurisprudential aspects of murders, Yusouf lingered on the endless possibilities of The Wound. Yusouf recapitulated the most recent case. The Craigavon murder posed no challenges to the police. The fish vendor had not even tried to escape. He stood at the the scene of the crime until the superintendent sent estate watchers to have him locked up while the police were on their way. The man had put up no resistance, saying 'yes' when asked, quite superfluously, if he had committed the crime. On the motive alone was he silent. The sole witness to the crime had turned out to be a deaf-mute Tamil labourer. The police had taken him in also, at first. But Yusouf asked the boys to let him be, he was not involved. (He had later turned out to be the estate clerk's servant.) The nature of the wound interested, almost perplexed, the Inspector. It was a deft wound, delivered not just lethally but expertly. It had gone through the external and internal jugulars in a straight line that ended after its object had been achieved fully. Yusouf had been certain that this was the man's first murder. And yet what finesse! That was the fish vendor in him surely. The man was used to cutting fishes' heads above the collar-fins. He must have been doing that for years. For Yusouf everything else in the episode was uninteresting. Everything else, such as the loss of one man's life and another's liberty. The Fishcut, he would call such wounds hereafter, Yusouf decided with self-satisfaction. The Fishcut.

Soma's parents were stunned. They could not understand what had happened. That their son, who hardly knew people, could have made an enemy of someone and murder him, passed their comprehension. Old Finando, already infirm, hobbled about the house muttering meaningless words. When the police came to inform him of the episode he had stared at them uncomprehendingly. Police, he said, there must be some mistake. He said he would come to the lock-up and identify the son, would come straightaway. But his legs gave. He sat down and found he could not stand up again. It was Seelawathi who went. She would go, she said, and show them that their son could not have done this foul deed. She went, running almost, behind the bicycles of the two constables who had come. Not my son, she kept repeating through her short breaths as she sped past the market stalls, the traffic. Not him. He doesn't hurt a fly. Can he murder? But the moment she arrived at the lock-up house, she knew she was wrong. The boy was grim and silent. 'Son, did you do this?' she asked him. Soma did not reply. Instead he turned his head away and began sobbing, sobbing uncontrollably. 'God!' Seela cried and slumped in front of the grilled door. She was brought back home in a police jeep.

Word of the murder engulfed Craigavon like a forest fire. A fire of which Jayasena's house was the white core. And after the body had been moved by the police for the post-mortem and the inquest, the attention shifted to Velu. Witnessing the murder had been a nerve-shattering experience. How could he explain to anyone what he had passed through? They would not, could not, understand. The one person who would have tried to understand was Soma. And he had been taken away.

The agony of facing a forest of gestured questions from the people crowding around him was unbearable. After a couple of hours of trying to understand and to explain, Velu shut himself up in his room. He knew they would bang at his door, but he could turn his head away from it.

'Poor boy,' someone said. 'What can he know?' Another suggested that he and the fish vendor had been good friends. 'That's the trouble with these boys,' a wiseacre expounded. 'They don't know their place. Why did he have to get mixed up with a Sinhalese fish vendor?' This weighty observation found a general murmur of support. 'Lucky for him that he is a deaf-mute. Otherwise, do you think the police would have let him off?'

Hermetically sealed by his deafness and a fastened door, Velu went up to the picture of Hanuman. 'Protect him,' Velu prayed to the deity. 'He is a worshipper of yours just as I am. You must protect him, please. Only you know why he killed the supervisor. Only you can save him.' With that silent prayer, Velu curled up in a corner of his room, trembling from the ordeal.

The rains, heavy and incessant, had brought gemming to a halt. Daud's illegal gempit had been reduced to a slippery hole. The step-niches Kandan had scooped out inside it were invisible now, rubbed away by the rainwater.

And so his legs carried Kandan to where he generally went when there was nothing to do: Mendis's tavern. Much of the cash he earned at the gempit found its way to the tavern. Mendis's recommendation to Daud had brought to him more than a fair share of Kandan's earning.

That day, Kandan had imbibed more than even his high standards. When he staggered home late that evening, he was in no condition to apply his mind to problems. He wanted to collapse on to his mat and sink into a deep sleep. He was thus more irritated than surprised by the large crowd surrounding their line. He stopped to think what it could all be about. A sudden death, perhaps. A youngster passing his way told him of the happening. Jayasena had been killed by a fish vendor in the afternoon. No one knew why. Only Velu had witnessed it. And Velu had drawn the crowd. Kandan moved on. Jayasena killed! It was unbelievable. Scenes flashed in Kandan's mind. Jayasena saying he cannot spare that tractor trailer for Amara. Kandan begging him to do so. Jayasena refusing. Kandan hitting him, hitting him hard. Jayasena flying into the latex drums.

Kandan entered his room to see Valli crouching on the ground. Theiva, who was sitting beside her, sprang to her feet on seeing her father. 'Akka has been crying the whole afternoon. She won't say why.' 'What's happening?' he asked. Valli sat up slowly, wiping the perspiration on her face. Asking Theiva to leave the room, she said, very softly, 'Appa, you have heard what has happened, haven't you? There is something else about it which you do not know.' Kandan narrowed his eyes to concentrate on what the girl was saying. 'That murder . . . Soma, the fish vendor. I know him . . . I know why he has killed Jayasena.' Kandan couldn't quite follow. She knows the fish vendor? Knows why he killed Jayasena? The girl continued, through tears. Her words came in spurts with her hot breath. Kandan absorbed them, reacting to each word, each sentence, a moment later than he would have, were it not for the toddy. She knows the fisherman. What does she mean 'knows'? She . . . No! Kandan was incensed. He raised his arm high in the air and swung it down on Valli's head. He hit her once, twice, thrice. Valli covered her head with her hands but did not try to run or evade the blows. 'Appa, but you have not heard me fully. Hear me. Hear me out.'

'Not heard you fully? Can there be anything more to tell? Can there by anything more humiliating?'

'Jayasena . . .'

Kandan steadied himself. Jayasena? Valli completed her sentence. 'Jayas . . . he did what? Valli! No!' Kandan doubled up in shock, grief and anger. Anger at the villain, at the fates, at himself. At the villain whose venality was boundless in its cynical cruelty. At the fates for revisiting the same family with such heartlessness. At himself for having hit his daughter who had endured an unspeakable experience at the hands of Jayasena.

'Save Soma somehow, appa. Save him please. He killed Jayasena for my sake.' The words sank slowly into his mind. Amara came to his thoughts, reproachfully. Peramayi's words rang in Kandan's ears. ('No one bothers about Valli. She is no child now.') His dead wife and his old mother joined his subconscious mind to make him feel an unbearable contrition for what he had done.

Kandan gathered his daughter into his arms, wiped the tears from her eyes, stroked her head where his blows had fallen and smoothed down the hair.

In the meantime, Craigavon had been converted into a cantonment. Nimal was so enraged by his assistant supervisor's murder that he went through and invoked the provisions of the criminal trespass law. This prohibited outsiders, vendors or anyone else, entering the estate without permission. The strict penalties to which 'trespassers' would be subjected were displayed prominently at the entrances to the estate and at a few conspicuous points inside as well. One of these boards warned the estate labour force that a resident worker who continued to live on the lines or anywhere else on the estate after dismissal would also be charged with criminal trespass.

Nimal obtained the Board's permission to pay a sum of ten thousand rupees to 'the family of the deceased assistant field supervisor as a measure of the estate's regret at the death in harness of an able member of its staff.'

'Thank goodness,' Nimal told his fellow superintendents at the Club, 'the murderer was an outsider. My task would have been considerably more difficult if one of my labour had done it.'

'They are capable of it too,' Wimalawardene assured Nimal. 'On Cork too, the workers are showing signs of resenting some of the stricter methods we are bringing into force under your guidance.' Tilakaratne did not like to be reminded that they were all now under Nimal's overall supervision. 'They have always been a sulky, scheming lot. I would never trust them,' he said. And Pieris, rarely for him, made a contribution to the subject. 'Unions,' he said in a voice hushed as to be this side of the waiter's hearing, 'are instigating them all the time, from behind the scenes. All the time. I hear three unions are meeting shortly to discuss the application of the trespass laws. They are saying it restricts the legal right to contact labour.'

'What nonsense!' Wimalawardene thundered. 'Legal rights indeed. Do you know, Nimal, in the good old days they had the Master and Servant Legislation which enabled government to deal with troublesome labour summarily. If a labourer left the estate without giving one month's notice, the police could arrest him and he would be fined or jailed and forced to go back to the estate from which he had tried to escape.'

Nimal did not know this piece of labour history but was not particularly interested. He knew the legislation was not in vogue now and there was no point in harking back to it. But Pieris's news about trade unions not having taken kindly to his trespass regulations worried him. He did not want a strike. He couldn't afford it. The Board would not like that at all.

'It was all the work of that A.E. Goonesinghe,' Wimalawardene went on. 'That man organized estate labour and started all the trouble.'

'He and two Indians,' Tilakaratne added. 'My mother, who is always speaking up for labour, says that without the efforts of a South Indian, K. Natesa Aiyar, and then of Nehru, estate labour in Ceylon would have remained unorganized.'

'I did not know Nehru had very much to do with estate labour in Ceylon,' Nimal said with genuine surprise.

'Oh yes. He visited the island in 1930 or 1931,' Tilakaratne continued, 'and brought a lot of Indian Tamil organizations under the roof of the Ceylon Indian Congress. His *Autobiography*, which my mother has made me read, describes all that.'

Nimal felt a familiar discomfort grow and spread inside him. He had felt it when reading Ronald Manners' letter. He felt it now. Nehru, a product of Harrow and Cambridge, had to come to Ceylon and helped organize labour. The very labour which he, Nimal Rupasinghe of Oxford, was now ranged against. Nimal felt an aesthetic defect in the situation. He would rather have been with a person who had been through Oxbridge in any venture whatever, than find himself leading his present company. Had he made a mistake? Was the situation irremediable? Nimal shuddered as his thoughts were interrupted by Wimalawardene's shout for more drinks.

Thaiyalnayaki Sriskandanathar was in high dudgeon. She had been in that state ever since the murder. Velu's presence at the scene of the crime had been reported to her by the servant next door and had sent her into hysterics. She packed all her jewellery into a box and insisted that her husband take it to Keselgoda and deposit it in the bank's vaults.

'Imagine,' she repeatedly said to her husband, 'we have had a murderer's accomplice working in our house all these months. Ayyo! What all he could have done to us!'

'We don't know what he was doing there,' Sriskandanathar tried to quieten her down. 'He may be quite innocent.'

'Innocent! Everybody says he was a friend of the fisherman's. In fact, I know that myself. The very first day those two met, I was there, watching. The fisherman asked Velu to follow him and they went away to some distance and then I could not see what they did. After that, every time the man came, Velu would rush out of the house with a big smile. Ayyo!'

'Don't worry, he will not be working here any more.'

'Have you had his room searched? There are some clothes of his here also. You better examine them. Maybe you will find something there which will be connected to the murder. Please search.'

Sriskandanathar was used to doing as he was told, in the office and at home. He went to the tiny space between the kitchen and their backyard garden that was Velu's 'room'. In a small plastic bag, Velu had left a change of clothes.

Sriskandanathar was reluctant to even touch the clothes. They seemed to him to be drenched in the man's sweat and grime.

Feeling the shirt pocket, Sriskandanathar touched a small piece of paper. Could it be a currency note? An idea went through his head and heart like a palpitation. If it is a big enough note, shall I . . .? The boy wouldn't dare ask. Even Thaiyal need not know.

But it was not a currency note. It was a lottery ticket. A one-rupee lottery ticket. Sriskandanathar pushed it back into the pocket with a mixture of contempt and hatred. How dare the lowly be so ambitious, was his unexpressed sentiment.

'Nothing there,' he shouted to his wife. 'Only a lottery ticket.' There was silence for a moment or two, and then Thaiyalnayaki's voice came back. 'A lottery ticket, is it? Can you bring it here?' The man was exasperated. He disliked doing chores at home, disliked being told by his wife to fetch and carry, but saying so could mean paying a much heavier price in terms of the peace of the evening. And so he took the ticket to his wife.

'The results of the sweep are out. The man could well have been lucky,' Thaiyalnayaki informed her husband, snapping the ticket from his hand. Sriskandanathar was entranced by the thought.

'Thaiyal! Can you . . . can you check?'

And check she did.

A woman's instincts are not to be lightly discounted. Thaiyalnayaki Sriskandanathar ascertained from Keselgoda that the ticket in her hands was one of twenty-five lucky tickets. It carried nothing less than a windfall of five thousand rupees. In the democratic anonymity that lotteries offer, she cashed the ticket and romped home in barely suppressed joy.

Husband and wife looked at each other and smiled. They smiled and looked at each other. Their shoulders quivered and their tongues went dry with excitement. The excitement that schoolboys feel when they have tried their first secret smoke, or schoolgirls when they have eaten forbidden sweetmeats in the school's back alley.

Thaiyalnayaki was not only an avaricious female. She was also an extraordinarily clever one. She had brought back with her from the sweep joint a rejected lottery ticket thrown away by someone. To her husband's unutterable surprise, she put the dud ticket into Velu's shirt pocket. 'He will never know now,' she winked. 'Ayyo, ayyo,' Sriskandanathar gasped with joy, 'ayyo, ayyo.'

Wilmot Inginiyagala of Ratnapura was a middle-aged, paunchy civil and criminal lawyer of repute. Like Inspector Yusouf, he too had cultivated specialized interests within his profession. Yusouf's study of wounds was matched by Inginiyagala's studies in the psychology of crime. An article by him entitled *Crime Passionel: Seven Case Studies in Motive and Method* had been serialized in a Colombo law magazine and had won him plaudits. Fellow lawyers envied him while magistrates treated him with respect. Inginiyagala had for long kept the rumour going that he had thrice declined an elevation to the bench because, he said, he believed in practising and not dispensing law.

Inginiyagala was not, however, dependent on his legal practice. He had inherited a sizeable estate of coconut groves from his father and had no need to work for a living. It was his interest in the subject that kept him in alpaca. Inginiyagala subscribed to a large number of journals on law—local, Indian, and British— and was able, with the help of his reading, to stay miles ahead of other members of the Ratnapura bar. His reading had worn out his eyesight so that he wore high-correction glasses. His wife was Ratnapura's crochet artist extraordinaire, giving lessons and demonstrations all the time. The Inginiyagalas were persons of leisure and its offerings. They were fortunate in that they both had certain active interests. Were it not for those, feudal decadence would have overtaken the family.

Inginiyagala had read of the Craigavon murder with some interest. But he dismissed the last sentence of the newspaper report with one word: Rubbish. The sentence ran as follows. 'While the motive for the estate official's murder has not

yet been conclusively ascertained, police believe it to have
been provoked by an insultingly low price offered for the fish
vendor's wares.'

The report had soon passed his mind. But Inginiyagala was
not surprised when, a couple of months later, his old acquaintance
'Captain' Sando of Keselgoda stood before him and said he
wanted to discuss the murder of the Craigavon official with him.
He had brought two Tamil estate workers from Craigavon, one a
deaf-mute and the other a middle-aged man.

'So you know something of it,' Inginiyagala said to Sando.
The 'Captain' explained that the accused was a pupil of his,
and the deaf-mute a friend of the pupil. Inginiyagala asked
the men to come into his office room and sit down. The
Tamils kept standing.

'Sit down,' he almost commanded them in Tamil. 'This is not
a courtroom and you are not the accused,' he told them. Sando
explained the events as fully as he had been able to understand
them after Kandan and Velu had met him. Inginiyagala listened
to his visitors with great care, punctuating their narration with
'That's it,' 'I thought so too,' 'See? I knew it, always.' When
Sando and Kandan had finished, Inginiyagala patted Kandan
on the back and assured him that he would take up the case
and do his best to reduce the sentence. That was all that he could
promise. The crime was patent, self-confessed. But he would
stress the extenuating circumstances which also ought to be patent,
self-evident, to any judge. 'Leave it to me, Perumal Kandan,' he
reassured the man. 'The boy will get off with a few years.'

'A few years!'

'Why does that surprise you? A murder is a murder. A few
years in jail cannot be avoided.' As the men were leaving,
Inginiyagala said to Kandan, 'You will, incidentally, have to tell
your daughter to forget about him. Better still, you had better
get her married off as soon as you can to some good lad on the
estate.' Inginiyagala met Soma in the lock-up soon thereafter,

met his parents, and informed them all that he would handle this case. He would be handling it free of charge, he told them.

Sitting down to an enormous meal of rice and curry that night, he asked his wife if she remembered the Sando case. Inginiyagala had been approached by Sando years ago. Restitution of conjugal rights, he had wanted. The man's wife had made off to Batticaloa with another man during Sando's absence during the war. It was not worth it, he had advised Sando, forget her. Marry again. Sando had agreed not to pursue the matter, but would never remarry, never. Were it not for my wife having joined that man of her own accord, Sando had said, he would have murdered him.

Mrs Inginiyagala did not remember the case at all. But not wanting to disappoint her husband, she mumbled, yes, she remembered. 'Well, that Sando came again today, after all these years.' Inginiyagala then gave his wife a summary of the Craigavon case. 'It's not just that the fisherboy avenged the violation of his girl. He was also being spurred by the mystique of "your womenfolk's honour", which Sando leavens into his pupils' egg-cup brains.'

Mrs Inginiyagala was dozing. She had gone through years of this and could no longer be enthused by legal points. Her husband went on. 'This murder is a strange hybrid. It is the classical *crime passionel*. It is also the exotic *crime machinal*, the mindless act of a robot, a robot programmed by its initiator to act and react in a given manner.' Inginiyagala dropped a mock bow at the summation of his argument and looked up at his wife for commendation. Mrs Inginiyagala was fast asleep in her seat, head bent, bifocals resting on the tip of her nose, mouth ever so slightly open.

Line seven was now aware of Valli's secret.

Sinnathal, her husband Adaikkan and brother Arumugam, constituted themselves into something of a jury. Their verdict was: *Guilty.* Valli and others in her family must atone. Sinna announced that, as a first step, the plan that Valli weds her brother, be forgotten. Arumugam must marry a 'clean' girl, she declared. Adaikkan was a bit shy-faced about it all but did not dare contest his wife's pronouncement. Arumugam affected an air of injured innocence. Valli smiled a bitter smile at this development. She had never intended to marry Arumugam anyway, she said. 'Never intended?' Sinna flared. 'And to think that it was I who looked after you and prepared your mind for adulthood and marriage. Never intended!'

'Hush, Sinna,' Peramayi intervened. 'The girl has been through a lot of agony. No one should be harsh with her. The same could have happened to anyone else, to you.'

'Not to me, thank you. I am never the one to go fooling around with Sinhalese fish vendors,' Sinna declared with the self-confidence of the lucky.

Valli went about her work in the house mechanically. There had always been that slight division between her mental and her physical activities. Her mind moved and had its essential being in one world. Her hands and legs, in another. But now, the division was total. Her thoughts with Soma, she went through her chores as if in a hypnotic trance. She had stopped going to work on the estate. Theiva did that full time now. After Valli described what had happened, the sisters had clung to each other and wept. 'Akka, don't you worry. All will be well, really,' Theiva tried to reassure her sister. Valli was too much of a realist to feel that all would be well merely because Theiva wished it. But the girl's words signified to her that there was someone who cared, someone who wanted all to be well with her. The two sisters moved closer to each other's minds and hearts than ever before. Theiva was determined to see her sister through the crisis. Her sister, whose experience she understood in its every nuance, physical and emotional. But Theiva, too, worked in a different spirit from before. Plucking was not fun any longer. She would work as much as the norm required and beyond, so as to earn the incentive bonus for additional poundage. The family needed all the money she could bring. She, who was now the sole earner.

But Kandan, despite the lucid interval when he was able to go with Velu to 'Captain' Sando and to the lawyer, was sliding. He felt he was like a tree that had been sawn through. A strong gale could push it off the base. And Sinna's fulminations were like one continuous gale. He could not endure that woman. Adaikkan and Arumugam had also begun looking at him as if he was a criminal. 'What have we done to you?' Kandan demanded of Adaikkan outside the line one evening. 'The fates have been cruel to us, have broken us. But why should you join the evil spirits?' The neighbour was quiet. He was abashed and afraid. You never know with slightly mad men, he told himself. Arumugam, who saw Kandan talking to Adaikkan, called his brother-in-law away. 'Why, why are you running away? Can we not talk? Are we not neighbours?'

'We are,' Arumugam said from a distance. 'That's the whole trouble.'

'Go to hell!' Kandan shouted behind them. 'And be damned!'

'Damned be you!' Sinna retaliated coming out of her room. 'You who brought death to your wife by your carelessness, and misery to your daughter by your drunken neglect.' Sinna's remark blanked out Kandan's mind. He could not think further, could not speak. He walked on, out and away from the complex of lines. He kept walking, past the tea bushes, the rubber trees. He reached and went beyond the estate boundaries. It was getting dark very fast. The rain started again. But Kandan did not feel it. A few estate workers saw him go past them. 'Kandan! Where to?' He did not hear them.

'I brought death to Amara, I brought it,' he kept repeating to himself. 'I have ruined Valli's life, I have. I, I, I.' Kandan's feet sought out the road to the gempit, through the slush and the rain. He reached the spot like the crazed stag chasing a mirage in fabled deserts. But unlike the stag's, Kandan's destination was real . . .

Rainwater was gushing into it. Mud and slime had crept into it. Kandan sat down beside the hole. The rushing waters flowed around him in circles and then curved into the pit. The sun began setting behind Kandan, behind the hillocks he had just crossed. And then a few stars blinked from beyond the clouds. Kandan looked up. The moon, nearly full, was right overhead. It seemed to be bending like a human face, over him. It seemed to want to speak to him. 'I brought death to Amara,' Kandan said to the orb. 'I have ruined my daughter's life.' Kandan thought the moon agreed with that, for it did not move. It kept looking down at him, inquiringly, almost critically. It was quite dark now. The rain had softened. The water in the gempit was high, just a feet or two lower than the rim. Kandan stood up. The thinning rain fell on his face. He felt it now, like soft needles. He looked down and got a start. He had seen that vision before. The water at his feet was glistening like a serpent's coil. It writhed there, coming over his toes, his ankles. Damnation! He lifted one leg. It constricted the other foot. He lifted the other. It would not let go. It glistened from a hundred shining scales. 'Ayyo!' Kandan screamed. He tried to jump and slipped, heading straight towards the mouth of the pit. Kandan's arms flew out as he went through. The pit which he had helped dig, sod by sod, sucked him in. It gripped Kandan as tightly as ten men or twenty hands. For a moment, Kandan looked up through the water. Pinioned to the bottom of the pit, Kandan raised his spinning head, saw bright specks, the stars. Bright chips, fragments of the moon. Gems! his mind said. Gems! And then, water flooding his lungs, his head, Kandan could see no more.

For almost three days no one knew what had become of the man. Valli and Theiva were desperate. Peramayi had resigned herself to the worst. 'I don't think we will ever see him again,' she moaned. She lay down in her room. Perumal was at his wits' end. Nothing he said seemed to console his wife. 'My eyes are too old now for tears,' she told him. 'But if I could cry, my tears would surpass the rain.' Perumal stroked his wife's forehead. 'Easy now,' he said.

On the fourth day, the rains stayed off and the ground breathed through its pores once again. A group of estate boys from Armagh, going through a shortcut to the estate school, noticed a protuberance in the slime inside the illegal gempit. The older boys among them were sure it was a human body. Someone ran up to the nearest field where labourers were working, for help. The workers came running. But no one dared lower himself into the pit, it was so treacherously slimy. Must wait for another day of sunshine, they said. Crowds of people from Armagh, the nearest estate, stood for long hours around the pit, speculating on whose body it could be.

Word reached Daud about the mishap. He arrived with Falil the following day. Some of the other diggers employed at the pit by Daud were summoned to bring the body out. Going down slowly, very slowly, they identified their fellow digger. 'Kandan,' the name went round. 'Kandan of Craigavon.' Slightly mental, they said he was. His wife died of childbirth some years ago. And his daughter had gone 'bad' recently. Mixed up, she was, in the recent murder at Craigavon. Definitely mixed up, though no one quite knew how.

Daud paid for a bullock cart to be hired to take the body to the man's estate. The cart-driver demanded thrice the usual hire. Carrying a corpse was not good for his cart or his business. But Daud was able to settle the bargain for twice the usual hire. Two of the other workers went with the cart. 'God knows what brought him to the pit in this weather,' the cartman asked the two diggers. They walked alongside, without a word. Both of them remembered their fooling Kandan about the star-gems, the moon-gem. 'Don't know,' one of them said at last. 'You never know with these half-mad men!'

The incident had unnerved Daud. A very ugly development it was. Daud got Falil to dredge the pit thoroughly after the bystanders had all left. The old gemmer was seated under a tree while the clean-up was on, contemplating whether he should not send a small sum of money to Kandan's family for the funeral expenses, when Falil ran up excitedly. His fists were clenched.

'Uncle,' he said, 'look at these. They came up just now, as we were cleaning the pit.' Daud peered into his nephew's barely opened palms. He had not seen many sapphires of the size of those seven.

Deep inside her, Sinnathal felt very sorry for the family. But egoism being what it is, she could not get herself to reveal her feelings too openly.

Peramayi had flickered like a sputtering candle for a couple of weeks after Kandan's body had been brought in. And then she went out—just like that! Sinna wept secretly in her room. Peramayi had been her neighbour ever since she could remember. And she had been much more than a neighbour, had been something of a mother. Sinna told her husband to help Perumal with the funeral arrangements, even advance the money. Adaikkan had grumbled, accusing her of confusing him about how they should treat that family. But he had given in. Arumugam, too, had joined. 'She should have a decent funeral,' Sinna told them all. 'Not like Kandan's, when so few came or helped.' Velu had organized Kandan's funeral single-handedly. Valli and Theiva had been senseless in their grief and shock. The gemmer had helped with a good sum of money and everyone had wondered who that strange hefty Sinhalese in enormous moustaches was who had come up from Keselgoda to assist Velu. 'We must do our duty by Peramayi,' Sinna advised. To set an example, she joined Valli and Theiva in bathing Peramayi's body. The estate barber, who functioned as the local undertaker, took charge of the funeral and burial. Adaikkan asked Perumal if he would prefer to have a cremation arranged, instead of the customary burial which is cheaper, no firewood being involved. But the old man was too dazed to reply. He merely shook his hands to indicate that he had no preferences And so a burial it was. A couple of crackers were burst and they carried her away on a bamboo stretcher, Valli and Theiva joining the funeral, though women did not generally do so. The man in charge of grave-digging on the estate burial grounds had dug the grave beside Kandan's still very fresh one. Water, coconut, rice grains and betel were sprinkled over the dried-up frame that had been the girls' grandmother. When the body was lowered into the grave the girls broke into unrestrained sobs. 'We have no one left now,' Theiva cried. 'No one.'

Fortunately, Theiva was wrong.

Kandan's death, closely followed by that of Peramayi, had brought Velu much closer to the family than ever before. The young man had sensed the isolation into which it had fallen, sensed the link between Valli and his jailed friend Soma. And, above all, he had begun to sense the beginnings of an attraction towards Theiva. The girl had begun to occur in his dreams very frequently, the more so since the day she and Valli had told him that he could have his meals with them. The Sriskandanathars having sacked him, Velu would not have known what to do, were it not for this offer of the two girls made in all earnestness and despite their great sorrow. Theiva served him his food, mean meal that it was, with a tenderness that touched him. It did something to him, something quite unique in his experience.

But Velu had no friend or companion with whom he could talk about this, either seriously or light-heartedly. Even marriage in the mechanical, 'given' sense in which it was known to people on estates could never have been discussed by him. Velu had but eyes to guide him, to prompt and stir him. But these were deprived the auditory assistance which everyone possessed of normal hearing and speech takes for granted. It was, therefore, an extremely difficult mental step for him to admit to himself that he was in love. He had to persuade himself that such a thing could happen, that it had happened to him, that the emotion was connected to what he saw in Theiva and to what his heart and his body compelled him to respect.

And Theiva too felt Velu's thoughts. The day she handed him his first plate of rottis she noticed him looking at her. There was gratitude and love in those eyes. Had Velu been capable of speech, the utterance of his eyes would have been weaker, diluted. But in the event, his eyes spoke powerfully . . . Theiva noticed that and was glad for it. Her sister's description of her feelings towards Soma had been too real and recent for Theiva not to recognize similar emotions where they existed. She responded to Velu's emotion instantly and with equal seriousness.

Perumal had a cousin, Kathan, in Glenville estate near Nuwara Eliya. Perumal and he were roughly of the same age. They had made a point of attending marriages and funerals in each other's families. Perumal, on the third day after Peramayi's going, had a telegram sent to Kathan. And Kathan came for the thirteenth day karumantaram ceremony, for which Sinnathal had got a reluctant Adaikkan to provide the money. He came with his son, Karuppayya, and a neighbour, Sannasi.

Perumal and these three persons assembled in the lineroom where the old priest and the estate barber had arrived to conduct the ritual. A pot was placed in one corner, containing water, milk and honey. It was decorated with turmeric powder and closed with a coconut, mango leaves and flowers. The pandaram did some ceremonies round the pot near which three bricks which he called the trimurti had been placed. Perumal went through the ceremonies with automatic motions, no thought or inquiry being bestowed on the goings-on. That, after all, was the secret of the priesthood's hold on the Hindu populace, was it not? The masses knew nothing, could understand nothing of the priest's panjandrums. The priest enjoyed his role. Smoke had filled the room. Everyone rubbed eyes, blew noses. But he was used to the smoke. It could not obscure *his* field of view. His field, which took in, particularly, Sinnathal, that comfortably architected woman and the two girls. What suppressed vivacity! The priest saw them closely through his reddened eyes. How wonderfully ripening those girls were! No wonder that fish vendor had netted the older girl. He was glad the other men would soon be gone to the stream when he would be left alone and could take his own time to return to the temple. At a signal from the priest the pot and bricks were picked up by the barber, Perumal and the other men to be taken to a stream close by. They were cast into the gently flowing waters. Later, the men bathed in the stream, ending the period of ritual pollution. The party returned to the lines and to the room which Perumal and Peramayi had occupied for decades and where Perumal was to live by himself hereafter.

That afternoon, Kathan, scratching his head from diffidence and embarrassment, went up to Perumal. 'You and I are old now. We cannot afford to have on our shoulders responsibilities for a day longer than necessary, can we? You had no responsibilities all these days. That was lucky. But now, with Kandan and your wife dead, the future of these two granddaughters of yours lies in your hands.'

Perumal's eyes went moist. 'Yes, Kathan. I am aware of that. Who would have thought I, in my old age, would have to worry about their future? What the future holds for them, I do not know.'

Kathan cleared his throat. When Kathan saw that Perumal was suggestible, his diffidence left him. In a strong tone of voice, he elaborated his point. 'You know I have brought with me this neighbour of mine, Sannasi. He is forty-six years old. He lost his wife some years ago. He has five children, the youngest of whom is five or six and the eldest, a girl, about sixteen. The girl, Meena, has to be married off soon. The children need a mother badly. I think it would be a good idea if Valli could be married to Sannasi!'

Perumal was disturbed by the proposal. Valli was barely eighteen, so beautiful, so full of youth. She should marry a young, healthy man, not a middle-aged widower. Kathan read his cousin's thoughts. His confidence became aggressive. 'Perumal, I know what you are thinking. But don't forget everybody knows of what has happened between her and the fish vendor. I can tell you she will not find a husband within the same caste easily. Sannasi is not young, but he is a very good man. He is a family man, who will look after Valli well. And, besides, he is going to India under the Agreement.'

At this last piece of information, Perumal sat up. 'He is going to repatriate, is he? So if Valli marries him, she would have to leave too?'

'Isn't that just as well? Look at our many difficulties here. We are poor and we are stateless. There she may be poor but she would have rights . . .'

Perumal was unimpressed. He did not know what rights meant. All he could see was that Valli, if she were to become Sannasi's wife, would be gone from him for ever. He told Kathan he would think the matter over and let him know.

'Yes, of course, you must think it over. But don't delay a decision too much. Remember we are not getting any younger.

Sannasi, a short but well-proportioned man with greying hair, stood at a slight distance all this while. He knew Kathan was discussing the marriage proposal. He had told Kathan before they set out from Glenville that he would be able to say if he was interested only after seeing the girl. After seeing Valli, he had whispered his willingness to the old man. And Kathan had lost no time in broaching the subject. Sannasi could see that Perumal had not said an outright no.

After the guests left that evening, Perumal called Valli to his side. 'Child, don't think I want to get rid of you. It isn't that. But you must think of your future.' He then told her of Kathan's suggestion. Valli heard her grandfather with rock-like composure. Could she have done otherwise?

As her grandfather spoke an option crossed her mind. She could take her life. There was any amount of lethal fungicide in the estate's stores to which she could help herself. But then another thought came close on the heels of the first, cancelling it totally. The other thought, which had been with her for a few weeks now was, in fact, not a thought at all. It was a piece of knowledge. She had known for almost two months now that Soma's seed had quickened inside her. If she had been able to endure the profound tragedy that had overtaken her in the loss of Soma and the death of her father and grandmother, it was only because of this knowledge and the strength it gave her.

As Perumal went on about the need for security and how he was past the age when he could provide it, Valli scarcely heard him. Her mind was moving at a momentum of its own. Soma's child must live. It must be given a chance to be born right, born into a house. Not under a tree, without a name or a nationality.

Perumal was most surprised when, moments later, Valli suddenly said 'Yes, father, I will marry him. Please arrange it at once.'

The marriage was taking place in the shadow of two deaths in the bride's family. And it was the bridegroom's second marriage. So the customary rituals of novelty and leisure, such as a prolonged engagement ceremony and a large wedding under a pandal, were dispensed with.

Perumal went, simply, with the two girls, Velu and Adaikkan (Sinnathal stayed behind) by bus over nearly a hundred miles to the bridegroom's estate Glenville, for the wedding. Unlike Craigavon, which was in the low-altitude south, Glenville, near Nuwara Eliya, was cold and windy. The visitors wrapped

themselves in sheets and scarves and were mildly amused at
the frosting of their breath. Velu, in particular, was intrigued
and pleased that any guttural movement he made converted itself
into an airy whiteness. This was the first time he could see a
use for his mouth other than the one use he knew, eating and
drinking. Of that use, too, there was substantial if not elaborate
opportunity in the marriage meal prepared by Sannasi's relations
and neighbours, Kathan supervising. They were housed in two
linerooms thoughtfully vacated by Sannasi's neighbours for the
girl's party. On the morning of the marriage they walked in
a small procession to the Glenville temple where the local priest
performed a brief ceremony. Sannasi tied a tali round Valli's
neck at the auspicious moment, and they all walked back to
the lines. Theiva stayed as close to Valli as possible, throughout.
The girls knew that the moment they dreaded, the moment of
farewell, was but a few hours away. There was none of the usual
merriment or pleasantry. It had all been very stark, very brief.
Back in Sannasi's lineroom Perumal gave his granddaughter
a couple of Peramayi's jewels and a small cloth no bigger than a
handkerchief that had been tied into a knot. It contained a pair
of gold earrings belonging to Amaravathi, preserved through the
years by the old couple for the day of Valli's marriage. Valli broke
down when Perumal gave her this. 'Father!' she sobbed, hugging
the old man, something she had not done in years. She was
surprised at her grandfather's boniness. His shoulder blades, his
ribs, jabbed her. Quickly regaining her composure, Valli said,
'Sit down for a while, father, and eat something.'

Valli had observed the rhythms of her new home for the
last few hours. Her husband's children were regarding her with
extreme caution. The eldest girl Meena was, surprisingly, the
friendliest. 'Come, Amma!' she told Valli. 'We will get something
for him to eat.' The girl was barely a couple of years younger
than Valli, and about the same age as Theiva. She had addressed
Valli for the first time and now that the marriage had been

solemnized, had done it consciously. But the word fell on Valli like a deadening weight. It not only fixed a name and a role on her. It dissolved her independence. And, more than anything else, it reminded her of the life within her life which was taking shape deep within her being, minute by minute, tissue by tissue, cell by cell. It was a boy, Valli was sure. It was to be a Soma. The parting, next day, from Theiva was indescribably painful. Their sorrow at parting was great, as was their self-conciousness in the presence of many strangers in that unfamiliar estate. And so the girls quickly checked their tears and, although it was not easy, assumed normal countenances.

Sannasi, understandingly, looked the other way as the Craigavon party bade farewell to Valli, his new wife. Sannasi walked with them to the bus stop outside the estate boundary and saw them off. Returning, he found Valli talking to his children in the lineroom veranda. Meena was trying to bridge the gulf between the younger ones and Valli. He could see that Valli had just about overcome her tears. He joined Valli in the veranda and gently put his hand on Valli's shoulder. She shivered at the touch but concealed her reaction at once. She would tell him, she decided. She would tell him that very night.

Sannasi took it very well.

'I am not surprised and I do not care. There are five children you have to look after, that are not yours. There can be a sixth that is not mine. We shall look after them all together.'

Valli was immensely grateful. She suddenly felt a concern for this man, her husband, a vague sense of responsibility towards him and his heavy load of worry. He needed her help, she told herself. And she his. She would stint nothing. And so, whatever he asked of her, including her body, she rendered ungrudgingly.

Sannasi got Valli's name registered as a worker at Glenville. Valli, Meena and Sannasi would go out to work. The family's income improved perceptibly, as did its tone. Sannasi was immensely pleased and grateful. He planned, every day, about

their future in India after they had all repatriated. They would go
to the Nilgiris, he told Valli. The work would be the same, as also
the climate and, what was more, they would be in India. Valli
heard him smilingly whenever he spoke of India, but without
comment. She could not visualize India, which meant nothing
special to her. She belonged here and at Craigavon. And as for
the little life that was quickening inside her, that belonged here
and nowhere else. It belonged to Soma.

But soon, after Valli's new life at Glenville had begun, all
estates and, indeed, the island itself, ran into most unexpected
difficulties. Supplies of food ran desperately short and rations
were curtailed. Until then a person's requirement had been
calculated as being three-and-a-half measures per week. But after
the cut, an estate worker received only half a measure free and
had to purchase three measures from the open market. The
prevailing price there being something like four rupees a measure,
he was left with virtually nothing.

The workers were forced to cut down on food, cut down on
proteins. Predictably their productivity went down.

Valli was undergoing a trial. The amount earned by her
husband, herself and Meena was just not enough to feed the entire
family. The four younger children cried and howled for their
usual quantity of rottis or rice. And Sannasi expected Valli to
somehow or the other materialize it. And so Valli would work for
as long as she could, pluck as much as she was able to during the
course of a working day. And she went further. She cut down her
own eating by less than half. The child in her womb needed
nourishment and Valli should have been eating more than her
normal regimen. But shortage is no respecter of pregnancies.
Her stomach burned with hunger, her head reeled with exhaustion
and weakness, and yet she forced herself. Meena helped her
spontaneously and Sannasi, too, saw that without Valli the family
would not have gone through that lean period unscarred. But his
one priority was the small children. A wooden obstinacy in him

made everything else subordinate, including his pregnant wife's health. He could have but did not tell her not to strain herself to work for all five days, and that too on a starvation diet. He had cut down on food too, Valli could see that. And so she couldn't fault him, although whenever she felt faint she worried for the child that was stirring inside her and despaired of her husband's children stirring all around her.

It was during one such siezure of painful exhaustion that Valli went to the resting shed for women workers near her plucking field. Father Gio, now in Kandewatte near there, drove up with a group of nuns to distribute milk powder to the women. 'What is your name?' he asked her in Tamil. When she gave it, he said 'That is a very good name. But I will call you Vyakulamary, Mary Anxious for her Child. Worry not. These nuns will be your friends.' He asked her then whether her parents were on that estate too. When Valli told him they were dead and that she was from Craigavon, Father Gio put his hand on her head. 'I am from those parts too, Vyakulamary. My heart is still there.' Tears filled Valli's eyes.

The shortage was on everyone's minds and lips. Sometime in December 1973, when the Maradeniya planters met as usual at the Club, Wimalawardene was seething with anger. Workers at Cork had told him through the union that they did not have the stamina to work for five days a week. 'What rot, I say, Nimal, what damn rot! They are just making it up, those union leaders.'

'The truth is that they want to go out of the estate to find work elsewhere at higher wages for the other days. I am not going to allow this.'

Tilakaratne informed the others that the average amount plucked had come down at Limerick from about thirty-five

pounds per day per plucker to about fifteen. Pieris, not to be
outdone, said Armagh had recorded a slide from thirty-five to ten.

It had become the convention at the Club for the other three
to make their points and then wait for Nimal to sum up the
case, give his pronouncement. Quite imperceptibly, eyes would
turn to him and footlights come slowly on. 'Well,' Nimal said,
'we cannot forget the fact that a superintendent is meant to achieve
the maximum profits with the minimum costs. The tactics for
achieving this have to be left to the man on the spot. These are
difficult times and we have to guard the company's interests very
cautiously. I personally think this business of nutritional levels
is overdone by doctors and do-gooders whose business it is to
talk about nutrition just as our business is to work for production.
But we have to admit that there has been a shortage and some
of the fallout will be on us. It is not going to be possible for us
to make the workers work for five days, as if nothing has
happened. I don't think Dick's line is safe. If we were to slam
the door at the union and say, no, they have got to report all
five days, we may land a strike on our heads, a strike when we
could have not three days' output but zero output. I don't think
the company would like that.'

Damn the dandy, Wimalawardene said to himself. Drops
the name of the company every time as if it belonged to him!
Wouldn't we all like to see a strike on Craigavon that plucks the
man's style from him like that much fluff.

Sublimating his thoughts Wimalawardene said, 'I beg to differ,
Nimal. I have been planting for decades. I know when it is that
we have to draw the line.'

Damn the dope, Nimal said to himself. Drops the decades
bit every time as if years spent on an estate are the only
credentials required. Wouldn't one like to see a strike take the
fat off his bones.

Nimal filtered his thoughts through a sieve of conversational
etiquette and replied, 'As I said, Dick, the man on the spot

will have to decide for himself, taking every local contingency into account.'

Wimalawardene felt he had won the point and ordered a refill of his parched glass.

And then, early in 1974, relations between the trade unions and the Maradeniya estates plummeted. Wimalawardene refused to meet the union's representatives, sending word that if any worker did not report for duty over one week continuously, his name would be removed from the checkroll. Tilakaratne and Pieris followed suit. Nimal was unsure of the attitude he should take. The very fact that his colleagues had acted in a particular manner made him inclined to act differently. Besides, he wanted the others to know that since he was head of the Group he would have to ratify their action. And before doing that he wanted to be sure that they were right.

The unions approached him last of all, with their charter of demands. A visitor's slip was placed at the desk, containing five names including a lady's, Martha Abeyesekere. The first name was that of Thambimuttu Sivaswami, leader of the largest union. Nimal asked them to be shown in at once. The five of them represented two trade unions and a Colombo-based social research body. Martha Abeyesekere represented the latter. Dressed in a simple light brown sari which contrasted with her fair skin, she struck Nimal as a woman of intelligence and resolve besides good looks. Nimal offered her the best seat in his room. She declined, saying, 'I think Mr Sivaswami who represents the union with the largest membership on your estate should sit there.' By that one move, Martha Abeyesekere had elevated the status of the visitors to a position of equality with the superintendent. Deft, Nimal thought. He went through their list. 'Item one, the estate should arrange to buy maize flour which, as a substitute, is available at comparatively cheap rates and distribute it to the workers to tide over the crisis. I agree to that.' The union representatives looked at each other with slight surprise and satisfaction. 'Item two, plucking rounds should be reduced from five days to three days and the wage rate increased so as to compensate for the wage days lost. I can reduce the days to three but I don't think the estate can afford an increase in wages.' The representatives tensed. 'How will the workers manage?' Nimal said he would not object to their looking for work outside on the free days. They remonstrated that all of them could not find such work. Nimal told them he was unable to help beyond that. 'Shall we go on to the next item?' he asked. The representatives did not reply. He proceeded unilaterally. 'Item three . . .'

Sivaswami, a tough-looking man in his forties whose parents had been estate workers themselves, interrupted Nimal. 'There is no point in discussing the other items if we cannot agree on the wages question.'

Martha Abeyesekere had been silent all this while but Nimal could see that she was reacting to the discussion like a barometer, tensing and softening ever so slightly but clearly, at every nuance in the discussion. In soft but clear tones she now broke her silence.

'Would it be possible for you to grant a wage increase to women workers? You know, for more than a century there has been a difference between men's and women's wages on the estates. A difference of almost twenty-five per cent. Women form more than half the labour force on estates, work longer hours than men, carrying heavy baskets on their backs, and queueing long hours before their bags are weighed. But they are still paid less wages than the men.' Martha opened her handbag and neatly extracted her spectacles and a sheet of typed-on paper. She glanced through the paper as if to make sure it was the right one before giving it to Nimal. 'Please look at these figures of disparity between men's and women's wages on tea plantations in Ceylon over the last five years.'

Martha continued: 'I know this is a general issue and is not connected with the immediate crisis. But it does not need extraordinary intelligence to see that this disparity contributes to the worker's difficulties at times like this.' Nimal read:

Basic Minimum Wages Including Allowances

Year	Males Rs	Females Rs	Difference Rs	Percentage difference
1969	4.67	3.65	1.02	21.8
1970	4.79	3.69	1.10	23.0
1971	5.09	3.83	1.26	24.8
1972	5.45	4.07	1.38	25.3
1973	6.17	4.55	1.62	26.3

Nimal's first instinct was to say that he saw the disparity but was not in a position to do anything about it. But the sophistication of his visitor compelled respect. Besides, Nimal had himself often wondered why the women were paid less.

Sivaswami intervened. 'We, in my union, have also considered the unequal wages to be unjustifiable.'

Handing the sheet of paper back to the lady, Nimal said 'Yes, the asymmetry certainly jars.' Sivaswami could not make Nimal out. Had the superintendent agreed or not? 'Do we take it that you are going to raise women's wages?'

'No, I can't quite say that. What I can offer to do straightaway, Mr Sivaswami, is to write to my Board and ask for permission to equalize the wages for the duration of the current shortages.'

'That will not be enough, Mr Superintendent.' Sivaswami was visibly disappointed. 'You do not seem to be aware that the workers do not have money for the next meal.'

Nimal fingered the bric-a-brac on his table. The talks were breaking down. Nimal knew that the Company had given him great discretion. The Board would most certainly ratify any wage increase he considered appropriate. But he wanted to play it safe.

And yet, a breakdown in the negotiations would be bad. Nimal was about to make a proposition when Sivaswami suddenly stood up. 'I am sorry, Mr Superintendent. There seems to be no meeting ground between us. I am afraid we will have to go to the workers and seek their verdict.'

'Does that amount to a strike, then?' Nimal asked with cold candour.

'It can.'

Martha, still sitting, addressed both Nimal and Sivaswami. 'A confrontation between labour and management will be disastrous at this point. Families will suffer incalculably.' Sivaswami cut her short. 'There is no point, Martha. They are inflexible. We have no alternative.'

No goodbyes, no handshakes. The trade unionists quit Nimal's room. All, except Martha Abeyesekere. Standing up after the others had trooped out, she removed her spectacles, folded them carefully and replaced them in her handbag. 'This is very unfortunate, Mr Rupasinghe. I was hoping you would be able to avert this.' Nimal, who had been taken aback by the action of the others, rose also. 'They left rather abruptly, didn't they?' Martha did not reply. Instead, she gave Nimal biographical information which he was glad to receive. 'I am not a trade unionist and so I am not here to bargain. But I believe in the trade union movement because I am a Trotskyite. I have been one ever since my university days. My party is not going to officially support a strike just now but we know the workers' cause to be more than just. We would like the confrontation to end constructively.'

Nimal, on an impulse, asked her where she had been to university. Almost absent-mindedly, as if it did not matter very much, Martha said 'Newnham College, Cambridge.' A shaft of unease passed through Nimal's mind. He had felt that shaft identically on a couple of occasions before. One was when Ronald's letter had come. Another, when he had heard of Nehru's interest in estate labour. And now this elegant woman was speaking to him about labour–management relations. Nimal's conscience was disturbed.

'I must not keep the others waiting. But I want you to know something that might surprise you. Two members of your clerical staff are members of my party. I have asked them to continue to report to work in case there is a strike and, if possible, act as a bridge between you and your workers. A bridge which could, perhaps, provide a way out of this impasse.' And with those words, Martha left Nimal's room. The news about the two members of his staff being Trotskyites worried him. In ordinary times he would have asked for their resignations. But these were not ordinary times. A Cambridge-educated woman had used the charm of her personality to not only neutralize him in relation to the two activists but had, in fact, made him vaguely dependent on them. Not many people, certainly not many women, had impressed Nimal quite as Martha had. For a few moments after she left, Nimal continued to think of her, the light smooth complexion of her skin, her very expressive eyes. And behind those looks, a mind of her own, and a commitment. How was it that he had never heard of this woman earlier? He remembered noticing that Sivaswami and she seemed to be quite friendly with each other. Was there anything more to their relationship than friendship and a broadly common cause? He suddenly felt jealous of Sivaswami. He will lead the workers to strike, will he?

S-T-R-I-K-E. The word spelt itself in Nimal's mind in bigger, ever bigger letters. He reached for the phone.

'Hello, Dick. The union chaps were here. They have just walked out. They do not seem to be interested in talks. I am afraid we have to be prepared for a strike call at any moment.'

'Oh, don't be afraid, Nimal . . .'

'I am not *afraid*, Dick. That was a figure of speech. I will speak to Tilakaratne and Pieris also. I am also getting through to the police in the meantime for security arrangements.'

'Don't worry, Nimal. I have my guns oiled.'

'I am *not* worried. I am merely making certain essential arrangements. And as for the guns, I hope you are only speaking metaphorically.'

'Eh?'

'Never mind.'

Nimal then got through to Inspector Yusouf.

'You are soon going to see a strike on these estates, Inspector. I would like my factories to be guarded by at least a dozen armed men.

'No problem, Mr Rupasinghe. We have already received intelligence of plans for a large-scale strike by estate workers starting any time this week. Reinforcements are expected and we have also been told that if necessary the Army can also stand by.'

'I see. Well, it is good to know mine is not the only estate to be affected.'

'No, not at all. I will be sending men to several estates tomorrow and the Maradeniya group will also he covered. I will send a jeep across which can be stationed on your estate wherever you want. And Mr Rupasinghe, if there is anyone you want us to round up as a precautionary measure, do let us know.'

The strike call was given the following morning. Work came to a halt suddenly and simultaneously on several estates. Men and women walked out of the fields leaving baskets and implements on the ground. Clerks in Nimal's office slunk out. A couple of hours after he had got word of the strike, a letter was delivered to him on behalf of Sriskandanathar. The man had applied for leave to take his wife to Jaffna as she had 'suddenly taken ill' that morning. Suddenly taken ill, indeed! Nimal was exasperated. The letter had been delivered along with the bunch of office keys only after Sriskandanathar had actually left. A fait accompli, if ever there was one. Everything suddenly fell very silent. Nimal could hear bird calls louder and clearer than ever before. Two clerks, Vijayakumar and Mahadevan, stayed behind. Slim, dark young men in their twenties, they worked in the accounts section of the estate office, the 'X-ray section' as it was called by virtue of its probing, reflective functions. The two men had very pleasant faces or, rather, pleasant expressions. Bachelors, they were uninvolved in life-and-death struggles. Clerks, they knew the condition of the estate's finances inside out. Vijayakumar was an 'Indian' Tamil. His father had worked on an estate as a kangani and ensured a high-school education for his only son. Mahadevan was a 'Ceylon' Tamil from Vavuniya, near Jaffna. They had both become very good friends, exchanging notes about their estate colleagues, keeping largely to themselves and being in touch quietly rather than secretly with Martha Abeyesekere and fellow Trotskyites. Their ideology itself was a quiet affair. They had been introduced to it by a mutual friend in Ratnapura. Classlessness had appealed to both of them because they had been able to relate the ideal to their own daily observations of want and exploitation on plantations.

Their relatively junior station had so far kept them from coming into close contact with their superintendent. But they had assessed Nimal, not incorrectly, as the sahib who stands no nonsense and is therefore to be preferred to the sahib who does not mind nonsense and is sometimes part of nonsense itself.

When Nimal saw them at their desks after the others had left, he knew they must be the Trotskyites. He was obliged to take notice of them. He was, in fact, obliged to do more. Communication between individuals on the same side of a crisis has a different timbre from ordinary conversation. Anxiety permeates thought and speech at such moments. It encloses the partners in the emotional tightness of the crisis. This is what happened with Nimal and his two Trotskyite subordinates.

'Sir, we will do whatever is necessary,' Vijayakumar offered when he saw Nimal fumbling with the keys to one of the cupboards that was generally operated by Sriskandanathar. And they did, too.

Every morning of the strike they opened the doors and

windows of the office, swept out the place, dusted the furniture. The office looked strange, empty and clean. Distant sounds of workers talking and being talked to would come now and then from the direction of the lines.

'Can you come in for a moment?' Nimal called out to the two men on about the sixth day of the strike when the silence became unbearable and he began 'hearing' his own thoughts. 'Are the two of you for the strike or against it?'

'We are for the strikers but not for the strike', Mahadevan replied with a smile.

'Very convenient. You have the best of both worlds, then!'

'Sir, you misunderstand us. We feel the matter could have been resolved without going in for a strike,' Vijayakumar volunteered.

'We feel,' Mahadevan resumed, 'that the strike can be called off even now without too much difficulty.'

'Provided?' Nimal asked with a more than necessary dash of cynicism.

The two men hesitated momentarily. And then Mahadevan spoke. 'Provided superintendents like you make a gesture that would appeal to the workers.'

'I notice you have said "workers" and not "unions".'

'Different unions can have different standards. But the average worker knows what his needs are and can recognize a genuine gesture when it is made.'

'I see. And what do you think that gesture should be?'

'A twenty-five percent wage increase and equalization of men's and women's wages.'

'Do you think I am a charity bazaar?' Nimal shot back. 'I have to maintain the productivity of the estate.'

'If we wished to increase productivity we would not starve the tea bush, would we, sir? We would fertilize it, spray it against pests, keep it in trim . . .'

'Spare me kindergarten analogies please.'

The young men withdrew.

The thousands of men and women on estates that went on strike that year to press for higher wages took a frightful risk. They were consciously bringing upon themselves and, much more significantly, upon their families an extraordinary hardship. And hence their decision to strike and their persistence in the strike was a truly remarkable act. Nimal was inwardly impressed, although on the opposite side of the strike.

'Do you think the unions are giving the workers a subsistence allowance?' he asked Vijayakumar and Mahadevan one day.

'No sir, they are not. Even if they wanted to do so, they would not have the money to feed so many people for so many days. Families are pawning and selling trinkets, utensils and just about surviving,' Vijayakumar explained.

Mahadevan, the more assertive of the two, suggested that Nimal visit a line. 'It could have a psychological impact. It might show them that the management cares.'

'Nimal had been going round the estate every few hours, driving the jeep himself, a constable sitting beside him. But he had avoided the lines. During the first days of the strike, the children and even some of the older inmates rushed out when they heard the whir of his jeep. But now they had stopped doing so. If someone was sitting outside the lines or if some woman was at the tap in front of the line, he or she just looked up at his passing vehicle with very weary eyes. The listlessness increased every day. Tea bushes grew into vast untrimmed hedges, the latex on the tapping panels of rubber trees congealed, factories gathered dust. And more unfortunately than all this, tension grew with each passing day.

The kanganis and sub-kanganis had been somewhat ambivalent at the beginning. Their hearts told them to join the workers but their heads advised them to stick to the management for whom they supervised the others. Most kanganis and sub-kanganis had therefore decided to sit on the fence and watch the situation for a while, watch whether the strike breaks the estate or whether the estate and the privation involved in the strike together break the strikers. The parallel hierarchy of talaivars, the workers elected to offices in the estate's trade union set-up, was, of course, at war. The talaivars had set their hearts on the strike and spoke contemptuously of the kanganis. The two hierarchies had log-jammed. But as the strike deepened, the kanganis joined their brothers. The workers' collective will alchemized their indifferences. Vijayakumar and Mahadevan gave Nimal as much of this picture as he was interested in hearing. And they kept in touch with Martha Abeyesekere. Nimal's father came up from Colombo, shortly after he heard of the strike, to be with his son. His doctors had advised him against it. But Edwin Rupasinghe had been adamant. Nimal, appreciating the gesture deeply, apologized to his father about being shorthanded for servants. 'Only Velayutham and one other chap come to work in the house. The others have joined the strikers,' he said, helping his old man out of the car.

'That's all right, son. Quite all right. How many servants do you think we have at home in Colombo?' Nimal felt guilty. He had got used to a standard of life higher than his father's. That his vastly reduced scale of facilities could be the norm elsewhere shook him, momentarily. 'Your heart has been none too strong, dad. The doctors have said you are not to have any shocks, any strain. Just take it very very easy.'

Later that afternoon, having put a great many cushions behind his father's back in the most comfortable sofa chair, and given him a copy of the latest *National Geographic* to read, Nimal told his father he must go to the office. 'For form, dad. There is no work, of course.'

Mahadevan told him, at the office, of kanganis having changed their minds.

'So the kanganis are now wholly with the strikers, are they?' Nimal queried the two men.

'Yes,' Mahadevan confirmed. 'They have also begun to say

that the management is not going to listen to the workers and that the government will have to intervene.'

'You can let them know that I am going to make other arrangements, if this situation continues.'

'Other arrangements?'

'Yes. This country is chronically unemployed. I can find workers from nearby villages. They could do basic jobs. I know of some retired kanganis who could coach them.'

'Blacklegs?'

'Why not? Aren't you something of a blackleg yourself?' Mahadevan was shocked but, before he could retort, the sound of an explosion tore through the air. Nimal dashed out and got into his jeep. Another explosion, even louder, deafened him. He drove towards what seemed like its source. But having gone barely half a mile down the road, he braked. It was no sabotage as he had feared a moment ago, no bomb. Loud crackers—louder than usual—were being blasted as part of a funeral procession. A worker's funeral. The men walking alongside the bier looked at Nimal grimly. A starvation death? Nimal quickly reversed. He drove straight home. Entering the drawing room, he wondered why his father had not put the lights on. Must be slumbering, Nimal thought. Edwin Rupasinghe, sitting on that comfortable seat, *had* been slumbering. But that was a while ago. Right now, he was where no human voice could reach him. Shocks were bad for him, the doctors had said. Shocks included blasts. Those two from the funeral were the last sounds Nimal's father heard. The rest was silence.

News of the strike on many of Ceylon's tea estates crept into the British and Irish press. The *Fabian*, a leftist weekly printed simultaneously from London and Belfast, focused on the strike at the Irish-owned Maradeniya group. It carried a picture of a woman tea-worker with a sackful of plucked tea on her back, juxtaposed with another picture of an enormous white woman with a trolleyful of goodies before a counter selling Ceylon tea in a Belfast supermarket. 'Teapickers' was the common title for the two pictures. The report itself was devastating. 'We like good tea,' it went. 'But if only we knew that the tea in each cup has been picked by chilblained fingers, carried on the backs of undernourished mothers, dried and fermented in class-oppression, we would like it less. And if we also knew that at this very moment the profit-lust of some British and Irish companies has driven tea-workers in Ceylon to a just strike which leaves their children hungry, we would like the "cuppa" not at all.'

The paper then went on to describe the strike in the perspective of colonial history. 'Ceylon did not have the capital for investment in plantations. We provided that. Ceylon did not have the labour to work those plantations. South India provided that. But while tea planting companies have been getting more than fair profits, the labourers have not been getting anything like a fair wage. It is the responsibility of the British companies, the British trade unions, the British Government and the British tea-drinkers to see that our taste for cheap tea is not indulged by the exploitation of a captive labour force.' The *Fabian* cited Paul Baptist, a Ceylonese doctor currently in London, as one of the chief sources of its information.

At the other end of the political spectrum, *Bugle*, a Conservative tabloid published from Belfast, tracked the doctor down in London and got him to agree to an interview. Paul agreed with some reluctance and, while the interview was on, regretted his decision. He was surprised by the undisguised hostility of the interviewer. Ronald Manners was a regular reader of the *Fabian*. And this despite the fact that his own specific position was more Christian than leftist in the conventional doctrinaire sense of the term. A 'Christian socialist' is how he liked to think of himself: socialist enough to be appalled by the expensive and inane merry-making at Christmas, and Christian enough to see injustice as injustice on either side of the iron curtain. News of the trouble on Ceylon's plantations had worried him. Nimal, his good but increasingly silent friend, was presumably in the thick of it all. The story in the *Fabian* confirmed his fears. The Irish-owned estates were badly hit. What would Nimal's role be? Ronald felt sure, with some regret, that Nimal would not be on the same side as the workers. Dr Baptist's statements interested him. Ronald was able to get Dr Baptist's London address from the editorial office of the *Fabian* and called on the doctor at his small flat in the East End of London. Ronald introduced himself as one who had read the *Fabian* article with great interest. Ronald noticed that the doctor and his wife stiffened at the mention of the article. Ronald went on then to mention that he had studied at Oxford with the superintendent of Craigavon. 'Oh! Paul knows Mr Rupasinghe fairly well,' the lady said, relaxing visibly. Dr Baptist explained at once the reason for his earlier caution. 'You see, not everyone has reacted to that article in the same way.' Paul then showed Ronald a copy of the Belfast tabloid. 'What impudence!' was Ronald's first reaction. But on re-reading it he felt Paul emerged from the queries a clear victor. He arranged, therefore, for the following excerpts from the interview to be printed in a church journal of which his father was in charge, the *Manger*.

Q: Doctor, do you regard the striking workers on Ceylon's tea plantations to be so undernourished that this strike could endanger lives?

A: I do. The strike could endanger the lives of the very old and of infants by depriving them of basic food inputs.

Q: A cynic might say that if on Ceylon's plantations you find very old people and infants, then the atmosphere on those estates conduces to a long life and to a cheerful expansion of families?

A: The same cynic might have advised Damien not to waste his time in Molokai since the fact that every year more and more people on that island were going down with leprosy showed that more and more people were being born and that, basically, everything with Molokai was fine.

Q: Do you see yourself as something of a Damien? Or
a Schweitzer, maybe?

A: I do not. But I do see the need for their spirit to inform
my country's health services.

Q: Our friend the cynic might ask you why it is that you are
not in Ceylon at this moment ministering to the striking
plantation workers.

A: He might be surprised by my answer.

Q: And what is the answer?

A: I had agreed to be interviewed about Ceylon's tea-workers,
not about myself.

Q: You might care to 'objectify' the answer to this biographical
question.

A: All right, if you insist. An epidemic of cholera broke out
some time ago on a plantation that is named after the Irish town
of which the great nationalist Terence MacSwiney was Mayor—
Cork. Well, the cholera microbe invaded Cork and brutally
laid low a good quarter of its workforce. Things had to be done
quickly to combat the epidemic and to prevent its recurrence.
The juggernaut had to be stopped in its tracks. But when the
chariot's bureaucracy is bent on extracting a nick of gold from
Baal's burnished flanks, when it does not mind the trampling of
its own kind by that lethally mobile ogre, then the Baptists of
the world are powerless indeed.

Q: I am not sure if I have got all the nuances of that
observation but the imagery was interesting.

The Baptists and Ronald met quite regularly thereafter at the
East End flat and at Ronald's home. Ronald was only slightly
older than any child of the Baptists would have been, in 1974.
They were drawn to him. 'Nature does not sustain vacuums
easily,' Paul hypothesized one Sunday morning. 'We seem to have
found a son after all. And he shares our views, our interests. Not
every son does that.' Constance heard him in silent agreement
from inside the little pantry with a gas range where she was

cooking lunch. They were expecting Ronald for lunch and also William Paine, the doctor who had brought the Baptists to England, and his wife, Marcia.

'Ah, the smell of steak in passageways,' Ronald quoted Eliot as he came in a couple of hours later. The guests partook of Constance's rice and curry meal admiringly. The brinjal, potato and beef curry had been cooked in a little milk. 'It should be cooked in coconut milk really,' Constance apologized.' '*Coconut* milk? What in heaven is that?' Ronald asked incredulously. Constance described how the milky sap from ripe coconuts is added to curries in Ceylon to give them that special creamy flavour.

'You can't get coconuts here, can you?' inquired Marcia Paine.

'No, you can't. But plain milk does just as well,' Constance informed her guest.

'Random mutation and natural selection,' Paul suggested. 'If you can't get x you can try z until z replaces x as the favoured variation.'

'I guess the isle of Ceylon has always been short in cows and profuse in coconuts,' said Paine.

'If an untravelled European,' Marcia said, 'were to close her eyes and think of what Ceylon looked like, the image of a wind-blown isle and swaying coconut trees would be the first to come to mind.'

'And that would be a not inaccurate image,' Paul assured her. 'The coconut tree *is* the most representative symbol of our culture and economy. The coconut tree, with the jack tree coming up as a close second. Everything in the coconut tree is used up, its trunk, fronds, flowers, water, kernel, shell and sap.'

'Some enterprising *menike* staying in England must have tried out plain milk as a substitute for coconut milk in desperation and found it worked. Now every Ceylon lady here uses plain milk,' Constance said.

After lunch, the group moved with their coffee cups on to

the small terrace which adjoined the Baptists' flat. It was unusually sunny, and from the terrace they got a wide view of the innumerable chimney tops of the low houses for which East London is famous.

Ronald's thoughts turned to Nimal, to the recent strike. It was strange, he ruminated, Nimal had almost never spoken of Ceylon with the kind of affectionate sense of belonging with which the Baptists spoke of it. And this despite the fact that the Baptists were not entirely Ceylonese.

A month or so later, Ronald received the following from Nimal:

8-3-1974

R,

Where does one begin?

You know of the strikes that took place here. Newspapers here and in England have been full of it. Well, the strike was called off after what has been described as an 'effective intervention by the Government.' The intervention has been followed by rumours of an imminent takeover of foreign-owned plantations by the State. The strike itself has been a great financial loss to my company. More than that, it has been a very great embarrassment. For this I hold the media responsible. But I ought not to inflict more details of these surface aspects of the matter on you. I have always liked sharing thoughts, not bare news, with you. News has been admitted only to the extent that it reflects or shapes thoughts.

I know intuitively that you have been concerned at the news of the strikes and, if I am not mistaken, have judged my role in it not too kindly. By way of a partial extenuation of my role I want to share a thought that has been with me for some time now. I have always been playing assigned roles. So have others. One is a planter and must carry a swagger stick. Or one is a trade unionist and must precipitate a strike even if compromise is possible. But, in reality, are we not being totally naive in imagining that these largely self-assigned roles are sacred and unalterable? The recent strike has functioned like a green room for me, where I have seen roles being peeled off like so many costumes and that much make-up, including my own. I have been preoccupied by the thought that my genes, environment and circumstances need not hold me in the thrall they have. I have to find an internal mobility of my own which needs no other source for sustenance or survival. Playing my role during the strike, I was confronted with the awful reality of this need one evening. An old plantation worker, Perumal, who had retired from service years ago, died while the strike was still on. Everyone believes he died because he could not eat enough and that his physical resistance sank so low that he was unable to survive a vicious attack of influenza. Perumal's death and funeral were turned into an extraordinary event by the trade unions. There was a large attendance at the funeral which was arranged with much secrecy. The idea was to startle me. Crackers are often burst at funerals of Tamils on estates. But for Perumal they obtained mighty big ones. Small bombs really. Well, the narration goes against me so far, does it not? It portrays me as the unfeeling executive who watches funerals of starving workers go by. But, R, is not reality more complex than that? My father, who'd been through three heart attacks had insisted on coming up to Craigavon to be with me during the strike. It so happened that Perumal's funeral took place on the very day father had come. He was in no condition to withstand decibel shocks. All of us, on edge as we were, assumed the explosion to be an act of defiance, sabotage, arson. Rushing to the spot from where the blast came I was relieved to see a funeral. But the explosion jolted my father out of his sleep so violently that his heart froze. The retired tea-worker's funeral had been a grand affair, fireworks, flowers, drums. But the retired QC's funeral was a quiet affair, R. I took the remains down to Ratnapura, the town nearest to Craigavon. He was cremated there with no fuss and almost no mourners other than myself and a couple of close relatives whom I was able to reach over the telephone. *Vae victis*

N

28-6-1974

N,

'My sincerest condolences' sounds so weak and hollow. But you know what I mean, don't you? I can imagine what you've been through in this grim combination of professional and personal crises. I have some idea of the bond between you and your father. You never spoke of him much but, when you did, I could see the strength and the *depth* of your relationship. I can imagine what his going—and the manner of it—must have meant to you, though you are not the one to let others get as much as a hint of it. I have met here in London an acquaintance of yours, Dr Paul Baptist, and his wife. They have asked if I would care to visit Sri Lanka, going with them when they return early next year. I have said I might do that, especially since the organization which runs the school I work in has offered to pay for my passage. Do you think I could study the working of schools under your charge, talking with the students, teachers and parents?

I have also heard a good deal about an Italian Jesuit who is said to have done a lot for plantation schools. I would like very much to meet him. Take your own time, please, to reply to this. There is so much, so much of it so awful, that you have to recover from.

R

The prospect of meeting Ronald Manners again pleased Nimal. Ronald's plans of studying plantation schools, presumably in tow with Father Gio, did not displease him either. A few months or a year earlier, the idea would have irked him. But now he was strangely placid about it. He wrote back almost at once, telling Ronald he would be welcome. He added, however, that his own continuance on the estate was unsure, what with talk of nationalization and the state of his own mind.

Nationalization had become by now a typical fairy-tale witch that scared little planter boys. Dick Wimalawardene gulped whenever the subject came up. Was he to lose his job? Rather cynically, Nimal paid Wimalawardene back in his own old coin.

'Don't worry, Dick. You don't have to be afraid. You'll only have to lose some of your perquisites. The job as such cannot be taken away.'

Perquisites. That long word had become part of Wimalawardene's waking and sleeping consciousness. It meant status to his mind and pneumatic bliss to every muscle, joint and pore on his skin.

Wimalawardene recalled in vivid three-dimensional detail the last occasion when that word was mentioned. Dictating a letter to the Board about the inadequacy of the terms of his service, he had faltered for the right word to describe his. . . . er . . . his . . .

Priyani Perera supplied the word, pronouncing it exquisitely, pouting her lips and pausing after the per-. 'Perquisite', 'exquisite' and 'Priyani' had fused in the sumptuously illustrated dictionary of Dick Wimalawardene's mind. And so Nimal's telling him of the likely loss of this trinity agonized him no end. Wimalawardene sank back in the abysses of his sofa when Nimal mentioned the word. 'Oh dear,' he said. 'Oh dear.'

Tilakaratne and Pieris were shaken too but not so severely as the superintendent of Cork. Tilakaratne itemized the disabilities when they all met at the Club on one of those depressing evenings. 'We would have to forgo the furlough, wait on some government functionary or the other for every pettifogging sanction, live in unpainted bungalows . . .' Pieris grunted approval of the range of Tilakaratne's list. Wimalawardene was sullen and silent. And then, when there seemed to be nothing more to say, Nimal spoke.

'No one has asked me what my reactions to the move are. I suppose you expect me to stand up and face the change like a man. I wouldn't blame you for thinking so since I have conveyed the impression of being a tough-minded guy. Well, let me tell you that my reaction to nationalization is not what you think it is.' The superintendents looked at each other discreetly as if to say 'Now what is he up to?'

'I am quitting. I have requested the Board to relieve me immediately and to place Dick in additional charge of Craigavon. The reason for my going is not disinclination to serve under the government. It is deeper. It is personal. I wish to reflect on how best I can play the hand that destiny has dealt me in terms of my temperament, my opportunities, my abilities, my handicaps.'

Nimal then told Dick that he did not have to worry about the transitional arrangements. Nimal had (he told them) made a thorough preliminary assessment of the assets and liabilities position and had advised the Board on how much it should expect as compensation. Dick would not have to do any elaborate calculations. The company, Nimal said, might even regard nationalization at this juncture as a blessing in disguise. 'The strike has displeased them and, besides, they have tired of managing remote estates through superintendents they cannot control directly.' Nimal left the Club before the others that evening. After he was gone, Wimalawardene brought a cigar out of his pocket like a prized secret and lit it with ritual deliberation. Thoughts and smoke rings wafted from his seat in larger and ever larger shapes. The happy prospect of being Number One warmed his cold forebodings of nationalization. He would be in charge of Craigavon, be the top man for the Maradeniya group itself. The Government would have to deal with him. The Board would have to deal with him. He might get a trip to Belfast in the bargain, with stopovers in London and Paris. Wimalawardene blew a very neat ring and then dissipated it mid-air by a shaft exhaled straight. Partitions, takeovers, leave a debris. A rich random rubble for the benefit of those with access. The fates, he thought, may be being very kind to him.

'He can quit,' Tilakaratne suddenly spoke up. 'A bachelor like him, with a vast fortune bequeathed by his father. He doesn't have to nurse a marriage, a home with children and parents.' Tilakaratne wanted to say 'an old mother who can't get on with her daughter-in-law.' But chose, instead, the other non-specific word, pronouncing it with a false matter-of-factness. Pieris also felt a compulsion to add his thoughts about Nimal. 'Lucky bugger,' he said.

'Language, Pieris,' Wimalawardene admonished his colleague, 'language.' Dick was in charge of the Club again.

Having been in constant touch with Valli, Father Gio's nuns saw to the confinement as well. Valli was taken to a hospital in Nuwara Eliya a couple of days before the expected delivery. A Sister Betty stayed over to be of assistance and support. Valli's thoughts were with Soma throughout this period. She wondered how he might look and feel in his cell. She wondered if he thought of her and if he knew of her marriage (as he must by now), whether he had understood her compulsions and forgiven her.

Sister Betty, plump, middle-aged and entirely grey, came from Galle. Her mother tongue was Sinhala but years of work in the diocesan branch at Nuwara Eliya had made her more than proficient in Tamil. Her work was among pregnant women and nursing mothers. The hospitals in the area knew her and she had admittance to wards, labour rooms. The staff and doctors in this hospital valued Sister Betty as an important bridge between them and the patients. She got the hospital to do all that was necessary for the patients and in turn ensured that the patients observed regulations, particularly those relating to hygiene and diet.

Valli confided in her. She had, in fact, spoken to no one at such length about her experience with Soma and Jayasena. Sister

Betty had heard her with interest but no curiosity, concern but with no demonstration of pity.

On the day the pains began, Sister Betty took over the situation completely. Masked like the doctor, anaesthetist and nurses, she held Valli's arms tight. 'Push, Valliamma, push!' she told the young mother to be. 'The more you push, the easier it will be.'

After what seemed an age in which each successive moment brought so much pain that Valli felt she would not be able to stand it any longer, the baby arrived. 'A strong baby boy,' Sister Betty told Valli. Relief and a sense of achievement came over her.

Sister Betty arranged to send word to Sannasi and, through Father Gio, to Theiva at Craigavon.

Sannasi and Meena came almost at once. He was polite about it all. Who could blame him for showing no elation? Meena was excitement itself. They could not spend much time at the hospital because of the children at home, and, after a couple of hours, were gone.

The baby was fair and had a surprising amount of curly soft hair on its scalp. Everyone in the maternity ward was curious about its good looks. Sister Betty overheard a couple of mischievous comments and promptly stilled them with a look. When the ward nurse brought the birth registration form to be filled up, Sister Betty asked Valli if she would like Sannasi's name to be entered against 'Father'. Valli thought for a moment. She looked at the baby. Visions of the collection centre at Crabeavon, of Soma trembling in her arms and she in his, flooded her mind. She shook her head. Sister Betty did not say another word. 'Leave it blank,' she told the nurse. Father Gio visited the hospital the following day. 'Aha, a bonny boy,' he exclaimed, lifting it gently and swaying the tiny bundle. Valli whispered something to Sister Betty. 'She wants you to name the child, Father.' 'Yes? Shall I give him a Christian name or a Hindu name?' Valli indicated that she left it to the padre. Father Gio held the baby up, held him very still. 'Let us call him Yesudas, then. Yesudas, servant of Jesus.'

Son of a Sinhala Buddhist father and a Tamil Hindu mother, illegitimacy baptised him Yesudas.

Wilmot Inginiyagala was disturbed. Not only had Soma continued in custody on account of magisterial diffidence, the High Court too had declined bail. The prosecution had suggested 'mysterious motives not precluding homicidal tendencies of an unpredictable nature.' The implication was that Somasiri might go berserk if enlarged on bail and do in some others. Inginiyagala's hypothesis of 'murder in the heat of passion' had not been accepted.

The veteran proctor's office room was a small affair. The desk was heaped up with case files folded into long narrow shapes so that they could be carried handily. Inginiyagala's diary had each page crammed with case numbers entered there by his clerk against the dates on which they were expected to come up for hearing. The walls were lined with racks holding law books, law journals and stacks upon stacks of disposed case files. A queue had already formed itself outside the room, of litigants, old and new, waiting to be either coached by the proctor for their roles in court or seeking to engage the proctor on fresh cases. Old men in topknots involved in land disputes, younger men seeking divorce proceedings, young women, some with babies in their arms, resisting divorce proceedings, relatives of undertrials held for crime.

Inginiyagala had an old clerk assisting him with his papers, Guruge.

'Can you give me the Somasiri Estate Murder file?'

Guruge, stooping and arthritic, was not too happy at what seemed to him to be an irrelevant requirement for that day. After all, that case was not coming up that day, or that week. The case files for the day had all been arranged in serial order on the proctor's table by him with such effort. Ignoring all those and ignoring the queue, the proctor now wanted some other file. Guruge rose slowly and walked past the small tables and chairs

cluttering the room to a cabinet. He opened it with a key that
hung on a chain fastened at the other end to Guruge's wide black
belt strapped round his sarong. He brought the file out and gave
it to his boss. Inginiyagala went through the dates scribbled on
the file cover, the dates of the several hearings, adjournments.

'Hmmm,' Inginiyagala grunted. 'What do you think of the
case?' he asked his old clerk. He did this occasionally, in order to
obtain what he called the vox populi. Peering up from above
the upper rim of his glasses, Guruge inquired whether this was
not the fish vendor's case.

'Yes, the same.'

'Oh, he does not stand a chance. All magistrates and lawyers
buy fish from that type of fellow. They would be dead scared
to let their wives meet such a fish vendor at their doorsteps.
I hear these fellows are very angry with this murderer. He
doesn't have a chance.'

'Hmmm. Right, let us start with the day's clients.' The queue
shivered into movement.

The deaths, first of Kandan, then of Peramayi and finally of
Perumal, brought Theiva and Velu together.

Witnessing the murder committed by Soma, followed by
Soma's arrest and Valli's marriage-of-compulsion and the three
deaths, Velu's mind acquired a dimension it had not known before.
He felt a responsibility towards the affected family which, made
tenderer by his feelings for Theiva, urged him to silent action.

Velu went to Keselgoda. To Sando.

The teacher was supervising the filling up of his sandpit with
fresh soft earth from the Kalunganga riverbed. He chided the
men who had brought the stuff on two push-carts for the stones
in the fine earth. 'Look at that stone and that one. Do you
want my boys to tear their skins? Can't you put yourself in their
positions and imagine what it would feel like to have stones
jabbing your sides while you exercise?' Sando's handlebar

moustaches, brown with a film of the riverbed earth being poured into the pit, quivered.

Hearing the shuffle of feet behind him, the master turned round. The young visitor brought his palms together and crouched in deferential greeting. 'Ah, Velu!' Letting the earth-filling operation be for the moment, he put his arm round Velu and took him to the stone slab near the pit.

'How are you, my boy?' Sando gestured. Velu's reply was a smile. Sando held Velu's shoulders, Velu's neck. 'Any problem?' Velu smiled again.

'It's no use like this. I know you have come to say something to me. Let's go to the School for the Deaf and Dumb. Someone there will help us understand each other.'

An hour later, Sando and Velu alighted from a bus in front of the School. The principal knew Sando.

'Hallo sir. Someone for admission? But we are full up and besides . . .'

'Not for admission, mahatmaya, only for help to understand each other.'

Mr Yapa took the men in and asked Sando to give him some background.

'I see . . . I see . . . hmmm. I think I can ask him now. Let us see.' And then Mr Yapa drew up his chair closer to where Velu had been sitting silently all this while. His hands drew patterns in the air. Velu gawked at them as one reads a crossword puzzle, understanding it but partially and yet totally fascinated. Slowly, the specialist was able to get messages across. They came through like signals through an obstructive storm. The vessel of Velu's understanding trembled in the excitement of self-discovery. Mr Yapa's intuitive knowledge of a deaf-mute's perplexity helped him to interpret Velu's silences as much as the grunts and nods.

After about fifteen minutes, Mr Yapa had decoded the message for Sando. Velu wanted to marry a girl, the sister of the girl who wanted to marry Sando's student. Could Sando speak of this girl and to their neighbours on the estate? In other words, could Sando help Velu get married?

A look of surprise came over Sando's face and was quickly replaced by a smile. 'Of course. Of course, I will. I owe it to Soma.' His eyes moistened. 'Come, my boy. I will take you back now and visit your estate as soon as possible.'

The principal conveyed this to Velu who at once bent to touch the feet of both men in mute thanksgiving.

Sannasi's family was a little shoal of shrimp that had floundered into the driftnet called the Indo-Ceylon Agreement of 1964. It waited, with hundreds of similar families in that vast mesh, to be drawn by invisible hands towards India. Some years earlier Sannasi had been told that he was 'stateless' and must apply for the citizenship of either country. Like everyone else similarly advised, Sannasi sought the citizenship of Ceylon, the country in which he and his father before him had been born. Sannasi received a card one day which informed him in very small English print that his application for the citizenship of Ceylon had been rejected. Similar cards were received by many others on his lines. What were they all to do? Avadai, a toothless old man, called by fellow workers on Glenville 'the wise one', addressed all those who had received the rejection cards. 'We came to this land because our own land could not sustain us.' Avadai wiped his mouth and continued. 'I remember how parched the earth was, how hungry we all were in our village of Avur in Pudukkottai. My father said, "Come, let us go and register at the Ceylon Office." And so we registered and came here. We came in order to be able to work, to eat.'

Heads, including Sannasi's, nodded in recognition of this familiar narration.

'And now, when we have lost all links with our native land, when we have sent our roots deep into this soil like the tea bushes planted by us, we are told, we are told . . .' Avadai broke down.

Younger hands, anxious to assuage and also to encourage Avadai to continue, reached out to the old man's shoulders.

'We are told that we do not belong here, that we must go back to India, that if we stay on here we will have no rights. Is this fair? Is this just?'

Heads shook to say, no, it's not fair, Avadai, not just. A couple of old women spoke too.

'Better to go back, to die in our motherland, than live like slaves here.'

'Yes, let's all go. We'll return to our villages. Our relations will give us our gruel. We'll survive on that. Let's not beg for rights here.'

Padavattan, one decade younger than Avadai, demurred. 'Brave talk, this. But let us face facts. We have no idea of what India is, what life back in the village means. Avadai, being older than the rest of us, remembers. But do you, Sami? Do you, Sengilli? Can you, Sannasi, plough a rice field? All of us have children. When we go back to our lines tonight, there will be a pot of food for them, for us. And it will be there tomorrow too, and the day after. But in India, you will not have that. You will have to hunt for work, move from place to place, young and old together, like nomads.'

There was a murmur. Emotion and reason, old rivals, sparred for the loyalty of the gathering.

Avadai spoke again. 'Even if Padavattan is right—and I know he is not—will they allow us to stay here? You may be able to drag on for a year or two. But then, sure enough, the day will come when we will be told our time is up. Padavattan, tell me, will you stay here to face that final indignity?'

The dissenter was silent, thoughtful. Congregations do not like silences. Padavattan's failure to meet Avadai's rejoinder at once clinched the argument as far as the Glenville congregation was concerned. A few of the men stood up, tying on their head-cloths in a gesture of finality.

'Let's all apply for India.'

'Yes, for India.'

Avadai had carried the day.

And so it was that Sannasi found himself paying ten rupees to one of the clerks in the estate office for help in filling up an elaborate form of application for 'Indian Citizenship and Travel Documents in Terms of the Indo-Ceylon Agreement of 1964.'

The agreement described 9,75,000 persons, mainly estate workers of Tamil origin, as 'stateless', apportioned 5,25,000 to India and 3,00,000 to Ceylon. In theory, there was an option available for every Avadai, Padavattan and Sannasi. They could choose either Indian or Ceylon citizenship. But in practice the Agreement was anything but voluntary. Unlike the group that had been persuaded by Avadai and other groups of that type, the majority opted for continued residence in Ceylon, the country where this group had lived and worked for the last one hundred years. The Ceylon quota soon became heavily oversubscribed. All those applying for a status quo after the first 3,00,000 were asked to take the Indian option. There was no other way. Avadai's intuitive understanding of the position was accurate. Padavattan's rational approach was not backed by the terms of the Agreement.

Forms, certificates, affidavits flooded estates like Glenville. Business in photo studios boomed as applicants for the citizenship of India were required to annex photographs to their applications. With all this paper work, the Agreement spawned form-sellers, form-writers, touts. Corrupt practices appeared like pustules in estate offices, in government offices and even in trade unions.

Sannasi had paid his way to his Indian passport, scarcely distinguishing between officially required fees that he had to remit at the Indian office and the bribes which intermediaries extracted from him. He had to do the same for Valli's passport.

And now, in Avadai's phrase, their time was up. The Sannasi family could stay on in the island only for a given length of time. The sands were running out for Valli, and with it, all hope of seeing Soma ever again was disappearing. Sannasi knew Valli's thoughts but left her with them. And, as for the child, he neither resented nor loved it. He was glad it had been given an un-Hindu name for that marked it out from the other children. Everyone on Glenville's lines knew now that Yesu was not Sannasi's child. But that was that. No one bothered about it any further.

Velu and Theiva were married almost immediately after the conversation in mime with Sando and Mr Yapa, Adaikkan and Sinnathal officiating for the bride's parents at the ceremonies.

The function was not without amusement for Craigavon. It is not every day that the only deaf-mute on an estate gets married.

'What! Velu getting married? He'd need help,' said one wiseacre to another with a wink. 'Rubbish! He's deaf, not blind' the other responded.

'Marrying Kandan's second daughter, is he? No sister of Valliamma would have problems with someone who can't speak to her. After all, that Sinhala fish vendor would never have spoken to the wench, would he have?' one husband joked with his old woman.

'Go on, what do you know of the difficulties of us women!'

But, by and large, there was gladness tinged with pity for the rather lonely young couple. Velu went through the ceremonies grim-facedly. He was afraid of making a mistake, of raising a laugh. He wanted to do nothing that might embarrass Theiva. When he clasped her hand as the priest required him to, he felt a hundred doves being released inside him. A smile came over his face which he quickly obliterated on noticing that Theiva's eyes were lowered, her head bent down. What was she thinking? Velu wondered if it could be that she was grieving for her grandparents, for her father. Or missing her sister. Or (and Velu broke into a sweat when he thought of this last alternative) was she already regretting the marriage?

He was reassured, moments later, when Theiva looked

up, smiled with her eyes and, seeing his worried look, seemed to say, 'I am fine.'

Valli could not attend the wedding. Sannasi's children had been left to fend for themselves during her confinement, making her feel guilty. If she were to be out again so soon thereafter, Sannasi wouldn't like it. And, despite her husband's non-aggressive nature, she was never without a feeling of being answerable and obliged to him. She felt all the time that he had done her a favour by marrying her, by letting her bring her baby into his family and that she must, therefore, cause him no additional trouble, no further worries. When, on receiving Adaikkan's letter informing them of the proposed marriage, Sannasi did not suggest that she go, Valli did not raise the subject. She merely suggested, over their lamplit dinner that night, that he send a letter of greetings. Sannasi grunted acceptance of the idea. All the children including Meena had gone to sleep.

Whether it was the talk of marriage, or the fact that all the children were deep in satisfied sleep, or that Valli's dinner had pleased him, Sannasi was a satyr that night.

Shortly before nationalization, Nimal quit. His decision had, earlier, been accepted by the Board with but a brief observation of regret. In a couple of private letters that he received from Belfast, Nimal was told that it was 'perhaps inevitable' that he should wish to leave in 'the changed circumstances' and that they were sure that he would do 'equally well' in his next assignment 'wherever that might be.' Nimal had no idea of where or what that might be. With his father's Colombo house an empty shell— emptier in some ways than his Craigavon bungalow with all its servants—and no office to attend to, Nimal turned untypically to self-pity and almost simultaneously to that ally of solitude and self-pity in the rich: liquor. Sitting quiet by himself, beside his father's law books amid dusty Victorian *objets d'art*, Nimal at first ruminated over his glass and, after a few months, began, softly but surely, to talk to himself.

Ronald had written saying he would not be able to come until much later; the Baptists were to be delayed, too. The vacuum grew. The one or two faithful servants in the house learnt to leave Nimal to himself (Rambanda, the late Sir Edwin's balding manservant, had received a gash on his pate by a plaster of Paris version of Venus hurled on him by Nimal who had been disturbed in the middle of a soliloquy with a perfectly well-meant 'Does the young master want some tea?') Occasionally, very occasionally, Nimal would go to a library. It was on one of those rare visits that he met a familiar figure, Martha.

'Hullo, Mr Rupasinghe.'

'Oh, hullo . . .'

'Do you come here often? It's a good library as libraries in Colombo go.'

'Huh? Yes, yes . . . no, not often. Sometimes.'

'You seem run down.'

'Do I? I don't feel run down. I'm all right, I guess.' And then, they met oftener. Nimal visited Martha's flat in Colpetty, a neat three-room affair with books on sociology and politics lining every wall and some exquisite sketches by George Keyt and pieces of old Kandyan craftsmanship. 'Beautiful, that brass betel-chopper and that . . .' 'Jewel box. It has no jewels in it, though. Only the house-keys.'

'I wonder why our people go in for westernized bric-a-brac when our own heritage . . .' and before Nimal could complete the sentence, a bout of coughing seized him. Martha fetched a glass of water and offered it to her visitor. Nimal could hardly hold it for his quaking. Martha brought it up to Nimal's mouth. Shame-faced but grateful, Nimal took a few sips. 'Thanks, thanks a lot. I will be all right in a minute.' They talked for over an hour, over tea, and then because of the lateness of the hour, over a makeshift dinner.

Early in 1977, Valli suggested to Sannasi that she visit Craigavon. She had a special reason, Valli said. She had thought it over carefully and had decided that when they repatriated to India later that year, she would not take Yesu with her. She would hand over the child to Theiva and Velu, to be brought up by them.

Sannasi turned his gaze to the toddler. Fair, strong-limbed, curly-haired, the child was like an exotic plant in his family. Valli's suggestion seemed to be eminently sensible. 'Do that,' Sannasi told his wife. 'I have no objection.' Valli went with Meena and two of the younger Sannasi children—and Yesu—to Craigavon in July that year. Theiva and Velu were thrilled with the idea that Yesu be given to them. And, to Valli's immense relief, Yesu took to Velu hugely. The child had not known the affection of any adult man and Velu seemed to Yesu to be a total novelty— a responsive man!

Sinnathal, looking greyer in the head and kinder in the face than ever before, saw the scene with friendly curiosity. And why shouldn't the child be so fond of Velu, she reasoned. Wasn't its father the only friend Velu had ever known?

Valli had brought gifts, little baubles. A plastic comb for Velu and a small hand-mirror for Theiva, all costing under five rupees. She had also brought a blouse piece made of pink artificial silk for Theiva. The money for these purchases Valli had saved from her own earnings and had shown the things to Sannasi before leaving Glenville. She did not want him to think for a moment that his wife was carrying away any of his household's belongings.

At line number seven, however, Valli changed her mind about giving the cloth to Theiva. Sinna had been standing at the door and Valli felt it would be wrong to leave their neighbour out completely.

'Here's something for you, Sinna.'

'For me?' The older woman asked with disbelief. Her eyes glistened as she opened out the cloth and held it up against her bosom. 'It's very nice.'

The moment had become a shade too sentimental for Valli

and Theiva and so they were both glad when Yesu, perched on Velu's shoulders, diverted everyone's attention by sending a warm bubbling cascade down his bemused pedestal.

Valli could not bear to see her old lineroom or the one her grandparents had occupied. Both were now lived in by two new families, Theiva having shifted to Velu's room. Memories of her father, of Perumal and Peramayi, were too sharp, too sad, to permit her to face those rooms with equanimity.

After Sinna was gone, Valli asked Theiva if she had remembered to keep their old group photograph, with the death certificate inside it. Yes, she had, Theiva reassured Valli and, springing up, brought it out of a trunk. '*You* must keep it,' Theiva told her sister. Valli took the picture, saw the certificates still in place, and put it into her bag. 'I will need it, I am sure, in India. What else will there be with me to remind me of Craigavon?'

Theiva and Velu, it was arranged, would join the family at Glenville on its final journey to Talai Mannar, the northern seaport from where a ship conveyed people across the Palk Straits to Rameswaram on the Indian side, a journey of twenty-six miles.

And they would bring Yesu with them.

It was only because Valli knew she would be seeing the child again that she was able to part with Yesu the following day. Even Meena, grown-up enough now to know what marriage and motherhood meant, was in tears when saying goodbye to the child.

Nimal Rupasinghe, chessman extraordinaire, had not returned to square one. That would have been bad in itself; the actual position was worse. He had been ousted from the board altogether. Logic, his old métier, lay in the dust, vanquished by the fates. Someone else, someone new to his life, was needed to lift Nimal out of his psychological and physical dumps.

Martha Abeyesekere's life, like Nimal's, had also been built on a foundation of logic. Nimal believed in class differences as constituting a natural order. Martha regarded the same differences as an evil meant to be eliminated by the operation of certain inexorable forces of history. No two belief systems could have been more different from each other. Nimal was the very thingness of class, born into a combination of feudal, colonial and capitalist interests, trained to be contemptuous of the 'lesser breeds'. For Martha such an attitude invited confrontation.

And yet . . .

Nimal was invited over and over again by his ideological adversary. Once or twice Nimal wondered if Martha's friendliness had some political purpose to it. But it was obvious that it didn't and he dismissed the thought, cursing his cynicism. Nimal knew that in his present situation there was nothing to be got from him. He was no longer in a situation of 'give' but, rather, its opposite.

Martha, all too aware of the change in Nimal's circumstances, was anxious not to convey any impression of being patronizing. In fact, in their early conversations, she kept up a point-counterpoint balance by discussing the subject of the strike. Not reproachfully or in a 'I told you so' vein but matter-of-factly, without any attempt at concealing her own position.

'I am convinced you could have averted the strike.'

'You see, Miss Abeyse . . .'

'You must call me Martha. And I would like to call you by your first name.'

'Sure. I am Nimal.'

'I know.' Both laughed.

'It's amazing how much you know of me and mine.'

'Not as much as I would like to.'

'Well, to come back to the strike, Martha, don't you think Sivaswamy left very abruptly? I was about to take a risk and concede the demand on women's wages!'

Martha was silent. She recalled the discussion in Nimal's office room. Her intellect siding with Sivaswamy and the others, her emotions had nevertheless prevented Martha from walking out with them. Her intellect and instincts had warred. Get up, Martha, what are you waiting for, Martha's mind prodded her. Wait a minute, this superintendent isn't the ordinary sort, he seems to be worth talking to, said another part of her being. And so she had stayed behind while Sivaswamy with the other unionists waited outside. Martha had anticipated Sivaswamy's cynical comment: 'So the dorai has been negotiating with you, is it?' With just the right note of irritation in her voice, Martha had replied, 'Every conversation is a negotiation.' And then, as they motored out of the estate, she put everyone at ease by amplifying: 'I have given away nothing. The talks have failed; the unions are free to chart their own course, which now means calling for a strike. Since you will all be involved in the direct combat I will exercise a watching brief and will maintain a line of communication with the superintendent in case it becomes necessary for us to use it.' Sivaswamy had remained generally impassive and, after a while, broken into an animated discussion with the others in Tamil (which Martha did not understand) on the preparations for the strike. As the car took them further and further away from Craigavon, Martha's thoughts travelled in the reverse direction—to her encounter with a man who stood on the other side of the fence and who yet seemed to her strangely close.

'Believe me, Martha, I was going to concede that demand.' Nimal's words pulled Martha back from her reverie.

'Yes, I knew that. I knew it even at that time. But then you see, Nimal, one sometimes finds oneself in situations where one has lost control over one's immediate actions. One is moved, activated, by some unseen hand like a player on stage or like chesspieces on a board.'

'I know that feeling. I know it only too well. I have deluded myself for so long into believing that whenever I have done anything in those situations, I have been exercising my free will. Actually, I have not. I have just been a puppet, wearing a mask.'

'When did you take it off?'

Nimal was thoughtful for some time. 'I think I took it off—or rather—it fell off, when my father died . . .' They were both silent for some time and then Martha got up and went away to another room, returning with a flat, hollow object in her hand.

'A mask, from Ambalangoda. Isn't it ingenious?'

Nimal took the mask, an old male face with the teeth missing, a squint in one of the eyes. Trying it on, he asked Martha how he looked.

'See for yourself in that mirror over there.' Nimal laughed loud and long in front of the mirror. 'So that's what I looked like, eh?'

'Ambalangoda,' Martha said after they had settled down to a drink, 'is where my father came from. He had a coconut estate there.'

'Tell me more about him.'

'You'd be bored.'

'No, seriously, Martha. I want to know more about . . . about you, about others. You see, I have lived such an insulated life, self-absorbed, self-opinionated.'

Martha too had never quite spoken of herself in any intimate sense to anyone. She fumbled for words, playing with a betelnut chopper nervously, as she spoke.

'You see, Nimal, my father had inherited a vast coconut estate near Ambalangoda and lived all his life on his absentee earnings. He spent much of his youth in England studying, ostensibly, but in reality just growing up as a little brown sahib.' The description touched a raw nerve in Nimal. Both he and *his* father had fitted that description.

'Nimal, do you really think I should continue?'

'Of course.'

Martha thereupon told Nimal about her father. Rodney Abeyesekere met her mother in London, way back in the early 1930s. Hilda Winterton, Martha's mother, had been a shop assistant in a bookstore run by a Jewish radical. Rodney, like many other Asians of his generation in London, had known the bracing winds of Fabian socialism. After a fashion, Rodney had become quite active in extra-curricular politics and even joined demonstrations led by Krishna Menon and the India League to canvass the independence of British dominions. During a brief courtship Hilda's predilection for the Left was assiduously pandered to by Rodney, but for reasons that were entirely unpolitical. Hilda looked upon Rodney as a representative of a whole people under colonial subjugation. If socialism had been a stimulation and a pastime for Rodney, it was an ideology with Hilda, one that interlocked with her workaday situation. Rodney and Hilda went through a civil ceremony of marriage when Martha was already on the way. Rodney had agreed to go ahead with a marriage not out of a sense of responsibility for what had happened but out of a sense of embarrassment vis-a-vis his leftist associates. Hilda had been liked by them all, taken seriously and shown respect. Hilda did not take long to find out that Rodney's politics was skin-deep and that he was, essentially, a pleasure-seeking individual who just happened to be Asian. Her opinion was confirmed when the three of them went over to Ceylon in the late 1930s. Martha, a little girl, was dazed by her new surroundings. The elephants fascinated her and the bhikkus awed her. 'What is *that*, mamma?' she had asked her mother on first seeing an ochre-robed monk.

Nimal listened to Martha's account with the attention reserved for film sequences. 'Is that your first clear memory?'

'Yes, but a fully-rounded memory dates to a slightly later period and I am afraid it is not very pleasant to relate.' 'Don't, if you would rather not, but you have no idea how important your experiences of childhood seem to me!' And so, with Nimal now sitting on the floor with his head cupped in the crook of his arm over Martha's chair, she continued the narrative.

Martha's earliest clear memory was of her first visit to the central

highlands where Rodney Abeyesekere had many planter friends.
The rapid changes of landscape from the paddy flatlands
to the undulating slopes of tea had dizzied her. But, at the end
of the journey, a bungalow with the most lovely things in it
awaited them. She watched, with her face glued to their guest
room window, rows of ant-like workers 'down there'. Hilda spoke
to her about them. 'They work hard; are very poor.' Martha
remembered having been woken up that night by voices raised
in a quarrel. Hilda, crouching on the ground next to Martha's
bed, Rodney pounding Hilda on the head with his fists. 'For
God's sake,' Hilda was saying, 'Stop! Aren't you ashamed of
yourself?' Martha recalled her father having replied, 'You bitch!
You'd have been rotting in London had it not been for me.'
Noticing that Martha had got up, Hilda had risen from the
floor, smoothed her hair and come up to the child to assure her
that all was well. But before she could reach Martha, Rodney had
pulled Hilda back by her plaits. Hilda screamed, Martha yelled.
Rodney had brought a mailed fist down on Martha's face.
The rest was blank . . .

'Why did he do that?' Nimal asked after a while.

'I asked my mother, years later, in London. She said it all
started over a trivial remark of hers, something to the effect that
the luxury of planters' lives sickened her.'

Until she was about fourteen, Martha and her parents had
lived in Rodney's lawn-encased villa in Colombo-7. At about that
time, Hilda took Martha away, very suddenly and furtively,
to London. Rodney, from all accounts, was shaken. For about a
year, as the two women found their feet in London, Rodney
moped in Colombo. Bravado about 'they can go to hell' gave
place to more sober reflections until he persuaded himself to
go to London. Hilda met him coldly, reminding him of his
duty towards her daughter. 'I can pretty well look after myself;
you know that. I have no interest in private property but I want
you to know that as long as you own property, you will have to

share it equitably with your daughter!' Looking older and greyer
than ever before, Rodney had told Martha that his home in
Colombo was her home. Martha had been quite moved. About
ten years later, by which time she had seen Martha through school
and college in Cambridge, Hilda had fallen grievously ill. Rodney
came to see her but found her in hospital, comatose. Doctors
attending on Hilda advised Martha to tell her father to return.
'It's hopeless, but the end may take weeks, months.' Rodney,
supported by a walking stick, returned to Colombo but not
before telling Martha: 'I have been lousy, a lousy husband and a
lousy father, but I want you to know there is no one, no one at
all, more precious to me than you. Come back to your father,
Martha, when it is time.' And so Martha did come back to a
large house and an estate that could support several generations
of the Abeyesekere family.

'But I wasn't interested in inheriting an estate. And so after my
father died, I wound it all up and started working in areas that
have interested me and for which I have been trained.'

'What did you do with the proceeds? I am sorry to ask
so personal a question, but we have already been over a large
field that is personal.'

'I gave over a third of the sale proceeds to the Institute where
I work, to finance research on Ceylon's plantations, with
an accent on labour. I am myself the first Fellow under the
scheme but, hopefully, in a couple of years from now others
will utilize the endowment. I made over another third to the
Ceylon Estate Workers Educational Trust to facilitate the
education, at any given time, of about a dozen female children of
estate workers. The remaining third I retained, buying this flat
and investing it in a manner that would bring me an income
every month. So that's it.'

'That must give you a sense of fulfilment.'

'Although I have acted in a manner consistent with my beliefs,
I can't truthfully say I feel fulfilled. Fulfilment is a much greater

possession, isn't it? So much more than the physical and intellectual is involved in being fulfilled.'

'I know what you mean.'

'Companionship matters.'

Martha's hand moved softly, tenderly, to Nimal's head, caressing it like an evening breeze over a lake. Strangely enough, this was the first time Nimal found himself physically and emotionally close to a woman. Nimal had always been totally different from his father, for whom promiscuity had been part of the process of growing up. Not that he had never felt drawn to the female form. He had, quite powerfully, on many occasions. The seductiveness of European cities after dusk had made evenings of singleness a torment for him. His companions had 'organized' themselves on a regular basis. But Nimal could never get himself to do so. Was it timidity, he had asked himself quite often.

Martha was therefore unlocking a door in Nimal's life that evening that had never been opened before. It opened gradually but gratefully. They ventured out together through that door into a vast and unexplored landscape that made their enclosed little Edens eminently worth losing.

'Zoop!' flew the cork from a new bottle of champagne opened at the Keselgoda Club one June 1977 evening by Dick Wimalawardene and his old colleagues at the Maradeniya Group, in honour of Victor Perera, the new superintendent of Craigavon. The group had changed little since nationalization. All the old planters had continued, Wimalawardene having held additional charge of Craigavon since Nimal left, until the arrival of Perera. The Club too had changed little. Portraits of the President and Prime Minister of Sri Lanka were the only additions to the room. 'All the best to you, Victor. You are bound to do well!' Wimalawardene blessed and prophesied. 'You are bound to excel your predecessors!' There was general merriment and the usual chatter about persons. Nimal, inevitably, figured in it. 'Haah!'

Wimalawardene exclaimed at the mention of Nimal's name. 'I am told, I am told . . .' and he bent over, suppressing his laughter, 'the man has got himself nationalized also! He is living with a Trotskyite dame these days. Imagine! A Trotskyite dame!' Amidst 'No?' and 'Really?' and 'Tell us more,' the Keselgoda cackle extended into the night.

Sannasi prepared assiduously for their departure. Their pots and pans and clothing went into two dealwood crates. A modest quantity of cloves and cardamom was purchased from out of the gratuity paid to Sannasi. He also bought himself a watch, the first he had ever owned. He could scarcely read the time but the glint of stainless steel on his wrist gave him self-esteem. It revalued him. Sannasi bought two new saris for Valli and Meena, to be worn on the actual date of their departure, and new clothes for the children.

But Sannasi had no idea of something that lay immediately ahead.

Nationwide elections had been held that year which gave an unprecedented share of parliamentary seats to the party representing the Tamils of Jaffna. The result had enthused nobody on the estates even though they shared a language. The life of the Tamils of Jaffna, the Ceylon Tamils as they were called, had never intersected with that of the Tamils of the estates, the Indian Tamils. The latter were infinitely poorer, mostly of lower castes, and much less literate than the Tamils of Jaffna. The electoral victory of the latter was no victory for the Sannasis of the Central Provinces. But the result, it was said, had shocked and angered the Sinhala majority. An outbreak of communal violence was feared. The Ceylon Tamils, it was said, would not be affected because they were far away. They were fortified, as it were, by geography. The estate Tamils, on the other hand, were in the midst of the Sinhala country, often surrounded by Sinhala villages, and would have to bear the brunt of the expected violence.

Sannasi did not understand the nuances of politics. And, in any case, he was too preoccupied with the departure arrangements to bother about esoteric matters like communal tension. A man who has crates to nail cannot dabble in political theory.

Ronald Manners had been in Sri Lanka about a week. He had not yet established contact with Nimal but, with the Baptists accompanying him, had gone in Paul's car (returned by the friends who had looked after it during the Baptists' absence) to the estate where Father Gio worked. They were to stay for a while there: Paul, to find his feet again and Ronald, to learn.

'*Dio mio*! The *dottore* looks younger than ever!' the padre exclaimed on seeing Paul. He bowed with a charming mixture of affection and respect to greet Constance. 'I have not done too badly, either,' he said replying to an inquiry from Constance as they walked towards the building where Father Gio was putting them up. 'The air is so much healthier in the hills than it is in Keselgoda.'

'But the political air, I believe, leaves something to be desired,' observed Ronald. Father Gio stopped in his tracks. 'Yes, my friend. It leaves a great deal to be desired. In fact trouble is expected at any moment.'

The family was at its evening meal, the younger children getting ready to sleep. Valli scraped the remnants from the pot of curry to serve Sannasi, when a series of explosions shook their lines. More explosions and shouts followed. Valli stood up and opened their door to peer out. Several columns of smoke had risen from fiery bushes. 'Ayyo, fire!' she said. Sannasi jumped up. All the occupants of the lines were out.

'They've come. They've come for us, the villagers.'

'Run, run. Gather your valuables and run for the tea bushes.'

'Ayyo! God help us! Ayyo!'

There was pandemonium. People knocked against each other,

babies yelled, women screamed. Men, women and children tumbled out of rooms, clutching pitiful objects of value—a sari or two, vessels, kerosene oil lamps.

But before the Sannasi family could run out, a lorry packed with villagers carrying staves hissed up to the lines and stopped. With one cry, the armed men atop the lorry jumped down and ran into the linerooms like an invading army. They hit anything and anyone that came their way. Objects, if they were of some value and not too heavy to be lifted, were put into the lorry. Poultry came in for special notice. Foodgrains could not be moved and so kerosene oil was poured on it and the grain set on fire.

Within minutes, the linerooms were ablaze, their occupants beaten, trampled and chased out. The younger women caught the huns' fancy. They were asked to huddle in a corner of the line's veranda where the tongues of fire had not yet reached. There the leader of the gang asked the women to strip. One by one. Stunned by the invasion, terrified by the fire that was licking its way to that corner, the women obeyed mutely. Six of the women were 'selected', beauty-contest-like, and ordered to mount the lorry. They included Valli and Meena.

Several dark hours later the women were abandoned on a slope of tea bushes beside a stream. Their honour plucked from them, the bitter cold of the night insulted their bruised bodies. The women knew one another. How could they not? They lived together on the same lines. But they had never known one another in their nakedness. They stirred where they had been left, in pain and in unspeakable embarrassment. Valli located Meena, unmarried child-woman. Barely conscious of what had happened but in extreme physical agony, the girl cried for water. Valli helped her walk in the starlight to the nearby stream. She washed the girl as each cried on the other's shoulder, in hot stifled sobs of pain and anger.

If the cold of the night hurt the women, it also served to clothe them in its darkness.

If it were not for the wives of some clerks, living in quarters not far from the scene, locating the women, they would not have rejoined their menfolk and children with a modicum of self-respect. These, curiously, were Sinhalese as well as Tamil. One of them, Mrs Amarasekere, heard that night from her servant, Kasi, of a few women having been carried away in a lorry. Mrs Amarasekere ran across to some of the wives in her neighbourhood and quickly arranged a search, with her servant as guide. They had spotted Valli and Meena by the stream and then the others. Saris were brought from their houses to clothe the women and a couple of hours later, arrangements were made to escort them to their lines.

Sannasi had crouched behind a rock with his children and seen Valli and Meena being taken away in the lorry along with the other women. Shock, fear and the need to protect the little ones petrified him. He had run, thereafter, carrying some of the children as far as he could. Like his wife and daughter he had crept back to the estate lines the following morning to see his newly made luggage crates gone, his watch missing. When, some time later, he saw his Valli and Meena in clothes he did not recognize, Sannasi sank to the ground, holding his head in his hands. Meena dropped beside her father, whimpering.

Valli's glance travelled to what remained of their lineroom. Everything was burnt or broken. An orange patch gleamed on the floor. Valli walked up to it and, bending, lifted the object—their passports—tied together in a pack. The raiders had found no use for them and flung them in a corner. They were singed but had miraculously survived the fire. 'Look', she told Sannasi. 'We still have these.'

The parish office telephone rang very early that morning. Father Gio was needed urgently at a nearby estate where lines had been burnt down. He jumped into his high-powered van and drove off, accompanied by a junior priest and two parishioners.

'I will be in touch. Please stay indoors,' he said to his guests as his vehicle drove out.

Within an hour the vehicle was back, with the junior priest at the wheel. Paul and Constance were needed at the estate where the dispensary was totally unequal to its task. Ronald was welcome, if he wished. On the way, they saw smoke rising from the direction of the estates. Shops in the towns they passed through were shuttered and there was no sign of life or activity on the way. They drove in silence, their anger and shock being kept in check by contemplating the hard work ahead.

As they approached the estate a group of stunned-looking workers milled around the vehicle. The crowd brought hands together in supplication. Constance peered out of her window. The women were wailing, gesticulating.

'I wish I could understand them, Paul. What is it that they are saying?'

'There isn't time enough now to translate, dear. We've got to move on to where Gio is.' Paul said something in Tamil to the people who were at once reassured and they drove on.

'Your arrival could not have been more timely, *dottore*!' Gio exclaimed as soon as he saw Paul enter the dispensary. The padre had been ministering to an old woman whose left arm had suffered severe burns. Estate labourers of all ages were, literally, strewn across the floor like pieces of garbage. There were at least one hundred figures lying around, each needing immediate and serious attention. Paul took the scene in, unblinking; Constance, her mouth covered by her hand in disbelief; and Ronald, white with shock and astonishment, stood petrified behind him. But before any of the visitors could make another move, a jeep crunched up to the dispensary's entrance. Three uniformed men emerged from it, exuding power.

The seniormost of them, in neatly trimmed moustaches that

moved with every word he uttered, addressed all three of them and Father Gio: 'I am under instructions to conduct you to the nearest police station for interrogation.'

After a moment's pause, Paul asked 'Does that mean you are arresting us?'

'There is no need for explanations; please get into the jeep.'

'What offence have we committed?' inquired Constance, with no effort at concealing her anger.

'Officer, do you have a warrant?' Father Gio asked, still standing near the injured woman, who by now had half sat up.

'No talking please. Do as you are told,' replied the personification of authority in olive green.

Constance, holding Paul's arm, entered the jeep first, followed by her husband and Ronald. Father Gio sat in the front, a uniformed escort on either side of him, the officer taking the wheel himself.

After they had left the premises of the estate and were well on the road towards the town, the officer spoke. 'You are not under any arrest. We have been told not to permit any outsiders in the estate areas so as to keep villagers at bay. Or else, there is bound to be more violence between them and the Tamils. And even though none of you are Sinhalese villagers, you *are* outsiders, and I cannot make an exception in your case. I will return you to your parish headquarters. Please do not venture out until normalcy has been restored.'

'But officer . . .' Father Gio was interrupted by the officer with a 'Please Father. No questions.'

When Theiva, Velu and Yesu arrived at Badulla, the important rail terminus from where they were to have gone to Glenville to join the Sannasi family, Valli and Sannasi and Sannasi's children were already there—waiting for the train that was to take them to Talai Mannar. Valli had given up all hope of seeing her child again, or her sister and Velu. Their simple plan of going

together to the seaport had been frustrated by the . . . Valli wept
inconsolably. They were going penniless to India, all their
belongings—and their self-respect—snatched from them. And
Yesu! The thought that she would never be able to see her child
again pierced her heart like a spear.

Valli was woken out of her reverie by her name called shrilly.
Turning, she saw Theiva, holding Yesu, running towards her.

'Valli! Akka!'

'Theiva! Yesu!'

The sisters hugged, kissed. Valli held Yesu so tight that the
child cried. 'This is the last your mother is going to be holding
you, child. Let her hold you tight,' Theiva said to the child.
Velu, who had followed his wife silently went up to Sannasi.
The situation, and Velu's handicap, precluded all conversation
between the men.

There were but fifteen minutes left for the coast-bound train
to depart.

'Akka, is this the end, the very end?' Theiva cried bitterly.
'When you go now to India, there will be no one left from our
family, Akka, I will be all alone!'

'Hush, Theiva,' Valli wiped the tears from her young sister's
cheeks. 'You have Yesu. And Velu. And . . . and when he is
released, you will meet Soma. As for me . . .' Valli's words were
drowned in the train's deep whistle. The sisters clung to each
other, Yesu between them. The child bawled. Hundreds of
other passengers, other repatriates to India, jumped into the train
which seemed poised to start. Sannasi came up to Valli and said
softly: 'It is time!'

The whistle blew again. Valli and Sannasi's children followed
by Sannasi boarded the compartment in which they were to travel
up to Talai Mannar, where the ferry that would convey them
to Rameswaram on the Indian shore bobbed impatiently at the
jetty. Theiva and Velu, holding Yesu now, moved up to a window
from where they could see the inside of the compartment. The

seats on the platform side had already been taken. The Sannasi family was at the far end.

They are already on the other side, thought Theiva, they are gone. Tears, more tears, clouded her sight as the train jerked into motion and, with loud grunts and puffs, was gone.

Determined to 'file' a story from Colombo on what he had seen and then meet Nimal to get his views, Ronald Manners arrived at the same Badulla station to take a Colombo-bound train. The train carrying repatriates, including Sannasi's family, was just then steaming out. Ronald, accompanied by Father Gio for assistance with the railways, was greatly affected by the sight of families being torn asunder by repatriation. Theiva, in particular, caught Ronald's eye.

'Father, do you think you could talk to that girl for me?'

'Yes, of course,' Father Gio was all too willing to try out his Tamil. 'What shall I ask her?'

'Well, you could perhaps ask who of hers has repatriated and what the separation means to her.' What began as a question developed into an extended conversation, with Father Gio becoming so involved in the narration that he forgot his interpretative duties. Ronald saw Father Gio's eyebrows go up in surprised recognition and then close in on his eyes in obvious regret, and heard '*Dio mio*' punctuating every other statement the girl made. At length, Father Gio turned to Ronald.

'I am sorry, my friend, I was lost in the story. You see, I have known this girl's sister who has just left for India. I—we—missed her by seconds. Vyakulamary—Mary Anxious for her Child—I had named her. This child—Yesu—is hers, now in the care of his young aunt—this girl Theiva—and her husband. He is handicapped, a deaf-mute. *Dio mio*, a sad tale.'

Before Ronald could fully absorb the details and ask for supplementary information, the padre had returned to his conversation with the couple and child. Presently, Ronald saw

Theiva kneeling and touching Father Gio's feet, followed
by the man.

'I have just told this girl that I shall call her Sahayamary—
Mary of the Good Support—so that she is inspired to look after
and support the child. Tchah! A sad story. The child's father is
a Sinhala fish vendor, in jail for having murdered a man—another
Sinhalese—who had violated the child's mother Vyakulamary,
the one who just left.'

Ronald looked at the small wretched family and felt an
uncontrollable sympathy for them.

'Can you ask them, Father, if they have enough resources
to look after the child? Is the child going to be taught to read
and write?'

Father Gio was inclined to answer the question straightaway
on their behalf but, realizing that Ronald would like the reply
to be in their words, went through the motions of repeating the
question and then relaying the reply.

'Sahayamary says they will both work and earn enough to
feed, clothe and educate the child, provided . . .'

'Provided?'

'Provided riots like these do not recur and God favours them.'

Theiva spoke again and Father Gio turned to the child with
a twinkle and muttered something whereupon Yesu lisped,
'Eka, deka, tunai.'

'What is Yesu saying?'

'Yesu is saying the numerals and saying them well, too. He is
saying them in Sinhala. Yes, in Sinhala. So Yesu, you are going to
speak your father's language, are you?' Father Gio lifted the boy
high up in the air. Theiva and Velu looked up with broad smiles
at the child kicking the air and enjoying the levitation. The sorrow
at their parting with Valli lost its edge, for a moment, in this
encounter with the padre.

'Come, Ronald, we should be getting you into your train.'

Ronald's train, in the meantime, had positioned itself near

them. Ronald boarded it, not without awkwardness and sorrow. Awkwardness at his life being so streamlined, so free of the trauma of final partings, of the cares of parenthood, real or foster. Sorrow at being shown a situation of distress at first hand and at being able to do nothing tangible to alleviate it. He took his first-class seat by the window with the tumult of these disturbing thoughts churning inside him. A real-life situation this, if ever there was one. Ronald Manners's train pushed out towards Colombo, erasing from his window's frame the image of a Tamil couple holding a Tamil-Sinhala child, beside an Italian Jesuit who was waving him godspeed.

'In that case, we belong to somewhat different churches!' Ronald Manners was speaking to Martha in her drawing room. She had just introduced herself as a member of the country's Trotskyite party. Ronald had arrived a few days earlier and was to meet Nimal at Martha's over Sunday. Nimal was late. This gave Ronald a chance to get acquainted with someone he could see enjoyed a special relationship with his old friend.

A male–female companionship such as Nimal's and Martha's is for all intents and purposes a marriage. And marriage alters the chemistry of both its partners in subtle but sure ways. If it does not, the marriage is bound to be under strain. Both Nimal and Martha had become somewhat different as individuals ever since they had begun to live together. And no one could have noticed the change in Nimal as strongly as Ronald did. They were meeting after years. Years wherein both had undergone experiences which waited to be told to each other in an explosion of narrative.

But Ronald beheld a different Nimal Rupasinghe. It was not that Nimal spoke differently or said things that were not expected of him. Conversation itself seemed to have left Nimal. He was distrait and seemed to rely wholly on Martha—for corroboration, for cues, for well-nigh everything. Even on the subject of the riots, Nimal seemed to lack views of his own. 'They have been dreadful,' Martha said. 'I do not know what would have happened if the army had not been called in.' 'But will this be the pattern each time?' Ronald asked. 'Will the estate labour be forever dependent on the army for its survival?'

The research institute Martha worked for had organized a meeting ('We do not want to call it a Seminar') on the subject. She asked Ronald to come and join the discussions. 'Do come; it might help Nimal decide to come too,' she told Ronald as he was leaving. There was a clear entreaty in the request, with Nimal at its core.

'Sure, I'll be there.'

Ronald and the Baptists were already there when Nimal and Martha arrived. Ronald had told the Baptists of his meeting with Nimal and of the sea-change in his personality. 'I couldn't have admired the pucca sahib image which he had so assiduously cultivated, but had he remained the same there would have at least been some interaction. Now he has just gone limp, totally limp. It's quite amazing.' Paul recalled his long conversation with the superintendent of Craigavon at the Keselgoda Club. They had talked of tobacco, opium, hypnosis and plantation workers. It all seemed so long ago . . . It was strange, Paul thought, that the man who had resisted being drawn into a discussion on estate labour was now attending a conference at which estate labour formed the only agenda.

Nimal was expecting to see Ronald but the Baptists were a surprise. 'Oh, hullo, Dr Baptist. Mrs Baptist. So good to see you again. Meet Martha. Martha Abeyesekere . . . a friend. Martha, Dr and Mrs Baptist were in Keselgoda when I was up at Craigavon.'

'So many terrible things have happened since then, Mr Rupasinghe,' said Constance Baptist. Martha and Constance looked into each other's faces with the silent rapport that links certain people together magnetically, from their very first encounter. Constance and Sujata Tilakaratne had 'clicked' similarly. The two ladies sat down in adjacent seats, Nimal sat between Ronald and Paul.

'Dr Baptist, I well remember our conversation at the Club.'

'You do? I pontificated on subjects that interested me without thinking of you.'

'On the contrary. Even if I did not contribute to the discussion, I was most interested.'

Paul Baptist's *tour de force* of so many years ago had impressed Nimal. Recalling it now, a chain of connected and yet unconnected thoughts rose in Nimal's mind. The doctor's mention of Graeco-Roman times had taken his thoughts to Sybaris, the ancient Greek city in south Italy, which had become a byword for luxury and for effeminate indulgence. Sybaris. Did he think of Sybaris because it rhymed with cannabis? His tutor in Oxford, Trevor Scott, would have enjoyed that coincidence. Scott had asked some of his students, Nimal remembered, to suggest the likely objective inspiration for Shakespeare's sonnet which has the lines:

> *Enjoy'd no sooner, but despised straight;*
> *Past reason hunted; and no sooner had,*
> *Past reason hated . . .*
> *On purpose laid to make the taker mad.*

Nimal had mentioned what seemed to be the obvious interpretation of the lines. 'Is not the reference in the culmination to orgasm?' Nimal thought of himself and Martha united like flotsam in a heaving ocean of timelessness. But Mustafa Pirzada, a West Asian scholar of English and Arabic poetry, who had been attending Scott's tutorials, differed. 'Your interpretation is too simple, too—what is the phrase?—too pat. I would like to suggest that the author of Othello knew a great deal of man's pleasure-seeking outside England and Europe. I would suggest the sonnet speaks of the use of opium or cannabis or khat by an English or European traveller to the Arabian peninsula or to north-central

Africa.' Nimal had murmured dissent. Pirzada had held his ground. 'Why should Shakespeare speak of making the taker mad if he was only referring to sex?' Nimal resisted the temptation, for reasons of form, to educate his Arab friend about certain modern connotations of 'laid' and 'taker' which would have clinched the popular interpretation. But wait, would they have? Nimal had second thoughts. Surely the connotations he had in mind belonged to the world of contemporary slang. Shakespeare had used them straight. Perhaps Mustafa was right?

Nimal's mind lingered on the subject of cannabis, LSD, drugs in general. What a heaven-sent boon they were! Unknown even to Martha, he had been administering to himself millilitres of the purest bliss. But he was being careful about dosages, very careful.

'Are you all right Nimal?' Ronald whispered into his ears. The question entered his mind like an alarm bell piercing one's morning sleep.

'Yes. Oh yes. Why did you ask?'

'Your hands were trembling.'

'Were they? There's nothing to it, nothing at all. Thanks, Ron.'

There is in the relationship between two men who have been close friends a depth which defies not merely description but also understanding—in the idiom of ordinary thought. There is in it a tenderness and a total absence of coarseness which, in the classic male–female equation, would be called love. But the word has been so aggressively and possessively patented by the man–woman equation that to apply it into a relationship between two men would amount to a plagiarism by nature of itself. And so it remains unnamed. Ronald, who had watched a nervous tremble of Nimal's hand for several moments, could not resist asking Nimal about it. Having got from Nimal an explanation which did not explain the phenomenon, Ronald placed his own hand on Nimal's. Nimal was only momentarily surprised. He turned towards Ronald with a look that spelt gratitude. But, only for a few seconds. Before conformity, that indefatigable goddess in starched white, could turn her steely eyes on them, Ronald withdrew his hand.

'Friends,' a voice came over the mike. A bald-headed and bespectacled academic who had been invited to chair the meeting addressed the gathering.

'We are meeting under the shadow of tragedy, a national tragedy. When one is so close to the event, it becomes difficult to be objective. Yet objectivity is the need of the hour. We have to consider the situation in the cool light of reason.'

The approach appealed to Martha, who straightened up in her seat with attentiveness writ on every muscle of her face. But Ronald and the Baptists were not quite impressed. The peroration went on for several minutes. Statistics were given, the 'progress' in the implementation of the Indo-Ceylon Agreement assessed, intricate analyses provided for 'shortfalls' in repatriation, the resultant stresses in the estate–village nexus were explored.

'Ladies and Gentlemen, I would now request you to respond with comments of your own.' For several seconds, there was no response. Then a soft foreign voice broke the silence. 'I am Ronald Manners, visiting from England.' Faces turned to where the voice came from. 'I happened to be present, along with Dr and Mrs Baptist here, at the scene of the riots. While I fully share the need expressed by the Chair for objectivity, I *would* like to say that the subject of our discussion is human beings and not numbers, human beings who have been reduced today to a game of numbers.'

There is in meetings such a thing as the collective mind. Individual perceptions are subsumed in a certain broad readiness to be led. The gathering looks to someone among the speakers to take the initiative and mould the meeting's preconsensual mood into a definite consensus of opinion. The controlled tension on Ronald's face and the urgency in his tone compelled attention. While the Chair had tried to 'set the tone', it was Ronald who now promised the gathering its joint articulation. The Englishman's temple veins throbbed as he continued. 'I come from a part of the world where there has been racial tension. And therefore someone might justifiably turn round and ask me if I have any credentials to speak in this country on ethnic matters. But there, I submit, lies the whole point. I would urge this gathering to consider the situation in its essential form which is its human form. Nowhere in the world, to my knowledge, have a *whole people*— grandparents, parents, youth, children—been told that they must up and get out. These people have lived here, not for some few years but for two or three generations; they know no other place. Residence for a fraction of that period in many countries confers on non-nationals automatic citizenship rights. This amounts to a reversal of history, a fold-back of a whole sequence in human progress, a turnabout in space–time evolution.'

Ronald now had the undivided attention of the entire gathering. 'The question of questions is: Does anyone have the moral authority to tell decades- and centuries-old residents of any place that they must quit? I am not going into questions of State. I have deliberately used the phrase *moral* authority. Now, would anyone present here today react to a Notice which tells him that the place where he has been living and working for years is not his and he must therefore leave? How would you react, Mr Chairman, or you, Mr Rupasinghe?'

The Chairman took his unlit pipe out of its oral home and pressed the cold tobacco deeper into the bowl. Nimal, sitting as he was right next to Ronald was startled by the personal reference. He looked up at his neighbour and, unable to meet Ronald's piercing glance, looked away towards the faceless audience.

'We would be astonished, on receiving such a Notice, into utter disbelief; we would need time to collect our wits.'

Someone in the audience tapped on a mike and interjected: 'Our friend from overseas is understandably worked up, since he was near the scene of the events. We all share his feelings but there is no need to become personal, or emotional . . .'

Ronald continued. 'If one is not to think of emotions now,

what else *does* one think of? I would urge with all the emphasis at my command that the core, the very pith of the matter is—feelings. Feelings of belonging, of association, of sentiment. These have been trampled upon. Assumptions of identity and domicile, which had taken firm root in the soil of this island have been plucked out. A sense of desolation and bewilderment prevails where once there was complete confidence. And today . . .' Ronald paused for a breath that was almost a sigh: '. . . today, to that desolation has been added—humiliation. For no fault of theirs, whatever. They know no politics and subscribe to no political ideology. Their lives are so completely occupied by the tedium of their work that they have had no time to think politically or even think of the morrow. Their daily life, their diurnal round, ends with that day. To ask such a people to think of what lies beyond the immediate present, would be like asking a child of three to do logarithms. And their experience of a few days ago amounts to corporal punishment being inflicted sadistically on such a child for its failure to comprehend the instruction. I would like to put it to this intelligent and well-meaning gathering: Is it not time for all of us to stop the cynical unconcern with which the majority, smug in its homes and hearths, has treated the exodus of thousands upon thousands of people?'

Ronald then narrated his experience at the railway station, of his meeting Theiva and Velu, and the fate as he knew it, of Valliamma. 'Mr Rupasinghe will be interested to know that this family, which has suffered from every crime in the book, was from his old estate, Craigavon.'

There was a gentle drizzle outside the building when the conference ended. A few umbrellas sheltered twosomes as they moved out and away into the evening. Some, like Nimal, Martha, Ronald and the Baptists lingered on in the foyer, talking. 'Sorry, Nimal, if I surprised or embarrassed you in any way,' Ronald told his friend. Nimal stared at the floor. Martha looked askance at both the men. She had agreed with every word that Ronald had said but was deeply worried over the effect those words would have on Nimal.

Just as Martha was attempting to give expression, however incoherently, to her thoughts, Constance was heard to say, 'What a surprise!' Everyone turned to see an ochre-robed figure approaching them from inside in the hall. The Venerable Seevali and Colin Samarasinghe had been at the meeting, sitting unobtrusively in the rear. The Baptists greeted the monk with a deep bow, introducing their English friend to him. Ronald folded his hands in the manner he had practised. 'Honoured to meet you, sir.' Constance then made a gesture to Martha and Nimal suggesting that they introduce themselves. 'After Mr Manners's observations at the meeting, no need remains for Mr Rupasinghe to be introduced, nein. Besides, I have long known of him although we have not met.'

Nimal continued to look dazed. His eyes turned to Martha, as if for guidance. Martha bowed slightly, without speaking, as Venerable Seevali smiled. The drizzle had almost stopped. 'It is beautiful outside, shall we venture to our cars?' said Martha. With everyone sharing the sentiment, the small group set out.

On the way to the parking lot stood a bo tree. Behind it and beyond was a small thicket of mixed foliage. Two squirrels scampered across the path in gay abandon and climbed up the tree. Seconds later, a large house cat, dirty-white and green-eyed, followed the squirrels. The pedestrian group unwittingly blocked the cat's pursuit, confusing and disorienting it completely. Everyone had noticed the chase and was pleased that it had been foiled.

'Lucky squirrels,' said Ronald. He felt a pang of guilt. Had he, Ronald, been too harsh on Nimal by talking about the Craigavon family?

Nimal continued to be in a reverie. 'Are you sure you want to go back home?' Martha asked him. 'Why don't you spend the night in the flat? I will drop you home in the morning.' Nimal merely shook his head. Martha left him in the large house with a distinct feeling of unease.

Nimal hardly spoke to anyone for the next few days. Ronald made an attempt to call Nimal. The phone remained unanswered. He contacted Martha. 'I feel terribly guilty about having made a direct reference to him at the meeting, and to his estate. Will you please tell him I feel sorry and wish to make amends?'

Martha would come in, spend some time and, finding that Nimal seemed to prefer solitude, she would leave too. The staff in the house kept severely out of Nimal's way fearing an outburst of temper.

But in reality Nimal was nowhere near anything as aggressive as that. Ronald's words at the conference had got enmeshed in his mind. Valliamma . . . that name kept going round and round in his mind. It resounded more determinedly when, one afternoon, Nimal gave himself a somewhat bigger than usual dose of the 'stuff'. He saw a skeletal hand playing on a piano keyboard, a tea bush growing enormous, two hands emerging from its sides, extending towards him, nearer and nearer as he ran. Run, son, he heard his father's voice call from somewhere. Run for your life, dive into the water, into the sea, swim away, the bush can't reach you there . . .

Rambanda heard the young master start the car and drive away. The old servant mopped his brow in relief. Gone to the white *nonna*, he was sure. May not come back for a couple of days.

Nimal's car went like a crazy bullet down the road to Mount Lavinia. Two cyclists were knocked down, sides of passing cars grazed. Buildings, trees, whizzed past Nimal. Whenever he looked into the rear-view mirror he saw in it—the tea bush, arms extended, reaching out for him. Nimal drove faster. But as soon as the surf came into view, he braked and jumped out of the car. Without looking back once he ran from where he had left the car, towards the sea. He stumbled, fell, and got up to run again. When he reached the water's edge, Nimal's heart pounded, his temples throbbed. He ran into the water. Oncoming waves pushed him back towards the land as if to ask 'What are you doing?' But that was only for a moment. Nimal pressed forward, until his feet were not on sand any more. Other waves followed, lifted Nimal high and brought him down again. The afternoon sun sent needles of light on to his face. Drops of seawater on his eyelashes refracted the light, scattering it into a million specks of iridiscence. Nimal tasted salt; the water rushing into his ears sang like a thousand conches.

An image came, fleetingly but clearly, of a certain deaf-mute conch-blower, the man's face, bewildered and questioning. Just then a wave wafted Nimal up, higher and higher. Clouds danced in the sky. A large bird gyrated above, training its beady eyes on the human figure that lay atop the ocean's angry froth. The wave sank, seconds later, pulling the figure down into its chortling innards. A long weed of drifting ipomoea wrapped itself round Nimal's hand. Nimal froze and tried to shake it off. It only clung tighter. Nimal by this time had no voice, so he screamed with the pores of his entire body. His waterlogged mind imagined the tea bush closing in on him. He heard Ronald talking about the girl, Valliamma. The water breathed the girl's name into Nimal's ears. As Nimal bobbed up he heard . . . VALLI . . . Going down he heard AMMAA . . . VALLI . . . AMMAAA. Nimal thrashed his limbs and tried to lift his head for a breath of air, a half-breath, a half-wisp of air. Within seconds, Nimal Rupasinghe was the property of the fathomless caverns of the sea.